'Even renown across two continents couldn't keep his wife safe - only grovelling to Hitler could do that. *Song of Buchenwald*, closely following the real-life stories of internationally-feted composer Franz Lehar, his family and colleagues, explores the impossible dilemmas they all faced to remain alive. It vividly imagines and retells a long-forgotten story of what it really meant to be Hitler's favourite composer.'

Peter Furtado - former editor of *History Today* and author of *History of Nations*

SONG OF
BUCHENWALD

a novel about the great
Austrian composer Franz Lehár
and Adolf Hitler

James Walker

Song of Buchenwald

Published by The Conrad Press Ltd. in the United Kingdom 2023

Tel: +44(0)1227 472 874
www.theconradpress.com
info@theconradpress.com

ISBN 978-1-915494-45-0

Typesetting and Cover Design by:
Charlotte Mouncey, www.bookstyle.co.uk

The Conrad Press logo was designed by Maria Priestley.

Printed and bound in Great Britain by Clays Ltd, Elcograf S.p.A

To my wife Jo, as ever, for her love and patience.

To James Essinger, whose idea it was that I should write this book, for all his valuable input throughout on what I have regarded as being a collaborative process between us.

Preface

It may be hard to believe, but there is extensive evidence that Adolf Hitler wasn't always a monstrous anti-Semite.

In his youth, living in the beautiful, cultured city of Vienna as a struggling artist, he was happy to sell his paintings to a Jewish art dealer, and, so this story recounts, happy to accept the support and patronage of the great Viennese composer, Franz Lehár, a man surrounded by Jewish colleagues and whose future wife was Jewish.

Hitler also fell in love with Lehár's music and this love never left him, indeed it grew stronger. Wagner may still have been the composer he most lauded, but it was Lehár's music he turned to for comfort, even in his final days in his bunker in Berlin.

Lehár, in his old age, after the Nazis annexed Austria and it became part of the Third Reich, looked to Hitler to protect his Jewish wife, and also to spare from the concentration camps his Jewish colleagues, especially the hugely talented librettist Fritz Löhner-Beda, who had a beautiful Jewish wife and two lovely daughters. Incarcerated in Buchenwald concentration camp, Fritz created an amazing song of courage and defiance in the face of adversity.

For all Lehár's efforts, while Hitler spared his wife, he otherwise refused to intervene, leaving Lehár a broken man as he learnt of the fatal consequences for so many of his Jewish colleagues, including Fritz, as well as their families. Yet Lehár survived the war and was able to be reunited with the fabled Jewish singer, Richard Tauber, with whom he'd collaborated so successfully for many years, while Hitler committed suicide in his bunker, and several members of his cabinet were found guilty of crimes against humanity, sentenced to death and executed.

James Walker February 2023

Prologue

Anton Lehár had been weeping, he simply hadn't been able to help himself.

Tears didn't come easily to him, but this was different. He had been utterly devoted to his older brother Franz Lehár, to whom he believed he owed so much, and now he was gone for ever.

He could but thank God for what had been a peaceful end in his own bed; a painless slipping away into the hereafter, leaving Anton at first in a state of numb sadness.

But then the full impact of his loss had struck home. It had done so with such power that it had forced him to his knees and tears had begun to flow.

Now, as he sat in a comfortable armchair next to his brother's open coffin in the spacious study of his former home, he was feeling calmer, giving him an opportunity for reflection. He knew he would miss him terribly and that his grief would continue to his own dying day, but there would still be so much to remember with a sense of both pride and love.

So, on this chilly autumn day, when his heart was full with memories of the past, he looked out of the window upon a large expanse of well-manicured lawn and neatly trimmed hedges, while musing on Franz's many musical achievements, of which the operetta *The Merry Widow*, which he had composed, was surely the finest.

Echoing in Anton's head, too, were the words *I love your music,* which Adolf Hitler, the man who had led Germany and Austria to utter devastation and disaster, had said to his brother on more than one occasion.

Anton was confident that a legion of people loved his brother's music, but he still shuddered at the thought that Hitler, of all people, should have been one of them.

Franz had been in poor health for some time, losing the will to live since the death of his wife Sophie the previous year. Six years his junior, all his life Anton had looked up to Franz, not just as his elder brother, but also as a friend and above all a supremely talented musician. Now, he pledged to promote his achievements to the end of his days.

It saddened Anton beyond measure that the last ten years or so of his brother's life had been so increasingly difficult, causing his well-earned reputation to suffer as a consequence. These years had also surely been amongst the hardest the human race had ever endured, which he thought said a great deal considering the death and destruction inflicted by the Great War.

Neither Anton nor Franz had ever imagined that the world in which they grew up and then prospered as young men would be swept away so completely by that conflict. What was then visited upon them in their more senior years as the forces of fascism took hold, plunging Europe into yet another war after only twenty years of relative peace, staggered Anton beyond all belief.

He fervently wished that it could have been otherwise and that the Austro-Hungarian Empire, which he and his brother had both called their own even into their middle age, had survived. It was, he knew, pure nostalgia but he still couldn't help but look back fondly at an empire in which many races, Jews included, had lived side-by-side in tolerant, even amicable co-existence under the rule of a benign emperor Franz Joseph.

Had his heir Archduke Franz Ferdinand, so tragically assassinated in Sarajevo, lived to succeed him, perhaps sparing the world such a disastrous war, Anton was also confident that he would have created a liberal, federal structure of government. With a fair wind this might well have enabled the empire to continue to prosper for many years.

So Anton couldn't help but look back to the heady days of his youth, recalling as he did so what hopes he'd had for a bright and prosperous future in a world of so many amazing innovations, which he believed could only be of benefit to mankind.

What he'd not however appreciated at the time was the darker side of this so that when war came it was more terrible than ever before. Indeed, it made him shudder to think that he'd lived long enough to know that entire cities could be obliterated in an instant by a single bomb.

Vienna at the turn of the twentieth century, embracing as it did the beauty of *art nouveau* in many of its new buildings, while enjoying a culture rich in musical and artistic accomplishment, seemed to Anton to embody everything that was best in human civilization. What also excited him most of all was that Franz had been at the very heart of this.

By 1902, while Anton pursued a military career, Franz had become conductor of the prestigious Theater an der Wien, while making progress with his composing, both of operettas and waltzes. Three years later, at the age of thirty-five, Franz composed the operetta *Die Lustige Witwe (The Merry Widow)* making him both rich and famous.

What neither Anton or Franz could possibly have envisaged was that this great achievement would also in later life become something of a curse. Throughout his adult life, Adolf Hitler remained a passionate and vocal admirer of Franz's music. Consequently, many people now associated Franz and his works with the Nazis. Now Anton's prayer, as he mourned his brother, was that this would not taint Franz's legacy, which he was determined to uphold. His fervent hope was that the name Franz Lehár would endure amongst the pantheon of composers, including such great names as Joseph Haydn, Wolfgang Amadeus Mozart, Anton Bruckner, Franz Schubert, Johann Strauss, and Gustav Mahler, who had endowed Austria with their genius.

The telephone next to Anton rang. He grabbed at the receiver. As he'd been expecting, it was Emilie, to whom he'd been married for forty-seven years. She said only, 'Darling, I'm so sorry. How are you?'

'Please don't worry,' Anton replied. 'Franz's death was… well, it was hardly unexpected. Of course, I'm very very upset. He wasn't just my older brother, he was my best friend too. You know, I've been thinking about old times, especially the première of *The Merry Widow* all those years ago. It was such a splendid occasion, and yet…'

1

The Viennese Theatre, Saturday night, 30th December 1905

On that cold winter's night, the First Act of *The Merry Widow* was about to come to an end. On stage the last few bars of its final number were being sung and acted by the operetta's stars, Louis Treumann, aged thirty-three, and Mitzi Günther, aged twenty-six, playing the parts Danilo and Hanna respectively.

As the music reached a crescendo and the curtain came down the audience applauded wildly. Then many of those present started to stamp their feet, shouting out 'Lehár! Lehár! Lehár!'

For a moment, nothing happened on stage, but the audience were not to be denied as they continued to applaud and shout 'Lehár! Lehár! Lehár!'

Thirty-five-year-old Franz Lehár had had his back to the audience whilst he conducted the orchestra. In response to this acclaim, he used his baton in an amiable fashion to beckon the orchestra to sit down, before turning to face the audience. The applause intensified as did the shouts of 'Lehár! Lehár! Lehár!'

Hesitantly at first, Lehár got down from the conductor's podium, then walked briskly onto the stage before standing to face the audience, which fell respectfully silent.

'Ladies and gentlemen, I thank you for your enthusiasm, but this is a breach of protocol. If I am to deserve any applause, I

13

should only be blessed with it at the end of the performance. But I thank you from the bottom of my heart for your enthusiasm! I only hope you are as enthusiastic after the end of Act Three, or I shall feel I have overstayed my welcome!'

The audience laughed and applauded appreciatively at these remarks before falling silent again as Lehár raised a hand.

'I thank you once more... Enjoy your drinks during the interval. As it says in the programme, we shall reconvene here in the auditorium in half an hour.'

He waved politely, and then withdrew from the stage as most of the audience began leaving the auditorium. A few remained, however, amongst them a thin, fresh-faced, sixteen-year-old youth with dark-brown hair and an intense expression, who remained entranced by what he had just seen.

Meanwhile, twenty-nine-year-old Anton Lehár, looking exceedingly smart in his officer's uniform, walked down towards the front of the stage from his seat near the back of the stalls. In so doing he passed the young man without giving him the least attention. Then he exited the auditorium through a door close to the stage and walked hurriedly along the corridor to what he knew was the door to his brother's dressing-room. He knocked gently on it.

'Come in!' Franz called out.

As Anton entered, he could tell that his brother was, not surprisingly, in quite an animated state of mind. A naturally gregarious showman, he was a picture of robust good health, handsome and authoritative in appearance, with a fashionably groomed moustache of impressive proportions. Anton was more slightly built, and in tune with the far more modest moustache adorning his upper lip, possessed an altogether more reserved personality. He went up to Franz and shook his hand.

'My dear brother, what a triumph! You must be so proud.'

This praise brought a smile to Franz's face as he put a hand on Anton's shoulder. 'Thank you, Anton. I know I can always rely on your support. And how's Emilie?'

He was referring to Anton's wife, who was eight months pregnant with their second child and needed to rest, otherwise she would have accompanied him to the performance.

'She's coping but still in some pain with her back, I'm afraid.'

'Oh dear. Still, do give her my fondest regards.'

'Of course I will...'

'You know, I'm slowly allowing myself to feel a tentative sense of triumph after spending the past three months feeling anything but confident. In fact I still worried that we were going to have an unmitigated disaster this evening.'

'Well, you were wrong to do so. Vienna has always adored a great love story.'

At that moment there was a loud knock on the door. Anton glanced at Franz, who nodded to him to open the door.

'Can we come in?' Mitzi asked. The undisputed queen of Viennese operetta, she was young, petite, vivaciously pretty, and above all blessed with a distinctively beautiful soprano voice. Next to her was her fellow star, Louis Treumann. A man with great charm, he was Franz's age but more youthful looking.

'Of course! Of course. You were both wonderful. Thank you so very much.'

'I was so worried,' Mitzi responded. 'I thought they weren't going to like it but they loved it almost from the beginning, even before I came on!'

'I personally thought it was a bit slow at the start,' Louis added. 'But when you appeared, my dear, everything sprang to life, as it always does.'

'You adroit flatterer! Though I suppose you're right.'

'Please, let's not get complacent,' Franz emphasised. 'We do, after all, have two more acts to go.'

The performance ended to more rapturous applause and several curtain calls with Franz coming on stage to acknowledge the further acclaim he received. Once more Anton then joined his brother in his dressing room, as did Louis and Mitzi, and they all proceeded to leave the theatre through its stage door with the intention of joining a party that was being held in Franz's honour at the Café Museum, a short distance away. At that moment, the sixteen-year-old youth who had been so entranced by the performance of *The Merry Widow* approached them nervously.

'Excuse me, sir...' he said, addressing Franz.

'Yes, young fellow, what do you want?'

'I wonder, sir, if you might do me the honour of signing my programme. I have a pen.'

'Yes, by all means. You enjoyed the operetta, I trust?'

'Most certainly, sir, I adored it! I've come all the way from Linz to see it.'

'But that's more than one hundred and fifty kilometres from Vienna!'

'Just over one hundred and eighty-four kilometres, in fact.'

Franz then proceeded to sign the programme, using the pen the youth had also handed him. Then he returned both to him.

'You seem very young to have come here on your own. Aren't your parents with you?'

'No, sir. My papa passed away two years ago, and my beloved mamma is at home in Linz, with my little sister.'

'I'm sorry to hear of your loss. I must say I'm surprised you could even afford the rail fare?'

'I saved up. You see, sir, I love Viennese opera and we hardly have any operas put on in Linz. I heard all about *The Merry Widow* and I so wanted to see it. I've been shovelling snow for my neighbours for more than a month to save the money.'

'So, where are you staying? I mean, it's the dead of winter. You can hardly sleep on a park bench.'

'I'm staying at the Danube rooming-house on Leopold Street.'

'Hm. Some of the chorus members lodge there and they always tell me how awful it is.'

'It's all I can afford, sir. I've got just enough money to buy myself some supper and my bed at the rooming-house before I go home tomorrow. I've paid for my return rail fare already.'

Impressed by the youth's enthusiasm, Franz decided to take cash from his wallet. 'Don't be offended, but here's twenty schillings. Hopefully, it's not too late for you to find somewhere better to stay and have a decent meal.'

'Sir, that's most kind of you...'

'And tell me, what do you want to do when you grow up?'

'I wish be an artist, sir. I want to paint watercolours and become a famous artist and live the life of an artist in Vienna.'

'Well, I very much hope you achieve your ambition.'

'Thank you, sir.'

'By the way, what's your name?'

'It's Adolf, sir... Adolf Hitler.'

Franz nodded kindly. 'Well, good luck to you, Herr Hitler young fellow, and now if you'll excuse me...'

'Of course, sir. It's been a great honour to meet you.'

When Franz and his party reached the Café Museum it was already full of members of the cast. They thronged around Franz and he enjoyed the adulation. His friend and fellow composer, Oscar Straus, was there, too; a man Franz held in high regard, and who wore a moustache even more impressive than Franz's. They were joined as well by the librettists Victor Léon and Leo Stein, who had written the lyrics to *The Merry Widow*. All three men were Jewish, as was Louis Treumann.

Franz and Anton were both aware of this. Neither of them was in the least anti-Semitic and nor did they recognise anti-Semitism as an issue in Viennese society at that time. Both of them were also proud of the fact that the empire encompassed many races, speaking different languages and enjoying different cultures, which in the main were able to co-exist perfectly equally. Indeed, having a Hungarian mother, they believed they embodied this multiculturalism.

Champagne had already been ordered, and once it had arrived and been uncorked and served, Straus was quick to raise his glass in a toast to *The Merry Widow*.

'I predict a world success,' he declared boldly. 'For one thing, the Vilja song alone is so memorable that I've been humming it to myself since I left the theatre.'

Yet despite the comparative success of the first night, Franz was in a sombre mood when he and Anton next met a few days later. In contrast to his outward self-confidence, there was a side to his character, exacerbated by some previous operatic failures, which was easily plagued by self-doubt.

'I'm not yet convinced that this operetta will achieve very much.'

'But Straus loved it and he's surely a good judge.'

'I fear that he was just being - how shall I put it? - professionally polite. Audiences are still disappointing, I'm afraid.'

Anton sought to reassure his brother. 'No, I think you're being too pessimistic. I thought he was completely sincere. Remember, it's still January and the weather miserable, which is bound to keep people indoors.'

Gradually, though, as word spread around the city that *The Merry Widow* was something special, box office takings improved somewhat. By Franz's thirty-sixth birthday in April, it had indeed been performed well over a hundred times. Sadly, even as Franz's masterpiece continued to perform to enthusiastic audiences, his widowed mother Christina passed away peacefully on 6th August. It was some comfort to him, though, that she had lived to attend one of the performances and witness his career fulfil its true potential. She had also told Franz what joy this had brought her, and he would be forever grateful for the encouragement she had given him in pursuing his career as a musician and composer, especially when she offered steadfast support during his early setbacks.

For a time Franz was understandably cast down by her demise, but by now the popularity of *The Merry Widow* was spiralling ever upwards. In fact, in little more than year, Straus's prediction of world success became a reality.

'My dear Anton, guess where *The Merry Widow* is soon to be performed?' Franz asked excitedly when they met for lunch at the Café Landtmann in the Ringstrasse, one of their favourites in the city.

'At the Emperor's Palace?'

Franz grinned. 'No, although that's an interesting possibility. London, the world's greatest city, that's where it's bound! It's agreed that there will need to be a few minor changes to the lyrics, so it has a best possible chance of success in front of a London audience, but the music will remain the same.'

Anton felt suitably impressed and offered his heartiest congratulations. 'And when will this happen?' he asked.

'All being well, in June.'

'That soon?'

'Oh yes, it's perfectly possible. Of course, the lyrics will need to be translated into English, but that's easily accomplished, and there'll be a cast of English performers. Better still, so long as it's well received it will then go to New York. I tell you, it could end up being performed around the globe!'

'We need to drink to this, Franz. Waiter, waiter!' Anton called out excitedly, as he spotted one within hailing distance. 'We need champagne, the best you have.'

2

In the years following the première of *The Merry Widow*, Franz continued to enjoy enormous success. The operetta was very warmly received in London when it opened there in June 1907, and later the same year an American production opened in New York.

At the same time he achieved personal happiness by entering into a relationship with an attractive Jewish woman, Sophie Meth. She was some eight years his junior in age, and they met after he decided to acquire a handsome villa in Bad Ischl, a stunningly beautiful spa town about 270 kilometres to the west of Vienna.

On the evening of 20th June Franz conducted the orchestra of the Viennese Theatre in a performance of his latest work, *The Man with the Three Wives*, which was enjoying a successful run. In a contented state of mind he then left the theatre via its stage door, only to be approached by a young man whom he vaguely recognised.

'Good evening, maestro. I wonder if you remember me?'

'I'm sorry, I don't think I do.., Ah, wait a moment, could you be that boy who approached me on the evening of the première of *The Merry Widow*?'

'Yes, that was me.'

'If I might say so, you look rather different now you're old enough to have grown a small moustache. Remind me of your name.'

'It's Adolf Hitler, maestro. I shall never forget that evening. It was the first time I'd ever been to Vienna. You showed me great kindness. Maestro, would you please do me the great kindness of signing my programme for this evening's performance? Once again, I have a pen with me.'

'I'd be happy to but tell me, what have you been up to since our previous meeting?'

'Sadly, my beloved mother Klara died last year on the first day of winter, December the twenty-first. Since then my poor sister and I have had to fend for ourselves, although we have fortunately both received orphan benefits. Paula is seven years younger than me. She was only eleven when our mother died. Our mother's death has been hard for us to bear; I've had to grow up quickly. Paula is being taken care of by one of our neighbours and goes to school in Linz. I came here earlier this year to try to make my fortune as an artist.'

'Really? And how are you getting on?'

'I'm afraid I've had no success selling my watercolour paintings. I've taken them to show many dealers, but nobody wants to buy them. I do have some money from my mother's estate, but it won't last for ever.'

'Why don't you try to get admission to the Academy of Fine Arts here in Vienna? If you did, it would bring you all sorts of new contacts.'

'I've tried, but I've been rejected.'

'I'm sorry to hear that.' Franz was silent for a moment, then said, 'Listen, young fellow, there's an art dealer I know, Sammy Morgenstern. He's a lover of the arts, a successful art dealer, and a good friend of mine. I have several paintings I've bought from him in my home. Sam's shop is at number twelve, Salzburg Alley. Do you know where that is?'

'No, but I'm sure I can find it.'

'Well, why don't you meet me there at twelve noon the day after tomorrow and I'll introduce you to Morgenstern?'

'You're very kind, Maestro Lehár. Thank you so much for signing my programme.'

'And where are you staying?'

'At the central hostel in the town centre. It's not bad. We're all hard-working men and people observe the lights-out notice after eleven o'clock at night. Even though it's a dormitory, I can get some sleep.'

'But where do you do your work? Don't you have a studio?'

'No, sir, but I'm allowed to paint in a corner of the basement, where the boiler is. Of course, it's pretty hot down there.'

'I'm sure it is. I admire your dedication.'

'Thank you, maestro, I hope it may one day bring me success.'

'Continue to work hard and I'm sure it will. So, young fellow, I'll see you at number twelve, Salzburg Alley, at twelve noon the day after tomorrow.'

'Thank you, maestro. I look forward to it.' Hitler then touched his forehead respectfully before walking off into the night.

The following day, as previously arranged, Franz met Anton at the Café Landtmann for lunch.

'Do you remember that young fellow who asked me to sign his programme on the night of the première of *The Merry Widow*?' Franz asked.

'Yes, I certainly do. I thought there was something a bit strange about him.'

'What do you mean by that?'

'He just seemed very intense.'

'Well, I don't know about that, but he appeared again last night outside the theatre and told me that he's now living here in Vienna and trying to establish himself as an artist. I've offered to help him by introducing him to Sammy Morgenstern, the art dealer I know well.'

'That's kind of you, but how do you know he's any talent?'

'I don't really, but he's clearly ambitious and reminds me of myself at his age. Anyway, helping him will cost me no more than a little of my time. Let Sammy be the judge of his ability.'

'So, how's work going?'

'Well, as you know, my latest operetta has been well received, and *The Merry Widow* continues to be a huge success.'

'Tell me, how many capital cities is it being performed in at the moment?'

'Four, I believe. That's New York, London, Berlin and Paris. I'm making more money than I thought existed in the whole world, and I get invited to all sorts of social functions that I don't especially want to go to. What I most enjoy is spending some time with my friends and doing my work.'

'Composition electrifies your soul. It always has.'

'How well you know me. Yes, I'm never so happy as when I've a tune in my head and I score it in my imagination and can hear it playing in the theatre. It's something I can't possibly explain, but it's absolutely wonderful.'

'Dear brother, I'm sure it is. How is Sophie?'

'… of whom, Anton, I know you still don't approve…'

'Let's just say that as a good Catholic it's taken me time to adjust to the idea of your having an affair with a married woman.'

'Except that it's much more than an affair, as you so put it. And, as you know perfectly well, she's been estranged from her husband since well before I ever met her.'

Anton immediately raised a hand in a conciliatory gesture. 'Of course, dear brother, I fully understand that. She has, I accept, both charm and beauty and I wish you every happiness together. I just don't want your reputation to be damaged.'

'Well, I don't think there's too much danger of that. Her home is still in Bad Ischl and for the time being our relationship continues to be discreet. In time, I hope she will be able to secure a divorce from her husband, and then that can change.'

3

When Franz arrived at Morgenstern's shop the following day, Hitler was already waiting for him. He was standing just outside its front door and Franz noted that he was carrying a brown leather portfolio.

'Good afternoon, Adolf.'

'And to you, maestro. Thank you again for this opportunity.'

'I'm happy to help, I assure you... Right, let's go inside.'

As they entered, Morgenstern's young female assistant came forward to greet them. She was fresh-faced and pretty, with long black hair tied up in a bun. She offered them a demure smile.

'Herr Lehár, how nice to see you again.'

'Good afternoon, Rebekkah. Is Sammy in?'

'Yes, he's doing some valuations of paintings sent in by hopeful aspirants. I know he'll be very pleased to see you, Herr Lehár.'

'Thank you, Rebekkah. This young gentleman here is an acquaintance of mine. His name is Adolf Hitler.'

'Nice to meet you, Herr Hitler,' Rebekkah said politely. 'Please follow me.'

She led them into a spacious gallery that had a tall ceiling and large windows, as well as numerous paintings and engravings on its walls. Morgenstern, who had a vigorous black beard, heavy tortoiseshell-framed spectacles and who wore a black skull-cup or *yarmulke*, was a few years younger than Franz.

Morgenstern was sitting at his desk, examining some paintings, of which there were two piles to his left and a much smaller pile to his right. He looked up and immediately smiled at Franz.

'*Mein Herr*,' Rebekkah said, 'Maestro Lehár and Mr Adolf Hitler are here to see you.'

'Good afternoon, Franz. This is an unexpected pleasure, I must say.' And with that Morgenstern came forward and shook hands with both Franz and Hitler.

'I apologise for interrupting your work, Sammy,' Franz said, 'but Herr Hitler is an aspiring artist and I told him I'd bring him here today in the expectation that you'd be good enough to take a look at his work.'

'No need to apologise, Franz. I can see he has a portfolio with him. I'll be pleased to examine it.'

'Would anyone like a coffee?' Rebekkah enquired.

'Yes, that would be very nice, Rebekkah,' Morgenstern responded and both Franz and Hitler agreed.

'Please permit me to assist you while Herr Morgenstern examines my portfolio,' Hitler added, fixing his eyes on Rebekkah and smiling at her.

'Why, thank you, Herr Hitler, that's very kind of you. Come with me then.'

At the same time she returned Hitler's smile with a somewhat flirtatious one of her own before leading him through a side door in the direction of the kitchen.

'Rebekkah's such a nice girl and efficient, too. I know I'll miss her once she marries.'

'Is she engaged, then?' Franz asked.

'Oh no, but it's surely only a question of time. So tell me, how did you become acquainted with this callow-looking youth?'

Franz duly explained. 'And sadly he suffered a bereavement last year when his mother died. His sister, who's considerably younger than him, is being looked after by neighbours. He's come to Vienna to try to make his way in the world as an artist. I've not the least idea how good his work is and I'm no judge, anyway, but I normally find with artistic people that if they're enthusiastic - as he is - it at least takes them some way.'

'Perhaps,' replied Morgenstern thoughtfully, 'but not necessarily very far. When all's said and done, there's something presumptuous about assuming that the world will necessarily want to pay for the marks one puts on a canvas or on a piece of cartridge paper. Well, let me take a look at his work.'

Morgenstern picked up the portfolio and glanced through it fairly briefly but with an expert eye.

'All right, I'm willing to buy two of these watercolours. They're not great, but yes, they have a certain energy about them that I like. More to the point, I have customers willing to pay for these kinds of works. Watercolour landscapes are becoming something of a rarity in Vienna as I find so many new artists think only of using oils, or tempera.'

At that moment, Hitler and Rebekkah returned, with Hitler carrying a tray that had cups and a pot of coffee on it.

'Adolf, I'm pleased to tell you that Sammy has agreed to buy two of your paintings.'

'Really?' said Hitler, setting the tray down on a table nearby. 'That's wonderful. Thank you very much indeed, sir.'

'It's a pleasure,' Morgenstern responded. 'I'll offer 125 crowns for the painting of the Vienna state opera house and the same amount for this picture, which you entitle "the courtyard of the old residency in Munich". Have you ever been there?'

'No, sir. I painted it from a photograph.'

'And so you imagined the colours?'

'Yes. Herr Morgenstern, I really can't overstate my gratitude.'

'Well, these are decent paintings and I expect I can sell them to my clients. How about creating some more watercolours of Austrian and German buildings? Painting architecture seems to be your strong point.'

'Thank you. I love beautiful buildings.'

'As do I, and so do many of my clients.'

'Thank you so much, Herr Morgenstern, for your kind words. If I may, I'd like to invite you all to have lunch at my expense.'

Morgenstern smiled. 'Young man, I'm paying you reasonably well for the two paintings, but if you go round inviting people to lunch, you'll soon be poor. You need to conserve your money.'

'I appreciate the offer, Adolf,' Franz added. 'Permit me to take us all to lunch, at my expense. I suggest we go to Café Central on Herrengasse.'

Hitler cried out at this suggestion. 'Oh my goodness! I've always dreamt of going there, but I've never been able to afford it.'

'Well, let it be my treat, young fellow,' said Franz, 'to celebrate the sale of your paintings.'

Morgenstern invited Rebekkah to join them, and having paid Hitler the two hundred and fifty crowns for the two watercolours and locked up the shop, they all adjourned to the famous Café Central, which exuded wealth and elegance. Because of Franz's growing fame, he and his guests were treated like royalty and all able to feel a sense of privilege, though nothing could insulate them from the smoky atmosphere created by so many of their fellow diners imbibing tobacco in one form or another.

They had barely ordered their meals when Hitler began to cough repeatedly whilst the expression on his face demonstrated that he was unhappy.

'I'm sorry, it's the smoke that's making me cough. I really don't like it.'

'You're not a smoker then, I take it?' Franz asked him.

'Certainly not, I think it's a most unhealthy habit... Please forgive me for saying that, though, if you...'

'Smoke?'

'Quite.'

'Just the occasional cheroot or cigar and certainly never at the dinner table. The same goes for you, doesn't it, Sammy?'

'Yes, Franz, there's far too much smoking in all Vienna's cafés, I think. But tell me, Adolf, what ambitions do you have, apart from becoming a successful artist?'

'I have no other ambition apart from that one, sir. Becoming a famous artist would for me be the summit of all my ambitions. My wish is to bring people joy through my art and to make a good living from it. That's really all I aspire to.'

'Even so, have you thought of becoming an architect? It's not a bad idea, as you draw and paint buildings so well.'

'I've looked into that possibility, sir, but it means studying for many years and I do not really find architecture an especially congenial profession. Besides, I have no money to fund my studies. Everything I earn that I can spare I send back home to help support my beloved little sister Paula. It was very difficult for me to say goodbye to her when I came to live in Vienna, but there was nothing for me in Linz so I had no choice.'

'Well, I think your concern for your sister is entirely to your credit,' Rebekkah commented.

'I'm glad you think so. Paula is truly the apple of my eye and I miss her very much. She has almost nothing so I send her what I can.'

'Well, I assure you, from this moment your sister need not have any more financial worries,' Franz declared. 'How old is she?'

'She'll be thirteen in January.'

'And is she still at school?'

'Yes, until she's fourteen.'

'Then I will make arrangements to give you some money every month for, let's say, the next two years, which you can send to her.'

Hitler looked astonished. 'Would you... would you really do that, maestro? It would be exceptionally generous of you.'

'Most certainly, I will. After all, it's hardly your little sister's fault she has been left without a mother or father. The world sees fit to consider my work important and pays me handsomely for it so this is the least I can do. I have no children of my own and now no likelihood of any, and your sister sounds to me an extremely worthy cause.'

'Well, I really can't thank you enough.'

'There's no need to thank me at all, except perhaps at some point by painting a picture I could display in my home.'

'But let me buy it first, please, so I can sell it to Austria's greatest composer at a profit!' Morgenstern added, jokingly. 'But tell me, Adolf, who most influences you? I mean, which artist do you most admire?'

'I'm a keen admirer of neo-classicism, but my favourite artist of all is Rudolf von Alt. His death in 1905 was a great tragedy for Austrian art.'

'I agree, but he was, after all, ninety-two years old, so he had fulfilled his potential in so many ways. Have you seen his self-portrait of 1890?'

'Certainly. I admire it very much. And also his famous portrait of the austere lady, which I think he did much earlier in his career.'

'Yes, in 1838. It's one of my favourite paintings of his. I possessed it once, nearly ten years ago, but I sold it after I received an offer for it I simply could not refuse... I'm impressed, young man. I've never met any other young artist who has mentioned von Alt right away when I ask them what their influences are. They tend to refer to the great painters of classicism, but, like you, I am an ardent Austrian and proud of our home-grown painters, including von Alt.'

'I myself am also very proud to be an Austrian and to follow humbly in the traditions of the great Austrian masters.'

Morgenstern and Hitler continued to chat amicably during the course of the meal, which Franz hoped boded well for an ongoing relationship.

Once it was over, Hitler also took the opportunity of again expressing his thanks in an appropriately fulsome way, which reassured Franz that he had been right to be so supportive of him. Glancing at his watch, he realised that he was in danger of being late for a journey he was about to undertake to Bad Ischl so having settled the bill for the meal, he was the first to leave.

'We must meet again soon, Adolf, to finalise arrangements for the payments I'm going to be making to your sister. Here's my card, with my address. You're welcome to visit me in ten days' time at noon. Now, I really must be going. My best wishes to you, Sammy, and also to you, Rebekkah.'

More than succeeding in establishing a working relationship with Sammy Morgenstern, Hitler had also been attracted to Rebekkah. By the way she had smiled at him and seemed relaxed in his presence he also hoped that this attraction was mutual, so a few days later plucked up the courage to return to Morgenstern's shop where he was able to speak to her. Morgenstern was in his back office with a client.

'Would you walk out with me this coming Sunday?' Hitler asked Rebekkah.

'Yes, Adolf, I'd be pleased to,' she replied, with a smile.

4

Vienna's public park the Volksgarten, four months later

It was a Sunday afternoon in late March and in the finest of Vienna's public parks with its ornate fountains and classical temples, there was a touch of spring in the air. In the period of time since they had first met, Hitler's feelings for Rebekkah had deepened to the point where he believed he was falling in love with her. He imagined, too, that his feelings were reciprocated, though any intimacy with Rebekkah had as yet been confined to some chaste kisses. Furthermore, he was acutely aware that he was in no position to make any proposal of marriage, as his money was fast running out.

As they walked together in the Volksgarten that afternoon, Rebekkah seemed distracted, which increasingly irritated him as he had previously enjoyed their conversations about a host of topics including art and architecture, encouraging him to believe that they had a great deal in common.

'Are you feeling all right?' he finally asked her. 'You don't seem yourself.'

'No, I'm sorry, Adolf. It's just that, well, I've given a lot of thought to this and decided that I don't want to walk out with you any longer.'

Hitler was totally stunned by this revelation. 'But why? I thought we were getting on so well and had much in common.'

'Even so, I just don't think we're suited. I mean not in a romantic way.'

'I see.' Hitler was now beginning to feel angry.

'Please try not to be too upset. I just thought it best to be honest with you before... I mean before you got a false idea of where our relationship was heading.'

'Is that I'm not good enough for you? I know I'm just a poor, struggling artist.'

'No, no, that's got nothing to do with it.'

'I don't believe you. Haven't I been attentive enough? Haven't I shown you every courtesy?' He was now speaking in a loud, angry voice.

Rebekkah sighed. 'I think you've just demonstrated why we're not suited.'

'What on earth do you mean by that?'

'I just mean that you get too angry and that frightens me.'

'No I don't. That's nonsense.'

'I'm sorry, but I think you do. But look, I'd like us to still be friends.'

'Oh, do you indeed, you Jewish bitch?'

'How dare you call me that!' Rebekkah was now close to tears.

'I'm sorry, you provoked me.'

'I was simply being honest and saving us both a lot of even greater heartache. I'm proud to be Jewish, by the way, and don't take kindly to your racial slur.'

'Well, it's your loss. One day I shall have a great career and be famous.'

'I somehow doubt that.'

'Well, if that's your attitude, good riddance to you.'

Rebekkah now began to cry.

'Look,' said Hitler, in a suddenly pleading tone, 'please don't do that. Just say you'll reconsider. I really care for you.'

'No, I'm sorry. My mind's made up. It's for the best, I know it is. But I still wish you every success, of course I do.'

Hitler was no longer listening. Instead, turning his back on her, he walked rapidly away.

'Adolf,' she called out to him, but he ignored her, and carried on walking until he had left the park far behind him.

He told himself that her rejection didn't matter and that her criticism of his character was simply wrong, but in truth she had deeply hurt not only his pride but also his sense of self-respect. What's more, although he insisted to himself that he'd only called her a Jewish bitch because she'd provoked him, he swore that he'd never again be foolish enough to fall for any Jewish woman, no matter how pretty she might be.

5

February 1913

Following Franz's display of generosity, the next four years proved to be a real struggle for Hitler as he scraped no better than a partial living, selling a few paintings to Sammy Morgenstern and other Viennese art dealers. Pride also prevented him from turning to Franz for further help until finally he grew desperate enough to swallow this. Franz's continued financial help for Paula was, Hitler knew, still making a big positive difference to his sister's life, but Hitler had ensured that all Franz's help went straight to Paula.

One afternoon as it was just growing dark, Hitler knocked on the front door of Franz's apartment. He was a thin, bedraggled figure with a sallow complexion, his overcoat worn in places, his unpolished shoes in urgent need of repair.

'Good afternoon, maestro, I'm sorry to trouble you.'

'Goodness me, Adolf, how are you? It must be two years since we last met.'

'I'm surviving as best I can, maestro, but to be frank it isn't easy. I wonder if I could take up a few minutes of your valuable time.'

'By all means. I do have to go out in about an hour, though.'

'A quarter of that is all I ask.'

Franz showed him into his expensively furnished lounge,

central to which was a large gas fire that was giving out a substantial amount of heat. For Hitler, it was a welcome contrast to the bitter cold of a bleak February day with snow lying on the ground. Franz motioned him to sit down and then asked if he would like a cup of tea or coffee.

'A cup of tea would be most welcome, thank you.'

'I'll just tell my maid Dorothy to make us some.'

Dorothy, who would never see fifty again, had been in Franz's employment for some years and was perfectly reliable. When it came to everyday tasks she was as good as a wife to him, but when in Vienna he still missed Sophie, who in the absence of a divorce continued to reside in Bad Ischl.

'So how can I help you?' Franz asked as soon as he returned.

'I have to confess that I'm so short of money that I have come here to ask if you would show me the kindness of lending me enough schillings to see me through to the end of the month.'

'Aren't you able to sell any of your paintings any longer?'

'I sell a few but unfortunately there isn't the demand that there once was. I'm working on some new paintings at the moment but I'm already behind with my rent and don't want to end up on the streets.'

'All right, I'm happy to help you. I have an idea, too. I'd like to commission you to paint a picture for me of my beautiful villa in Bad Ischl.'

'Maestro, the opportunity to create such a painting would be a great honour for me.'

'Well, consider yourself appointed to the job. I can give you an advance of a thousand schillings today.'

'Thank you, maestro, that's most kind of you.'

'I want you to see the villa in the flesh, so I will cover the cost of your train fare to Bad Ischl and once there you can stay in the villa for as long as you need to as my guest. As it happens, I shall be going there at the end of the month so we can travel together.'

Once again Hitler expressed his profound thanks and within moments Dorothy appeared with a tray.

'Have you heard from your sister?' Franz asked Hitler as the tea was poured.'

'Paula writes to me almost every week.'

'And how is she?'

'She still misses me and I'd like to return to Linz soon to see her. Every one of those one hundred and eighty-four kilometres feels painful to me.'

'I quite understand that, but look, once you've seen the villa and completed your preliminary drawings, I'll happily give you a further advance and you can travel back to Linz.'

'That's so kind of you, maestro. Once again, you're my saviour.'

'It's the least I can do, really.'

6

Three weeks later

Hitler now faced a dilemma. At the end of February, just before he was due to travel to Bad Ischl with Franz, he'd received notification that he was required to undertake a period of national service in the Austrian army, beginning at the end of May.

He'd known for some while that there was a likelihood of this happening but had put it to the back of his mind, in the hope that having moved addresses frequently in Vienna he'd somehow succeeded in evading this summons. Now it had finally caught up with him, it wasn't that he was opposed to military service per se, but rather that he no longer felt any enthusiasm for doing so in the Austrian army.

The longer he had lived in Vienna the more he had become disillusioned with the Austro-Hungarian Empire and its multicultural identity. As a consequence he was now seriously considering leaving Austria altogether in order to live in Germany.

Once he'd finished the work of sketching the villa in Bad Ischl, a task that took him just a couple of days, he duly travelled to Linz by train. Upon his arrival on what was a Sunday afternoon, he then went straight to the house where his sister Paula, now aged seventeen, was still living with her guardian,

40

Magda Schneider, who was a widow. It was to be his first meeting with his sister in five years.

'Hello, Magda. It's me, Adolf, Paula's brother,' he said to her when she answered his knock on her front door and at first gave him rather a blank stare. 'I trust Paula received my letter telling her that I would be coming.'

'Adolf, of course. I'm sorry, I just didn't recognise you at first. You've grown up so much! Yes, she did receive your letter and she's been so excited at the thought of seeing you again. Do come in.'

'Paula, Adolf is here,' she called out as Hitler entered the hallway.

Paula appeared at the top of the stairs, no longer the child that Hitler remembered but rather a young woman with looks that instantly reminded him of their late mother.

'Adolf!' she cried out, rushing down the stairs and then practically falling into his arms with happiness. 'It's just wonderful to see you, beloved brother. I can hardly believe you're here.'

'Dearest Paula, how lovely you are.'

Over supper, Hitler told Paula and Magda how fortunate he was to have someone as famous as Franz as a patron, before going on to share with them the difficult position he found himself in because of being called up for military service.

'To be honest with you, I don't want to serve in the Austrian army.'

'Why ever not?' Magda asked him.

'Bluntly, I've come to despise the empire. It's weak and decadent. What I have in mind is moving to Germany and living in Munich. I've heard so many wonderful things about the country and have come to believe it's the greatest on earth.

Munich's only about three hours from here by rail. I'd like to visit it soon for just a couple of days and I wonder, Paula, if you'd care to accompany me?'

'I'd love to, but I have my work. As I've told you in my letters, I'm a shop assistant now.'

'But as I've just said it would only be for a couple of days. We could go on Friday afternoon and return on Sunday. You could go sick, couldn't you?'

'Yes, all right, I'd love to come with you. That is, so long as you're sure you can afford to pay for both of us?'

'Thanks to the advance I've received from Lehár, I'm quite sure I can.'

Six days later, Hitler and Paula were strolling together in the main city square of Munich in front of the Frauenkirche, Munich's cathedral. It was late morning so they agreed to seek out a suitable café.

Having found one overlooking the river Isar, they enjoyed the coffees they'd ordered and Hitler began to enthuse about the city.

'I feel Germany's history and splendour here and that this is a place in which I can be truly happy. What's more, in the event of another war between Germany and France, I'll willingly join the German army. I'm not afraid of death on the battlefield and I think I'd enjoy being a soldier. Of course, I'll never lose my artistic temperament, but I expect there's room for that in the army, too. I just know I can't fight for the Austro-Hungarian Empire. I will not risk my life or my health for people who are not either German or Austrian.'

'Do you really think a war is likely?'

'Yes, from everything I've read, I think it's inevitable. It's just a question of time.'

'But don't you think war would be a terrible thing?'

'No, not at all. It would be an opportunity for the German Reich to secure its destiny as the greatest nation on earth.'

'Well, I don't know about that. Anyway, if you come to live here in Munich I'll see just as little of you as ever.'

'Once I've established myself here, you could come and live here, too.'

'Yes, perhaps I could, but, you know, I don't think Austria is that different from Germany. After all, we speak the same language.'

'To an extent I agree. Who knows, if the German Reich does fulfil its destiny and the Austro-Hungarian Empire continues to decay so it is no longer tainted by lesser nations, Germany and Austria could one day be united in a Greater Reich with a pure identity. Ideally, they certainly *belong* together.'

'So, your mind's made up that this is where you want to come and live?'

'Most certainly.'

7

Bad Ischl, April 1913

With the coming of spring, Anton and Emilie arrived to stay with Franz and Sophie at their villa in Bad Ischl for a week, in response to a longstanding invitation that had enabled Anton to arrange leave from his military duties.

One morning, during the course of their stay, Franz was sitting at his piano in his study, composing, when there was a knock on the door.

'Yes, who's there?'

'It's me, Anton. May I come in?'

'Why, of course. And there's no need to knock. You're my brother, for heaven's sake.'

'I don't like to just walk in when you're composing. I like that tune I heard through the door. Is it a new *Merry Widow*?'

'No, I doubt it. Just a few random ideas I'm toying with at the moment.'

'Well, I'm sorry to disturb you.'

'You haven't, I assure you. Do sit down.'

Anton did as he was asked and Franz then asked him if Emilie was enjoying her stay.

'Yes, very much. She told me only this morning how much she appreciates the peace and beauty of this place. We'd like to go for a walk by the river this afternoon, if you and Sophie would care to join us?'

'Yes, that would be very nice. By the way, I've received a letter this morning from Adolf Hitler. You know I mentioned to you that he was here not so long ago to make drawings for the painting I've commissioned from him. He just stayed a couple of nights in the guest room.'

'Was he good company?'

'Well, Sophie and I only really saw him over dinner. He worked hard, I think making lots of sketches of the house in the two days he was here. He was perfectly polite to Sophie and they seemed to get on, but even so, I wouldn't say he was especially affable.'

'Any idea why?'

'No, he just seemed rather self-absorbed, even - I'm sorry to say - troubled.'

'From what you've told me, his artistic career hasn't exactly blossomed.'

'True enough. Anyway, here's the letter.' And with that Franz went to his desk, picked up the letter and then handed it to Anton.

My dear Maestro Lehár, I hope this finds you well. I'm working hard on the painting, and I hope to finish it in about three weeks, whereupon I plan to come to Bad Ischl to deliver it to you personally. I am at present in Linz. but after visiting Munich recently with my sister Paula, I've fallen in love with Germany and intend to go and live there after I deliver the painting. I intend to live as an artist in Munich and I would be grateful if you could favour me with further commissions. I shall send you

my address there as soon as I know it. Please remember me to
your charming lady wife.

Yours in art and friendship,
Adolf Hitler

Once he had finished reading Hitler's letter, Anton asked
Franz, 'Will you give him any more commissions?'

'I rather doubt it. I only gave him the one I did because he
came to me for a loan, saying he'd fallen on hard times.'

'Then it's hardly surprising he's decided to make a fresh start
elsewhere. For all we know he may have needed to escape his
creditors and that's what was troubling him during his stay.
I'm fond of Germany myself, though I can't say I've any desire
to live there. The Kaiser is too much of a Prussian warmonger
for my liking.'

'I agree. I draw all my inspiration from Austria, my homeland, and especially from Vienna. In my opinion, Germany's
less beautiful, and there's no doubt in my mind that its people
tend to be much bossier. When it comes to music, too, whilst
I admire Beethoven, I prefer Mozart. You know, it's always
struck me as a great shame that our national anthems use the
identical melody, when I like our lyrics more...'

Franz returned to his piano and started to play the opening
bars of Austria's national anthem, singing as he played.

'Austria, be blessed forever,
Glorious nation of our soul,
Let her beauty perish never
Immortalised in our fair scroll.'

Franz added: 'Our words are so much better, don't you think, than the German words, *Germany, Germany, over everything/ ruler of the mortal world*. That's so aggressive!'

'I agree. It's just what I don't like about it as a country.'

'Anyhow, I shall respond to Adolf's letter wishing him every success in Germany.'

8

December 1913

Oscar Straus, Franz's fellow composer and friend, who had accurately predicted a world success for *The Merry Widow*, was once again hosting a Christmas party at his apartment in Vienna to which Franz had been invited.

Straus was always generous with the food and alcohol he provided and anyone of importance in Vienna's musical community could be expected to attend. It was also an occasion that Franz had come to enjoy for its conviviality in the company of so many friends and colleagues.

Occasionally, too, he was drawn into rewarding conversations with someone he'd not previously met, and on this particular evening Straus introduced him to a man who was to play an important part in his career for the next twenty years and more.

'Franz, this is Fritz Löhner-Beda, whom I don't believe you know. He's a very talented young writer.'

'It's a great pleasure, maestro,' Fritz said. 'I've seen you at the theatre on several occasions and I very much admire your work.'

Franz was struck by his vigorous handshake and engaging manner, and as they fell into conversation Fritz was forthcoming in telling him that he'd been born in Bohemia thirty years previously, had once been a lawyer, and was of Jewish extraction.

'My family moved to Vienna when I was just five years old. When I was sixteen, they changed their surname to Löhner from Lowy to make the name seem less Jewish. I didn't really approve; I feel no shame about being Jewish. Indeed, I regard it as being a club to which it's a privilege to belong, not that people who don't belong are in any way to be blamed for that! Still, I can't really blame my parents for not wanting to make our Jewishness too obvious.'

'And how did you get into the legal profession?' Franz asked.

'After leaving school I studied law at Vienna University. While I was there, I was a member of the Jewish student association. I came to regard the profession as stultifying my talents as a writer. I've always been obsessed with words. I love the German language. It's so astonishingly rich. I also like concocting rhymes; the more outlandish the better, as far as I'm concerned.'

'Yes, and I love composing music that makes the most of the rhymes in the lyrics. So how did you start out as a writer?'

'I'd saved some money from my time as a lawyer and decided to give myself three months to see if I could find any writing work. It went surprisingly well, almost from the beginning. I've written a fair number of satires, sketches and poems. I only make a modest living from it, but I enjoy writing infinitely more than practising the law and I've absolutely no intention of going back to being a lawyer.'

'I admire your tenacity.'

'Thank you. I've had an idea for a story, which could easily, I think, be adapted into an operetta. It's only a light-hearted story, but, after all, many great operettas have such stories.'

'Yes, that's true, but it's what the audiences want, I believe.

So, what's this story about?'

'A young astronomer, a stargazer - I thought in homage to you, maestro, I would call him Franz - has been bringing up his sister, Kitty, after their parents' death. His visit to her finishing school is eagerly awaited by Kitty and her three closest friends. Her friends all flirt with him outrageously, and he gets himself into such a series of romantic messes that he ends up being engaged to all three of them!'

'An intriguing premise! I like the idea of an operetta about an astronomer.'

'Thank you, maestro. Yes, Kitty's friends are all quite mad about him, and indeed quite mad generally, including one of her friends, who is quite ready to renounce her previous admirer, who's also fallen for Kitty. But that's only the start of the intrigues, which grow ever more complicated when the three girls' parents hire a detective to investigate Franz's financial state. Many feminine wiles and plot stratagems are required to bring matters to a happy ending. Mind you, I need to write it first! So far I've only worked out the overall plot.'

Franz smiled. 'And I would need to sit down at my piano and think of some tunes. As you can probably imagine, I'm always being asked to provide Vienna with another *Merry Widow*. I've so far failed to do that, so perhaps this astronomical story may offer the project I'm looking for. Now, Fritz, I wouldn't expect you to write the libretto on a speculative basis, so drop me a line about some reasonable sum you would expect to get paid for the commission, and I'll see what I can do. Send me the libretto when it's finished.'

'It will be a pleasure, maestro.'

'You know, I always know when I like an idea someone

50

presents to me, because I start to hear tunes in my head that might fit in with the libretto.'

'You mean even before you've read the libretto?'

'Yes, believe it or not, I have a tune in my head now - I'm not sure where it came from, but then I never am - in which a man and woman in *The Stargazer* operetta meet for the first time.'

'Really? how does the tune go?'

'Like this...' Franz began to hum a lively melody.

'Bravo! Did that literally just come to you?'

'Well yes, it did. I'm lucky that that happens to me.'

The two of them continued to chat, pleased to find that they had a natural rapport that in the event was to hold them in very good stead for many years to come. What they could not know, though, was that by the time Straus held his next Christmas party, it was an altogether more subdued occasion, as Europe had plunged into a terrible war.

9

Sunday 28th June 1914

There had been talk of war between the so-called Great Powers in Europe for some years. It had led to a series of alliances in the hope that this would prevent such a catastrophe. All the while, Germany had laid its plans, in the event of war, for an invasion of France through Belgium, whilst at the same time modernising and expanding its military capacity both on land and at sea.

Though there were many who rightly feared the prospect of war, many others, including Adolf Hitler, were excited by it. What no one could predict, however, was what the catalyst for such a war would be, nor when it would occur, until a fateful Sunday in Sarajevo, the capital of the Austro-Hungarian Province of Bosnia and Herzegovina.

It was a pleasantly warm day, which began badly for Archduke Franz Ferdinand, the heir to the Habsburg throne, and his wife Archduchess Sophie, when a bomb was thrown at their car. However, it missed and they were uninjured. Others were less fortunate and out of concern for their welfare the couple insisted on visiting them at the local hospital. It was a laudable but fatal decision.

As the expensive-looking phaeton automobile in which they were travelling was driven down a side road, it passed an alleyway from which nineteen-year-old Gavrilo Princip leapt out, firing a bullet into Sophie's abdomen and another bullet into Franz Ferdinand's neck. Princip then dropped his gun and ran off, disappearing down a side alley.

'For heaven's sake! What happened to you?' Sophie said to her husband, before sinking from her seat, her head falling between his knees. He leant over her.

'Sophie! Sophie dear! Don't die! Live for our children!'

He then sagged down himself, his plumed hat falling from his head, as Count Harrach, who had been standing on the running board of the car, seized hold of the collar of his uniform in order to hold him up.

'Is your Imperial Highness suffering very badly?'

'It is nothing,' the archduke responded repeatedly but his voice was barely audible and he soon expired. Sophie, too, was dead before they could get her to hospital, leaving their three children, a girl and two boys, orphans.

The domino-like effect of this terrible assassination then plunged most of Europe into war within a little matter of five weeks. The German declaration of war in the Odeonplatz in Munich on 2nd August was greeted with jubilant acclaim by a large crowd, amongst whom was Adolf Hitler, cheering along with the rest.

10

Franz was in the study of his apartment in Vienna, sitting at his piano, and doing his best to concentrate on composing a piece of music for *The Stargazer*. He found it hard to concentrate, though, as his mind kept straying into thoughts of war and what its consequences might be. Then he heard the doorbell ring. He ignored this, knowing that his maid would answer it, and a few moments later as he continued to play this piece on the piano, Anton walked in wearing his military uniform.

'Hello Franz, I like that music you're playing. Is it new?'

'Welcome, Anton, it's for that new operetta *The Stargazer* I mentioned to you. Fritz Löhner-Beda provided me with the libretto, which is excellent. I predict a success, although not on the scale of *The Merry Widow*, especially at this of all times.'

'Hm, you've mentioned Löhner-Beda's name before, too. He's a lawyer turned writer, isn't he?'

'Yes, that's right. I think he's seriously talented. So, I see you're in uniform.'

'Yes, I have to report to my regiment later today.'

'So you'll be fighting?'

'Unquestionably. For all I know, my dear brother, this may be the last time you see me alive.'

'Don't even begin to talk like that. Have you any idea how

long this war is going to last? There's talk of it all being over by Christmas.'

'I fear that that may be far too optimistic, now what started out as merely a war between our empire and Serbia has escalated into an appalling, all-out war across the continent, involving Germany, France, Russia and Great Britain, too. At least it's some comfort that that devil, Princip, is now languishing deservedly in jail for his wicked crime.'

'I live in the world of composition, not politics, but I just feel this is a dreadful calamity.'

'Yes, I agree. Too many people throughout Europe have been hungry for war and Princip's insane deed presented them with the perfect excuse. Too many people seem to have forgotten what war is really like: the agonising deaths, the squalor, the foul food, being cut off from one's loved ones and maybe never seeing them again, the waste of money and the wholesale squandering of resources.'

'That I can understand but why are so many, who should know better, blind to this?'

'There's a prevailing view that going to war is a glorious thing, like a sort of international football competition. The fact that people usually come home safely from football matches, by railway train or in an automobile even if they lose, rather than in a coffin, seems to have escaped the notice of many of the would-be players.'

'For a military man I think you're very cynical about this matter.'

'No, I've merely studied the wars that have taken place over the last half-century and taken due account of advances in technology, especially the effectiveness of the modern machine gun. Obviously, I realised when I joined the army that I might have to fight one day. I love Austria, even though I think we are ruled by fools. One thing I can predict, and I don't expect any reward for doing so: if this war is lost it will mean the end of the Austro-Hungarian Empire. A new Europe will be born, and goodness knows what *that* will be like.'

Franz shook his head in dismay at the very thought of this. 'And will we lose?'

'I'm no fortune teller, so I really do not know. Rightly or wrongly, we've saddled ourselves to the German Reich, so if that falls Austria will fall with it.'

'... which could mean the end of the Europe we know and love, couldn't it?'

'Yes, if the very worst happened the established order could be completely overthrown. Certainly, the stakes could hardly be higher.'

'But I was thinking more of the cultural repercussions. I mean if everything falls into the abyss, will anyone still have time for light-hearted, dare I say frivolous, operettas?'

'I wouldn't worry too much on that account, Franz. Once the blood-letting is over, people will want to find refuge in escapism more than ever.'

'Then I'll do my best to keep the theatre I know and love in good health, and perhaps when this madness is over, people will see I've done the right thing.'

'I'm sure they will. More than that while the war lasts there's likely to be an increased demand for catchy tunes that are either patriotic or lift morale.'

'True, I'll give some thought to that. Anyway, dear brother, take the greatest care of yourself. I really don't want to lose you.'

'Like any man I can only place myself in God's hands and hope for the best.'

The two men embraced, for all they knew for the last time.

11

14th August 1914

In his enthusiasm for the German Reich to fulfil its destiny as the greatest power on earth, Adolf Hitler didn't waste much time in seeking to volunteer for military service. Along with many other similarly minded young men he was happy to queue for as long as it took outside the recruiting office of the Bavarian army.

Here he fell into conversation with the man immediately in front of him who also appeared to be in his mid-twenties and said his name was Becker. He was blond-haired and more robust looking than Hitler, and revealed that he was an agricultural labourer on a farm not far from Munich.

After waiting as patiently as they could for about half an hour, Becker was then called forward by the recruiting officer who was seated behind a desk and gave him his name, date of birth and confirmed his German nationality.

'And you want to fight for your country in the war?'

'Yes, sir, more than anything else in the world.'

'Good man, consider yourself recruited. Go to see my colleague in the room through the door on my left.'

Becker then gave Hitler a smile before departing in that direction, and he stepped forward to confirm his name and date of birth, being 20th April 1889.

'And what's your nationality?'

'German, sir.'

'I notice you speak with an Austrian accent.'

'Yes, sir. It's true I was born there, but I came to live here in Germany some while ago and think of myself as German. Certainly, my loyalty is to the German Fatherland and the Kaiser.'

'Hm, so it follows you want to fight for the German army?'

'Very much so, sir, that is my dream.'

'All right then, you're in...'

Hitler clicked his heels respectfully. 'Thank you, sir! Thank you for enabling me to fulfil my destiny!'

The recruiting officer snorted. 'We aim to please. Do your best to aim to kill.'

As Hitler headed in the same direction as Becker, he felt an immense pride. The eyes of the man Franz Lehár knew as a watercolour artist blazed with thrilled excitement.

Hitler had no doubt that, at the age of twenty-five, he had finally found his destiny.

12

Promoted swiftly to the rank of major, Anton Lehár was soon given command of an infantry battalion on the Russian front in Poland. Then, within months, he suffered such a severe wound to his left leg as a result of shellfire, he thought it would require amputation if his life was to be spared.

'Anton, Anton, are you awake?' He was vaguely aware of a familiar voice speaking to him. He opened his eyes to see Franz's anxious face looking down at him.

'Dear brother,' Anton said weakly, 'it's so good of you to come.'

Franz smiled at him. 'As soon as I heard what had happened I was determined to do so without delay.'

'You find me in a sorry state, I'm afraid. The doctor says my leg will have to be amputated.'

'We'll have to see about that. I've been in touch with a couple of specialists. They should be here within the hour if they want their fees paid.'

'You shouldn't have gone to such trouble. What about the expense?'

'Nonsense, you know I can afford that.'

'I'll have to pay you back.'

'No you won't. You've been wounded fighting for your country while I continue to compose. Regard it as a gift in gratitude for your courage, or I'll be most offended.'

Anton winced in pain. His throat, too, was desperately dry so he gestured towards his bedside cabinet where a glass of water was standing. Franz immediately placed it in Anton's hand, enabling him to drink deeply from it before becoming so overcome by the agony he was in that he wanted to cry out.

'You're still in much pain, aren't you?' said Franz.

Anton nodded and Franz placed a comforting hand on his shoulder.

'I won't leave you, Anton, I swear it.'

Over the coming days Franz was true to his word, remaining by Anton's side day and night, taking his temperature, encouraging him to eat, and above all to find the will to live.

Furthermore, within the hour two specialists did indeed arrive at Anton's bedside, waking him from a fitful sleep. With their greying beards and long frock coats, they reminded him of the wise men from the Bible, and after a painful examination of his leg, they began conferring with one another. Then one of them, who wore spectacles, spoke to him in a solicitous voice.

'Major Lehár, we believe that your leg can be saved. We will talk to the doctors here in order to agree the necessary treatment.'

Anton's sense of relief at this news was immeasurable as slowly but surely, with Franz's help, for which he knew he owed him so much, he began to make a recovery. Long months of convalescence lay ahead, but Franz was a frequent visitor, and Anton was finally left with only a slight limp. By the autumn of 1915 he was even able to return to duty, serving this time on the Italian front as a lieutenant-colonel.

'I fear this will be a drawn-out and very bloody conflict,'

Anton told Franz one day in June 1915, almost a year after the archduke's assassination.

'But can we still win?' he asked him.

He shrugged. 'I don't know, but win or lose I'm certain we'll continue to pay a terrible price...'

'Yes, I know the casualty figures are unbelievably high. When I think of all those brave young men who've already sacrificed their lives it makes me want to weep.'

'War has become a matter of industrialised slaughter and men are but cattle fit for the slaughterhouse. Think of the power of the machine gun and the shells fired by heavy guns.'

'You know, this war has depressed me so much I've struggled to compose anything apart from a few worthless marches.'

'But what about that soldier's lament of yours. How does it go? *Drüben am Wiesen...*'

'Um... yes, that's not bad, I suppose.'

'It's become popular with the troops, I believe.'

'... Which pleases me, but I've been needing to get back to what I'm best at even if it does nothing to help our country in a time of war.'

'Don't be too hard on yourself, Franz. There's nothing better than music for sustaining morale and your operettas have brought pleasure to millions of people.'

'Even so, I can't just rest on my laurels. After all, I'm still only forty-five. It's good that Fritz and I are still making progress with *The Stargazer*. He's such a talented fellow, you know. When the opportunity arises, which I know might not be for some time, I'd like to introduce him to you.'

At Christmas 1915 Anton was able to enjoy a period of leave

with Emilie and their children, Johann and Maria, which was a welcome escape from the harsh realities of war. He wasn't too sorry either when his wounded leg caused him to suffer a nasty fall as this gave him a perfectly valid excuse to extend his leave until the middle of January.

Two days before rejoining his regiment he was pleased to attend the première of *The Stargazer* at the Theater der Josefstadt in Vienna, along with Emilie and their children. Although he thought it thoroughly entertaining, he couldn't help noticing that it was not as enthusiastically received by the audience as *The Merry Widow* had been, something which he was sure would not be lost on Franz either.

While Emilie took the children straight home, he attended the first night celebration at the Café Museum. He was prepared for Franz to display a measure of the self-doubt which had affected him when *The Merry Widow* was first performed, but in the event he was perfectly relaxed and philosophical about *The Stargazer's* prospects.

Having Fritz Löhner-Beda by his side surely assisted his mood, too, for the moment Anton was introduced to him, and felt the strength of his handshake, he was conscious of being in the presence of someone with a positive and energetic personality.

Fritz was still in his early thirties at the time. Anton noted that he was already going bald and was no more than average height, but behind his spectacles, his eyes were still sharply focused on him and he had a warm, friendly smile.

'So good to meet you, major,' Fritz said. 'How is your leg? Franz has told me how badly wounded you were.'

'Well, I had a recent fall, which set me back somewhat, but

I'm much better now, thank you. Without it, I'd already have rejoined my regiment and so wouldn't have been able to enjoy this splendid evening. Many congratulations.'

'Thank you, thank you. I must say, it's a great honour to be able to work with your brother.'

It was quickly apparent to Anton that there was a great rapport between the two men and that their personalities complemented each other. He had confidence that they would go on to even greater achievements together, and the next two decades were to prove that this was well founded.

13

27th September 1916

Franz and Fritz Löhner-Beda were both deeply disappointed by the poor reception *The Stargazer* received from both critics and the public during its initial run at the Theater der Josefstadt. As a consequence it was taken off after a mere seventy-nine performances, but then the decision was made to make some revisions to both the lyrics and the libretto before starting a second run at the Theater an der Wien.

On the day of its first performance at this new venue, the two of them arrived early within minutes of each other and were both understandably in a nervous frame of mind. Franz went straight to the conductor's dressing room and Fritz soon followed him.

'Good evening, Franz, fingers crossed for tonight's performance,' Fritz said, putting his head round the dressing room door.

'Thank you, Fritz. You're welcome to come in for a few minutes.'

Fritz accepted this invitation and Franz showed him a chair where he was able to sit down.

'I realise, Fritz, that putting on an operetta in the middle of a war that's claiming untold thousands of Austrian lives every day has not been easy, but I still think it's been worth it. Here's to a more successful run second time around.'

'I'm most grateful you were even prepared to consider it after its initial reception.'

'Hopefully, the changes that have been made will make all the difference. God knows, amidst the nightmare, people need entertaining more than ever... By the way, I've been meaning to ask whether you've been called up yet?'

'I failed a medical because of my defective eyesight, but I've been told that with mounting casualties the government's desperate for more men, so the chances are they'll lower the bar before this whole ghastly business is over. In the meantime, let's hope enough Viennese come to see *The Stargazer* to give you a tidy profit on all your work. I love the music. I really do.'

'Thank you. I really haven't been at my best, creatively, since this nightmare started. How can I be when the composition of anything but military songs seems a terrible self-indulgence? But my brother Anton has told me that I shouldn't feel like that and that I'm making my contribution.'

'Is his leg still bearing up?'

'He's still serving as a lieutenant-colonel and has a desk job as head of the department for infantry and cavalry weapons. He'd have liked to be with us tonight but is too busy.'

'He's a brave man... Anyway, I just wanted to say that whatever happens tonight there's nothing as wonderful as hearing singers singing my lyrics to your amazing music.'

'That's kind of you, Fritz, but let me return the compliment by saying that you don't need my music for your lyrics to be remarkable. You know, I adore your song, *I lost my heart in Heidelberg*.' And with that Franz began humming the first few bars.

'I'm glad you like it so much. Yes, it was the first thing I wrote that made me any real money.'

'Well, let's hope we can still make some real money from this operetta, but I want you to think about writing me something even more ambitious than *The Stargazer*, and perhaps more serious, too. At least it should have plenty of serious passages. a piece with a foreigner in it, a foreign emperor or king, perhaps?'

'I'll be happy to give that some thought.'

'Please do. What this appalling war is surely teaching us is that, if we don't as a species all work together and collaborate, whatever nation we live in, we're all going to end up exterminating ourselves.'

'I couldn't agree more. Being Jewish, I know we've been on the receiving end of a lot hatred and discrimination down the centuries and I'd like to see that finally come to an end. Mind you, perhaps that's a naive hope.'

'Better to live in hope than hatred. I have a bottle of schnapps here. Care to join me in a glass?'

'I'd be happy to.'

Franz went to a cupboard where he took out a bottle and two small glasses, which he proceeded to fill. 'I propose a toast to the Jewish people and also to our future collaboration.' The two of them then touched glasses.

'To the Jewish people! Prosit!' Franz said.

'Prosit!'

'I suggest, too, that we agree to donate our royalties for this first week of the run to the national fund for the welfare of Austrian soldiers.'

'Yes, that's an excellent idea. I agree.'

In the event this second run was little more successful than the first, something that Fritz attributed to the public's increasing enthusiasm for dance operettas such as *The Gypsy Princess* and *The Rose of Stamboul*.

'I'll still give some thought to that further work you suggested,' he told Franz, although as it happened it was to be a number of years before this came to fruition.

14

Early October 1916

After more than two years' service on the western front, Hitler, now a Lance-Corporal, could count himself fortunate still to be alive and unwounded. To an extent, this could be attributed to the fact that he had been made a regimental messenger, for the most part serving away from the front line, but this didn't mean he was totally safe.

One morning, much like so many others, he was waiting with two other messengers, for orders, when he was called over by his sergeant, George Salzmann.

'Hitler!'

'Yes, sir?'

'I have an important job for you. Come here right away.'

Sargent Salzmann was standing at the entrance of a dispatch hut. At that very moment a shell scored a direct hit on same, killing him outright. The blast was also such that it killed the two other messengers waiting with Hitler as well.

Hitler was luckier, although the blast still knocked him off his feet onto the muddy ground and he let out a groan of pain as his left thigh was hit and his wound began to bleed profusely. Another soldier rushed forward to assist him.

'You're hit! We'll get you some medical help.'

'What about my compatriots?' Hitler asked groggily.

'I'm sorry, lad... they're all dead.'

'Oh, God, why was I saved when providence took them?'

'I don't know about that, but if you don't get help you could bleed to death. Consider your salvation a blessing from Almighty God.'

Medics were quickly summoned. Hitler was taken away on a stretcher to a field hospital where he received emergency treatment. The following day he was told that his wound was severe enough to justify his evacuation to a hospital in Germany.

'It will aid your recovery,' the doctor told him.

'But I want to return to duty as soon as possible.'

'And you'll stand a better chance of doing just that if you're able to recuperate properly.'

For most of the next two months he received treatment at a Red Cross Hospital in Brandenburg before being discharged. However, although he considered himself fully fit, rather than being sent back to his regiment he was sent instead to a depot in Munich, which made him angry. He decided that he had no choice but to write to his commanding officer, Hauptmann Fritz Wiedemann. He wrote:

... It is intolerable to me to be kicking my heels here in Bavaria, while my fellow comrades-in-arms continue to risk their lives at the front. I beg therefore to be allowed to rejoin them at the earliest opportunity...

Duly impressed by his desire to continue to place himself in danger, Wiedemann arranged for Hitler to resume his former duties at the beginning of March 1917.

'Welcome back, Lance-Corporal,' Wiedemann told him. 'You are a credit to the regiment.'

'Thank you, sir. I'm delighted to be back. I would have regarded it as cowardice not to be able to put myself in danger along with my comrades-in-arms.'

15

Tuesday 15th October 1918

After his return to his regiment in March 1917, Hitler continued in his role as a messenger until in August 1918 he was awarded the Iron Cross First Class for his bravery in singlehandedly capturing a group of French soldiers hiding in a shell hole. His regiment had, by then fought well in many battles throughout the course of the war and Hitler felt justly proud of it, however much the tide of war might now be turning against the German Reich.

By October the German army on the western front was in retreat, but not yet beaten, and in Hitler's regiment morale continued to be fairly good, although many including Hitler were beginning to fear the worst. Hitler knew that he was lucky to still be alive and healthy when so many of his comrades-in-arms had died. Whatever might lie ahead he also had an inner confidence that he was going to survive, but this was about to be tested.

It had been an ugly war in so many ways with both sides being prepared to use gas as a weapon. On this particular Tuesday, Hitler had no premonition of danger as he woke in his trench and had breakfast. Autumn rain had arrived so conditions were muddy but not especially so, and as he looked at the clouds above they were broken and high, allowing some sunlight to break through. Suddenly he heard a loud explosion and saw a yellow cloud heading towards them at ground level. He flinched in fear.

'Gas! Gas!' more than one man around him screamed in panic. Unfortunately, there was no time in which to escape its effects and seconds later the cloud enveloped them all.

Hitler began to cough violently as did those around him. Worse still, he soon realised that he was unable to see properly. As he then fell to his knees in the trench, the prospect of being permanently blinded filled him with dread. He'd been a witness to pathetic lines of men, their eyes covered in bandages, being led away, and he now realised with horror that he was likely to become part of just such a line.

As the gas began to dissipate he still couldn't see. He tried to call out in desperate need for help but no sound came out of his mouth. Had the gas made him dumb as well as blind? It was all too awful to contemplate.

Evacuated back to a hospital in Germany he made a gradual recovery, regaining his sight and also his voice by the time that the news arrived that Germany had surrendered unconditionally. This came as such a dreadful blow to him that he suffered a relapse, albeit a brief one, so that on 18th November he was discharged.

He had entered the army with such hope of a great victory, and played his part bravely in four long years of conflict, only for everything he'd fought for to end in disastrous defeat. It was a shattering, life-changing experience. The grim reality of war had hardened him, too. In truth, he'd never possessed much, if any empathy for the suffering of others, and now he really had none at all.

16

Bad Ischl, early September 1919

The war had duly brought down the Austro-Hungarian Empire along with the Habsburg dynasty that long reigned over it. The result was that Austria was reduced to such a relatively small amount of territory that the questions were even asked about its economic viability. For his part, Franz was just relieved that the war was finally over, although scars inevitably remained with beggars all too visible on the streets and all too many men to be seen without limbs or with white sticks because they'd been blinded. And then, too, there were the more invisible scars because so many men had been left mentally traumatised, whilst women had been left widowed, or lost their fiancés.

Since the war's end, Anton had remained in Hungary as a military commander, and Franz had recently received a letter from him bearing the news that he had been promoted to the rank of major-general. Anton's letter also expressed the hope that Hungary might be able to restore its monarchy, a struggle to which he stated that he was fully committed. Franz admired his brother's tenacity but couldn't help thinking that he was pursuing a lost cause.

Now as he sat at the breakfast table with Sophie, he found himself perusing an unexpected letter he'd received from a man he'd rather put to the back of his mind during the long years of war and its immediate aftermath.

'This letter is a surprise, I must say.'

'Who's it from?' Sophie asked.

'That artist fellow, Adolf Hitler. You remember, he stayed with us the year before the war. His painting of the villa is in one of the guest bedrooms.'

'Oh, yes. He's survived the war unscathed then?'

'Not exactly. He says he was the victim of a mustard gas attack and temporarily blinded.'

'Poor man.'

'Well, at least he's recovered. I can't say I like the tone of his letter, either. The war's left him a bitter man, I'm afraid. Here, read it for yourself.' He then passed the letter to her.

My dear maestro,

I hope this letter finds you well. I recall with pleasure my short stay with you back in 1913 and I wanted to take this opportunity of thanking you again for your kindness to me during the years I spent in Vienna. I hope you continue to enjoy my painting of your villa as I will always continue to take pleasure in your wonderful music.

Towards the end of the war, while serving in the German army, I was temporarily blinded and hospitalised but I'm pleased to say that I've made a full recovery. I have to add that I am utterly incensed and distressed at knowing that the brave army to which I devoted four years of my life has been stabbed in the back by the Versailles Peace Treaty. Is Germany's destiny always to be nothing but suffering? Nothing but betrayal? Nothing but ignominy? Yet Germany is the greatest nation on earth! The Romans, for all their military might, could never defeat us and never ventured north of an impromptu border that they made, in their fear to advance further, between their own kingdom and Germania. We are a nation of warriors, and what has happened to us? We have been betrayed! The German army surrendered even though it was never defeated. Even worse than this, I now believe that we have also been betrayed by the Jewish weevils who are part of our government. They inhabit, or should I say, fester, in so many positions of power in German society, business and industry. Only one percent of the German population is Jewish and yet how malign and pervasively wicked is the Jewish influence on our society!

When I was a young man in Vienna I saw nothing wrong with Judaism. Thanks to your endeavours on my behalf, my work was patronised by Herr Morgenstern. I was glad of his patronage because I needed it and I appreciated what he did for me. Now, as I look back on those days, they seem to me the days of my ignorance of Jewish ways before my long-over-due enlightenment.

I shall now be devoting my life to politics rather than art but I say again how appreciative I continue to be of all your help to me in the past. I shall also always remain a great admirer of your work and I look forward to your composing many more splendid operettas.

With kind regards,
Adolf Hitler

Fritz exclaimed, 'This is just an insane rant against the

Jews. Doesn't he recall I'm Jewish? I certainly never hid that from him.'

'I don't know. It's tactless of him if he does, and I find his views abhorrent. I shall acknowledge his letter but make no comment on what he's had to say.'

'I sincerely hope he doesn't go far in politics if his intention is to spread anti-Semitism.'

'I quite agree, but I can't imagine he'll enjoy any more success as a politician than he did as an artist.'

17

Friday 12th September 1919

The truth was that despite the goodwill that the likes of Sammy Morgenstern had shown him, Hitler's hatred of the Jews had begun to take root even by the time he left Vienna. In particular, he had come to admire the beliefs of Georg *Schönerer,* a fanatical German nationalist, who advocated the union of Germany and Austria and argued that Jews could never be German citizens. Further, Hitler also admired the anti-Semitic views of Karl Lueger, who was Mayor of Vienna when he first came to live there.

Yet it took four long years of war, a humiliating defeat along with the chaos that followed it, together with what he saw as the unjust terms of the peace treaty imposed on Germany at Versailles, to transform him into a virulent anti-Semite, capable of describing Jews as weevils.

Still a serving soldier, and by July 1919 acting as an army intelligence agent, Hitler was given the task of infiltrating the German Workers' Party, which had been founded by Anton Drexler who was an anti-Semitic, anti-Marxist nationalist. Impressed by his policies, Hitler decided to become a party member and attended his first meeting on 12th September 1919.

He had also begun to demonstrate his skills as an orator and was invited to address the admittedly quite small gathering of about thirty people in a not particularly large, nonde-script hall in Munich. Drexler and one other party official were seated on either side of him, and it was Drexler who introduced him.

'My fellow workers,' Hitler began once he'd stood up to mild applause. 'I am one of the hard-fighting soldiers who were betrayed by our government. We offered our very lives for Germany, but were stabbed in the back when peace was declared. So, let us never forget that the German army was undefeated! I blame our leaders for their indifference to our fate! They have been contaminated by foreign infiltration and by the pernicious influence of Jewish elements. The Jews live in Germany like parasites destroying our nation from the inside! They do not care what happens to Germany, for they are part of a sinister international sect that conspires to break our nation's heart. I say that one of our most funda-mental objectives, something unshakeable in our hearts and in our wills, must be the removal of the Jews from Germany altogether!'

A member of the audience stood up. 'And how do you propose to do that, Herr Hitler?'

'Right now, it cannot, alas, be done, but it should be our objective! The will of the people must be obeyed and the will of the people is that Germany must be made great again after this appalling humiliation. If the people truly unite, the Jewish poison will soon be purged from the blood of our nation. We true Germans are all flesh of one flesh; we are all blood of one blood! We do not want foreigners in our nation, nor Jews, nor any people who dilute the true and heroic blood of the German heart and the German soul.'

Then another member of the audience asked an even more awkward question. 'But you yourself are Austrian, are you not, Herr Hitler?'

'Yes, but that matters little. I am in the process of getting my Austrian citizenship revoked and becoming German. Besides, all Austrians of pure Austrian blood, such as I am, are Germans at heart. Moreover, anywhere where German is spoken as its first language is truly part of the greater Germany!'

This time, there was vigorous applause for Hitler in the hall and several members of the audience cheered.

Within two years of attending his first meeting, Hitler had replaced Drexler as leader of the party and it had changed its name to the National Socialist German Workers' Party, to be known throughout Germany as the Nazi Party.

In July 1921, at a larger hall in Munich, Hitler made his first speech to the party faithful in his new role and on this occasion was introduced by Josef Goebbels, who was to remain his faithful henchman to the bitter end.

'Our beloved leader, Adolf Hitler, the hero of Germany, will now speak to us.'

He then left the podium and shook hands with Hitler who walked slowly towards it. Then he stood at it very deliberately in silence for about half a minute before starting to speak.

'Greetings, fellow members of our movement! The National Socialist German Workers' Party is the most ambitious, most vital and most forward-thinking political party in Germany and in the world! It is now more populous than it has ever been! It is now stronger than it has ever been! It is now more vigorous than it has ever been! It is now more perceptive than it has ever been! It is now brimming with more confidence than it has ever had before! Follow me, and I shall make you not only masters of Germany, but also of the entire world!'

These words were greeted by thunderous applause from the audience, and by the time he stepped down from the podium Hitler truly felt that he was now beginning to fulfil his destiny.

18

By 8th November 1923 Hitler was ready to launch a *coup d'état* against the Bavarian government. Supported by some two thousand party members, some of whom were armed, he marched to the Marienplatz in Munich where he was confronted by the police. Fighting broke out, leading to the deaths of sixteen party members and four policemen. The police succeeded in gaining the upper hand and Hitler decided that he had no choice but to flee the city. However, three days later he was arrested and put on trial for high treason.

The trial started in a Munich courtroom before a special People's Court on Tuesday 26th February 1924 and lasted until 1st April that year. Hitler denied the charge of treason and when the time came to address the court, he was vigorous in his defence.

'I say to this court that as one after another of my colleagues was arrested and brought to Landsberg prison, I came to a decision that we should march. Let me emphasise that these were honest men whom I knew to be absolutely innocent, and whose sole crime was that they belonged to our movement and shared our philosophy, and whom the government was simply afraid of for speaking their minds.

'Thus I have come into this room, not in order to explain things away, or lie about my responsibility; no indeed! In fact,

I protest that some of my colleagues have declared they bear responsibility for what happened when in fact they had no responsibility for it at all. I alone bear the responsibility. I alone, when all is said and done, wanted to carry out the deed. The other gentlemen on trial here only negotiated with me at the end. I am convinced that I sought nothing bad. As I say, I bear the responsibility, and I will shoulder all the consequences. But one thing I must make clear: I am no criminal. On the contrary, if I stand here before the court accused of being a revolutionary, it is precisely because I am against revolution and against crimes. I admit all the factual aspects of the charge, but I cannot plead that I am guilty of high treason; for there can be no high treason compared with that treason to the Fatherland committed in 1918 and all the betrayals of the German people that have occurred since then.

'I declare that I am no more or less than a good German, who wants only the best for the German people.'

Hitler's conviction was inevitable, but although the court could have sentenced him to death, or for that matter deported him to Austria, instead it imposed the comparatively light sentence of five years' imprisonment. Taken to Landsberg prison, he received a friendly welcome from its guards and was allowed special privileges including the use of a private secretary, Emil Maurice, who soon arrived at the prison to help Hitler begin work on an important project he had decided to undertake.

'Welcome. Emil, as you can see this is a comfortable enough cell; quite spacious, with a view of the river, and plenty of books to read. Now, we must waste no time in my beginning to dictate to you the book that I have dreamed of writing for years.

It will be my political testament and shall, I am convinced, infuse patriotism and ardour into the hearts of all noble and loyal Germans.'

'Adolf, I am proud and privileged to be here with you at this moment. What is the book to be called?'

'*Four and a half years of struggle against lies, stupidity and cowardice.*' Then Hitler smiled. 'No, that is too long, of course. *My Struggle* will do well enough. Now, let us begin.'

'I'm ready, Adolf, and so is my shorthand.'

'Thank you.'

Hitler then began to stride around the room before pausing to gather his thoughts and then beginning to dictate in a confident and fluent manner.

'As from the first of April 1924 I am serving my unjust sentence of detention in the fortress of Landsberg am Lech following the iniquitous verdict of the Munich people's court.

'After years of uninterrupted labour, it is now possible for the first time to begin a work which many have asked for and which I myself felt would be profitable for the movement, so I have decided to devote two volumes to a description not only of the aims of our movement but also of its development and to destroy the fabrications which the Jewish press has circulated about me. In this work I turn not to strangers but to those followers of the movement whose hearts belong to it and who wish to study it more profoundly. I know that fewer people are won over by the written word than by the spoken word and that every great movement, like ours, owes its growth to great speakers and not to great writers.'

Hitler looked at his secretary. 'You have that, Emil? You have my words?'

'Yes. I am just finishing writing them down. One moment, please, Adolf.' Hitler gave him an impatient stare. '... All on paper now, please continue.'

'Volume one: a retrospect.
'Chapter One: in the home of my parents.
'It has turned out fortunate for me today that destiny appointed Braunau-am-Inn to be my birthplace. for that little town is situated just on the frontier between the two States, Germany and Austria, the reunion of which seems, at least to us of a younger generation, a task to which we should devote our lives, and in the pursuit of which every possible means should be employed...'

By the time Hitler was released from prison for good behaviour a mere eight months later, his book *My Struggle (Mein Kampf)* was ready for publication. Sales were initially modest but greater days lay ahead, both for the book and for its author.

19

Spring 1924

Despite the comparative failure of *The Stargazer* Fritz Löhner-Beda's career had continued to progress, although he and Franz were yet to work again on any other projects. Fritz had also become increasingly well known in Vienna as a professional writer of genuine talent with a large personality to go with it that made him popular amongst his peers.

One Tuesday Fritz went to his favourite restaurant, The Star of David, for lunch and sat at his usual table. Seeing a beautiful young waitress whom he vaguely thought he recognised, he beckoned her over.

'Good afternoon to you.'

'Good afternoon, sir.'

'I'd like to order some lunch. I always have the same meal when I come here. I'm terribly conservative when it comes to food. I'd like a bowl of matzoh ball soup, some potato latkes and a steak, medium rare, please... I don't think I've seen you before.'

'No, sir, I only began working here last week.'

'May I ask your name?'

'It's Helene.'

'Well, thank you, Helene. So, could you please bring me a bottle of mineral water? I don't drink anything stronger this early in the day. In fact, I don't drink anything stronger much of the time. I'm mostly boringly sober.'

'That's a virtue, sir. I have a friend whose husband is an alcoholic and it absolutely ruins their married life.'

'I'm very sorry to hear that.'

'I'll bring you your lunch soon, sir.'

A few minutes later, she did so and Fritz thanked her for her service.

'Forgive me for asking, sir, but would you be Dr Beda?'

Fritz laughed. 'I believe that's my nickname in certain circles. My name's actually Fritz Löhner-Beda and I assure you, I'm no doctor.'

'It's just that I believe I've seen you at the theatre. You're a songwriter, aren't you?'

'Amongst other things. Your lovely face was also vaguely familiar to me so our paths must have crossed.'

Helene smiled at him. 'I've only seen you at a distance. You see I'm a dancer... And I sing, too.'

'Ah, I might have seen you on stage then. So how come you're working here?'

'I'm between shows and need the money.'

'Of course.' Then he leaned towards her and spoke in a quiet voice.

'I know you'll think this very forward of me but I really wish you could join me for lunch. Of course, I realise that's impossible. Would it be unreasonable for me to ask when you finish work here today?'

'My shift ends at five o'clock, sir.'

'Then might you extend me the privilege of buying you coffee and cake at the Café Central after your shift? It's only a short walk from here.'

'Yes, I know where it is. Well yes, sir, that would be very nice. Thank you.'

'No, Helene, thank you. By the way, please call me Fritz. May I come and meet you outside here after you finish your shift?'

'I'd rather you didn't. I don't want my colleagues or my boss to see that I'm meeting a gentleman customer. Let's just meet at the Café Central, if that's all right with you?'

'Yes, of course.'

At five o'clock, still wondering what had quite possessed him to invite a girl who looked to be half his age to come for coffee and cake with him, Fritz found a secluded table to one side of the café and then waited. A few minutes later Helene arrived. She had changed from her waitress uniform into a pretty but modest-looking sky-blue dress which, if anything, enhanced her looks.

At first they were merely polite to one another, ordering coffee and cake and then waiting to be served; but once they had been, Fritz felt compelled to say what had been on his mind since lunchtime.

'You know, from the moment I saw you in the restaurant, I knew I just had to talk to you. If I might say so, you really are extraordinarily beautiful.'

'Oh, sir, you really flatter me.'

'No, I really don't. I mean it. I'm not the flattering kind. May I ask if you have a beau? That is, if that's not too forward a question on our brief acquaintanceship.'

'It certainly is a forward question, sir, but no, I don't. I live with my mother, not far from here - my father died about five years ago - and my mother being rather unwell, I have quite enough to do with doing my work and running the house. I don't have time for much frivolity.'

'Not everything in the matter of a man meeting a beautiful woman needs to be frivolity. I like you very much.'

'You don't know me at all, sir, so how can you say you like me?'

'I like what I see and what I hear, certainly. Besides, I'm sure we can easily address the problem that we don't know each other. I'm a married man with one son, Bruno, who's nearly five, and I will soon be forty-one, I freely admit it. But sadly I've been estranged from my wife for two years now, and I don't see much of Bruno, either. They've moved away from Vienna, you see. As you also know, I'm a songwriter, but there are other things I write, too. Screenplays for films, for example. In fact, I write anything I'm paid to write. I'm a hired freelance hack, so to speak. Perhaps my best achievement to date has been to write the libretto to the operetta *The Stargazer* by Franz Lehár. It wasn't quite the success we hoped for, but there will be other opportunities for us to work together, I'm sure.'

'Well, my name is Jellinek, I'm Jewish...'

'As am I, but do go on.'

'And I'm just a simple chorus girl who loves to sing and dance. I'm much younger than you, of course.'

'I realise that. How much younger, if I might ask?'

'I'm twenty-two.'

'So do you think I'm far too old for you? I was quite the athlete in my younger days but as you can see I have become a little stout with the passing of the years. Too much cake, I fear.'

'No, I wouldn't say you're too old for me. I rather like older men, in fact.'

'So tell me, what do you like to sing?'

'Songs from operas and operettas mainly.'

'So would you do me the honour of singing something for me?'

Helene looked shocked. 'I can't possibly, not here in this café with all these people around!'

'Sing quietly, then, just to me.'

'All right.'

Softly she began to sing to him, looking into his eyes as she did so.

'I dreamt I dwelt in marble halls
With vassals and serfs at my side,
And of all who assembled within those walls
That I was their hope and their pride.
I had riches all too great to count
And a high ancestral name,
But I also dreamt, which pleased me most,
That you loved me still the same,
That you loved me
You loved me still the same,
That you loved me
You loved me still the same.
I dreamt that suitors sought my hand,
That knights upon bended knees
And with vows no maiden's heart could withstand,
They pledged their faith to me.
And I dreamt that one of that noble host
Came forth my hand to claim.
But I also dreamt, which charmed me most,
That you loved me still the same

That you loved me
You loved me, still the same,
That you loved me
You loved me, still the same.'

'That was really beautiful,' Fritz said. 'You have a wonderful voice!'

'You really think so?'

'Most certainly, Helene, you have a great talent. I know that aria: it's from the opera *The Bohemian*.'

'Yes! It's one of my favourite operas. I've seen it twice in Vienna.'

'It's one of my favourites too, though I've only seen it once.'

'Perhaps we were at the same performance!'

'Yes, perhaps so. You know, I might be able to help you further your career as a singer. I know a lot of influential people, including Franz.'

'You're a very kind man, Herr Löhner-Beda...'

'Do call me Fritz, please.'

'Yes, yes of course.' Again she looked into his eyes and smiled. 'I must say it would be wonderful to have a leading role in one of Maestro Lehár's operettas, such as *The Merry Widow*.'

'Yes, I know how popular it is, but I'd like to let you into a little secret. I don't like it very much. The first twenty minutes are rather tedious; as an audience we're expected to care about the fortunes of a totally imaginary, not especially engaging, principality staffed by pompous officials. The story then becomes a little more interesting when we meet the Count and Hanna and up until the end of the first act it gathers quite a momentum. but then in my opinion it grows tedious again.'

'Well, I hope Maestro Lehár never finds out that you dislike his most famous work!'

'I've no plans to tell him, I assure you. I do find the music in *The Merry Widow* wonderful, yet I feel that an operetta should not just be about the music, it should be about the story as well. I have little respect for the story of *The Merry Widow*. The two main characters, Danilo and Hanna, have been lovers in the past but have become estranged for various reasons. By the end of that first act it's obvious they're going to be together at the end, and there are two more acts to go which, in a rather contrived way, delay that inevitable conclusion.'

'Yes, I don't disagree, It's the music in *The Merry Widow* that really carries it as an operetta.'

'So, would you do me the honour of having dinner with me tomorrow night?'

'I... I'm not sure.'

'So you do think I'm too old for you?'

'No, it's just our meeting like this is quite a shock. You're far above me in society. As I say, I'm just a chorus girl.'

'Nonsense, you clearly have talent, and can I assure you, I'm not trying to buy either your time or your affection. I'm a gentleman, Helene. Nowadays, I'm also rather too busy with my writing to have much time for any romantic adventure, but you are so absolutely lovely and so charming that I would give up any of my writing time to spend it with you.'

'I see.'

'Yes, I know we've only just met. All the same, we both know that a gentleman is aware very quickly if he really likes a lady, and if he is serious about her, or if he just sees her as an opportunity for a flirtation to distract him from his work, and I wish to assure you, Helene, that I am serious about you.'

'Very well then, I'll be pleased to have dinner with you.'

20

Summer 1925

Fritz and Helene were soon very much in love and as soon as he was able to secure a divorce from his first wife, they decided to marry at a synagogue in Vienna in 1925.

A lovely wedding song was sung for the occasion and once it had finished, the Rabbi addressed the congregation:

'Shalom! We are gathered here today to celebrate one of life's greatest moments, the union of two hearts. In this ceremony today we will witness the joining of Fritz Löhner-Beda and Helene Jellinek in marriage. Today we have come together to witness the merging of these two lives. For Fritz and Helene, out of the routine of ordinary life, the extraordinary has happened. They met each other, fell in love and are finalising it with their wedding today.

'Fritz and Helene, life is given to each of us as individuals, and yet we must learn to live together. Love is given to us by our family and friends - we learn to love by being loved. Learning to love and living together is one of the greatest challenges of life; and it is the shared goal of a married life. Yet we also must remember that it is not humankind which created love, but God.

'Blessed art Thou, O Lord God, creator of all things. A good marriage must be created. In marriage the "little" things are the big things. It is never being too old to hold hands. It is remembering to say, "I love you" at least once a day. It is never going to sleep angry. It is standing together and facing the world. It is speaking words of appreciation, and demonstrating gratitude in thoughtful ways. It is having the capacity to forgive and forget. It is giving each other an atmosphere in which each can grow. It is a common search for the good and the beautiful. It is not only marrying the right person, it is being the right partner.

'Now, do you, Fritz, take this woman Helene Jellinek to be your lawful wedded wife, here in the sight of God?'

'Yes, with all my heart.'

'And do you, Helene, take this man Fritz Löhner-Beda to be your lawful wedded husband, here in the sight of God?'

'Yes, with all my heart.'

'Then I pronounce you man and wife. May God Almighty bless your wedded union forever.'

Fritz and Helene kissed lovingly, gazing into each other's eyes, and Fritz then smashed a glass goblet that has been wrapped in paper under his right foot to symbolise the act of marriage.

Later that same evening, having gone to a hotel on the first night of their honeymoon, they were quick to make love to one another.

Fritz was quite in awe of Helene's beauty as she stood naked before him, finding it hard to believe his good fortune. That such a goddess of a young woman should have fallen so madly in love with him when he would never see forty again was definitely the stuff of dreams.

He liked to imagine that it was just his natural charm, intelligence, and good humour that had so attracted her. Yet he was not so vain as to discount the likelihood that his growing wealth as well as the circles he moved in, along with his capacity to advance her career as a singer, might well have played their part. Whatever the truth of the matter, he was more than content to glory in her beauty and enjoy her flesh to his heart's content as their love-making proved every bit as satisfying as he had ever dared to hope for.

When it was over, they lay naked in bed together, her head resting on his chest, and his arms around her, feeling a happy afterglow of sated desire.

'Have I ever told you that I love you very much?' he said to her.

'Only about a thousand times, darling.'

'How remiss of me. A thousand times isn't nearly enough.'

'I'm a very lucky woman. You're such a lovely, gentle man.'

'Didn't I always assure you of that?'

'Yes, indeed you did. I'm going to love being married to you, Fritz Löhner-Beda.'

'And I to you, wonderful Helene.'

Helene then brought her lips towards his as they started to kiss again.

The following morning, Fritz was the first to wake and couldn't resist studying Helene's beautiful face as she continued to lie asleep. Then she opened her eyes.

'Good morning, darling wife. I trust you slept well?'

'Yes, very,' she said sleepily.

'You know I always used to dream that a woman like you might exist, but I never really thought it possible. I really am the most fortunate of men.'

'And I am a fortunate woman.' She then lifted her head and kissed him. 'I'm so, so glad we met, and even happier now we're married.'

'Darling Helene, do you know when my life properly began?'

'No, when?'

'Only on that blessed day when I met you at the Star of David restaurant.'

21

As the nineteen twenties drew on, Fritz was able to renew his musical partnership with Franz, when in partnership with Ludwig Herzer he wrote the libretto for the operetta *Frederica*, telling the story of the younger days of the great German poet Goethe, which was first performed in 1928. The success that they enjoyed with this encouraged them to continue their partnership with a further operetta, and by the spring of 1929 Fritz and Ludwig had completed their work on this, so the three men agreed to meet at Franz's apartment in Vienna. In the event Ludwig was indisposed but gave his blessing to them proceeding without him.

'So, maestro,' Fritz said with one of his usual beaming smiles, 'I have with me the manuscript of the libretto Ludwig and I have been working on. We've given it the title *The Land of Smiles*.'

'So, please enlighten me: what's the story?'

'One moment, Franz. I have something else here, I want to show you.' He then reached into his case and took out a copy of Hitler's book *My Struggle*, which he showed to Franz.

'Have you seen this before?'

'*My Struggle?* I've heard of it. Of course I've heard of it. Who hasn't? But I absolutely refuse to read it.'

'Franz, you should read it. He means business. It's nothing more or less than a manifesto from a man who plans to take over the whole world if he can. It's not even a question any longer of his argument that Germany is where German is spoken, absurd as *that* is.'

'Yes, one might as well say that the United States is England because they speak English there!'

'Exactly. In this horrible diatribe he even explicitly states that the German nation has a moral right to expand into other territories. But, maestro, that's not what worries me most. It's what he says about Jews.'

Fritz then turned to a particular page in the book and asked Franz to listen before reading from it.

'*There were very few Jews in Linz. In the course of centuries the Jews who lived there had become Europeanised in external appearance and were so much like other human beings that they were even looked upon as Austrians. The reason why I did not then perceive the absurdity of such an illusion was that the only external mark which I recognised as distinguishing them from us was the practice of their strange religion.*'

'It's bad enough that he should suggest that Jews are not like other human beings but listen to this...'

At that moment there was a knock on the door and Sophie appeared, looking cheerful. She and Franz had finally married in 1921 and since then had enjoyed a peripatetic existence between the Vienna apartment and the villa in Bad Ischl.

'I'm sorry to interrupt but I was just wondering whether Fritz would like to stay for dinner? The cook's making Wiener schnitzel with noodles.'

'Thanks so much, Sophie, but I really need to be getting home,' Fritz said. 'As you know, Helene's expecting any time now.'

'Of course. Do give her my very best wishes.'

'I will.'

'But what's that book you have there? You look very worried. Is something wrong?'

'Yes, you could say that. This is Hitler's book *My Struggle*. I was just reading an extract to Franz.'

'But why on earth would you want to read that filth? Why would you even bring it into our home?'

'Believe me, Sophie, I detest it as much as you do. but we can't afford to ignore him. We need to know our enemy and how his mind works.'

'But surely you mean how it *doesn't* work? Hitler's clearly insane. Why bother reading the rantings of a lunatic? He's really such a dangerous man, especially for people like us.'

'Quite, but insane as Hitler's become, it's perfectly possible he may one day become the leader of Germany. Just listen...'

'What soon gave me cause for very serious consideration were the activities of the Jews in certain branches of life, into its mystery, which I penetrated little by little. Was there any shady undertaking, any form of foulness, especially in cultural life, in which at least one Jew did not participate? On putting the probing knife carefully to that kind of abscess one immediately discovered, like a maggot in a putrescent body, a little Jew who was often blinded by the sudden light.'

'Oh my God,' Sophie exclaimed. 'That's awful.'

'Yes, he actually calls us maggots. It's difficult to imagine a more odious or dehumanising term. So, what do you think of that, Franz?'

'I believe that we need to take him very seriously indeed. His trial in front of the so-called "People's Court" in Munich caught the public's imagination in Germany. Many see Hitler and his party - or his "movement" as he persists in calling it - as the saviours of Germany. They think that he speaks up for what he considers to be unspeakable wrongs done against the German people, which, I suppose, from some perspectives, is a reasonable stance to take.'

'A reasonable stance?' Sophie exclaimed. 'The man doesn't have a reasonable bone in his body.'

'Maybe not, but to some extent I agree with Franz. Germans do have much to complain about. The Treaty of Versailles was bitterly unfair to Germany and has caused the Germans utter economic disaster. The idea of the victors that if you impoverish a country you somehow punish it satisfactorily is absurd. Countries aren't like individual criminals. Surely, if one impoverishes a country, all one does is make it resentful and more likely to try to want to win next time around... And, what's more, I fear there *will* be a next time around.'

'Oh please, God, no,' Sophie responded.

'Should Hitler should ever manage to win power, which I hope to God he won't, then it's all too possible. But it will only happen if the Germans become so desperate about their plight that a majority of them decide to support his mad nonsense.'

'Well, let's pray they never do,' Franz exclaimed.

'Unfortunately, I fear they might. What terrifies me most

about *My Struggle* is that it isn't, by and large, written in a hysterical way. Yes, it's full of mad rhetoric that's anti-Jewish, anti-capitalist, anti-communist and pretty much anti-everyone who isn't thoroughly a pure-bred German Nazi, but Germans are very susceptible to that kind of thing. I've seen newsreel footage of Hitler speaking. He has a look in his eyes when he speaks that I admit could be addictive. It makes you feel that he is someone who really cares about the situation in Germany. But never mind all that. What really frightens me is this stuff he says about Jews.'

'A maggot in a putrescent body, you mean,' Sophie said angrily. 'How dare he write about us like that? He's a vile, little man.' She was now close to tears.

Rising from the piano stool where he had been sitting, Franz embraced her. 'Don't cry, my love. All will be well. You'll see.'

'I only hope you're right, darling. Now, I must leave you get on with your work.'

They shared a brief kiss before Sophie began to leave the room but upon reaching the door she turned round.

'Just promise me one thing, Fritz. Once you've finished with *My Struggle*, throw it in the trash where it belongs.'

'I will, Sophie. I promise.'

'Thank you.'

'She worries too much,' Franz said once she had closed the door behind her.

'Sadly, think she has every reason to worry about Hitler.'

'You know, I find it difficult to believe he's really like this. He was on such friendly terms with Sammy Morgenstern and Sammy's told me he has sometimes written to Hitler, sending greetings.'

'And has Hitler replied?'

'Only once, I gather. As I recall Sammy telling me, it was a long time ago now.'

'It's the war that's changed him, I expect. Yes, I can see why he feels that the German army was stabbed in the back. But the real problem is that Hitler has come to the conclusion that the war was caused by the Jews in the first place and, even worse, that Germany's surrender of an undefeated army was inspired by the Jews as well, but it makes no sense. Here in Austria and in Germany, too, we Jews are thoroughly integrated into society. I believe we're part of what makes both countries tick.'

'Fritz, my friend, I really don't think you have anything to worry about. Hitler is nowhere near coming to power in Germany.'

'Not at the moment, but what if he were to ever do so? I've no intention of emigrating and leaving Austria. Apart from anything else, I don't have any relatives outside the country. Also, Helene loves it here and would hate living abroad, even if it was possible, and having to learn a whole new language is never easy. Frankly, I need my mother tongue. I'm a writer. I can't suddenly transplant myself to America and expect people to read what I write in English, a language I can speak a little, but not to such an extent that I could *write* in it.'

'You know, you worry too much, my friend. Do put that absurd and wicked book away. I'm sure in time it will be forgotten, and very likely Hitler will just be a tiny footnote in history.'

'I do hope you're right.'

'I'm sure I am. The Germans aren't stupid. Yes, they're an emotional race and prone to some nonsensical ideas, but there are plenty of real Germans who would no more follow Hitler's nonsense, and be vindictive towards the Jews, than they would abandon eating sausages. Now come on, let's use this time for the purpose we've allocated to it. Tell me the story of *The Land of Smiles*.'

'Yes, of course. By the way, Sophie's a remarkable woman. Spirited, full of integrity, loyal. You're a lucky man, maestro.'

'Yes, I am. And as are you, Fritz.'

'Oh yes. Never a day passes when I don't count my blessings for having met Helene. Anyway, here's the scenario. In her own way, the heroine of the new operetta is also a remarkable woman. She's a beautiful Viennese lady called Lisa. She knows her own mind, and passionately wants to love and be loved. She's much admired in society. Her close friend Gustav, an officer in the Austrian army, asks to meet her. He tells her he's lodged a deposit with the army, as army regulations say he must, because he's planning to get married. She, completely guilelessly, asks him who the lucky woman is. Gustav, surprised, replies, "Well, you, obviously."'

Franz laughed. 'I see.'

'Lisa is astonished and, in a song that I think could work really well with the right music, says that she cares for Gustav as a friend, but doesn't feel that way about him and doesn't want to marry him. They sing a lovely duet in which they accept that their friendship is still something worth having. Moving on: a Chinese delegation happens to be visiting Vienna at that time and Lisa, through her official role in society, meets the Emperor Sou Chong. He's a complete charmer and experienced at winning the hearts of women. He sings to her, including a lyric about taking tea with her, and also a more serious romantic solo entitled "I'm always smiling". In it, he says that, because of his position as Emperor, he needs to be positive and smiling in all situations, but no-one cares what lies deep within his heart.'

'I must say I like that. I can imagine the kind of melodies that would really work in it.'

'And I can imagine you'd produce something really wonderful. It would be just the kind of song at which Richard would excel.'

Fritz was referring to Richard Tauber, the brilliant Austrian tenor who had been performing Franz's operettas for the best part of ten years and had become a close friend.

'Yes, I agree, it would very likely be perfect for him. All right, tell me more.'

'So, Lisa falls head over heels in love with Sou Chong and, when he asks her to come back to China and marry him, she says yes. Gustav's heart is broken, but in true noble Austrian style he's magnanimous and vows to Lisa that he will stay her friend. And so Lisa goes to China with Sou Chong and is all set to marry him when she discovers not only that he has other wives already, so she will have to be another one of several, but also that her very presence in his life is an affront to the gods.'

'The Chinese gods, you mean?'

'Quite. So, Sou Chong's ministers, who are presented as comical pedants, are always berating him for not remembering the wisdom of the traditions of China. Of course, there's only so much they can say to him as he is the Emperor, but they're quite determined in what they're saying. At this point the story gets more complicated, because Gustav has decided - somewhat implausibly, perhaps, but this is after all an operetta - to travel to China himself to pay his respects to Lisa.'

'So, he meets her there, I take it?'

'Yes, and while he's there he meets Sou Chong's younger sister, Mi, who sings a comical, but nonetheless sincere and, I hope, affecting lyric about the constraints of life of a young Chinese woman and why she can't have much fun. When she meets Gustav she falls hopelessly in love with him.'

'Excellent! So how does the piece end?'

'Lisa rebels against the subservient life Sou Chong has in store for her. She ardently wants to leave China, but he forbids her from going back to Vienna. This, not surprisingly, opens her eyes to his authoritarian nature. Gustav meets Sou Chong. The two men get on pretty well, considering that Gustav is in love with Lisa, and that Sou Chong's sister is in love with Gustav.'

'Quite a dramatic quartet of love! I think the Viennese will adore it!'

'I so hope they will, maestro. Well, Gustav so impresses Sou Chong with his Viennese gallantry and magnanimity towards Lisa that the Emperor finally decides to let Lisa go, and Gustav movingly and sincerely compliments Sou Chong for his gentlemanly manner towards her.'

'Fascinating! But don't tell me any more. I can't wait to read the libretto!'

Franz then propped the libretto on the music stand on his piano and started flicking through it. 'I must say, my friend, your handwriting is far better than mine. I need a secretary when I dictate letters nowadays because no-one can understand my writing... Ah, I see, here is the scene where Gustav tells Lisa he wants to marry her. Let's look at this, shall we?'

Fritz, excited by the idea that Franz might be about to start composing some music *ex tempore* there and then, leant forward towards him.

'So, this is the start of the song… Yes, I understand, Gustav has just made his proposal and been rebuffed, albeit in a friendly way. Lisa speaks to him, although I suppose she's actually going to be singing this.'

'Yes, she would be, maestro.'

Franz began to speak the words from the libretto, but then began *ex tempore* composition of the melody whilst starting to sing the words to the melody.

> *'This isn't the very first time,*
> *And certainly isn't the last time,*
> *That two friends must say just what they feel*
> *And yes I'm sure we both can see*
> *Our romance is not to be,*
> *But we'll stay forever loving friends.'*

He then hummed a tune to himself and tried out some notes on the piano, thinking about how the song might work musically, before looking up to the ceiling in a kind of ecstasy of creativity as it all came to him. Then Franz repeated the same words, only now singing the tune.

Fritz, admiring the maestro's genius, tried to forget his dire words of warning about Hitler, wanting to believe that his fears would never come true. Perhaps, after all, they never would and all would be well, except that, remembering his experiences as a serving soldier in the Great War, he understood perfectly well that cruel realities could often destroy even the best of dreams.

22

10th October 1929

Franz decided that *The Land of Smiles* should première in Berlin at the Metropol Theater rather than in Vienna, with Franz conducting the orchestra, on the grounds that it would be likely to attract bigger audiences. There was also every reason to be confident that this would be the case as *Frederica* had premièred there the previous year and enjoyed a profitable run.

Anton had been living in Berlin since the early 1920s after being forced to leave Hungary following an unsuccessful attempt, in which he had been heavily involved, to restore the Habsburg Monarchy there. He and Emilie were therefore delighted to be in the audience for this special occasion, and as they sat in their seats in the front stalls and Anton glanced around him, he noticed someone enter one of the theatre's boxes, whom he immediately recognised. He then turned to Emilie.

'Do you see who's just arrived? He's in the box to our left. Can you see?'

Emilie looked in the direction in which Anton had pointed and then gasped a little. 'It's Adolf Hitler, isn't it?'

'Why, of course. I must say, he's come a long way since his days in Vienna as a struggling artist...'

'But, nasty little man that he's become, surely all in the

wrong direction. How many seats has his party got in the Reichstag now? Only ten, isn't it?'

'Twelve actually, but that could still change in his favour, I'm afraid. He has some of his henchmen with him, too, I see. I think I recognise Josef Goebbels. Since Hitler made him his party's leading official in this city two or three years ago, he's been trying to stir up a lot of hatred towards Communists and Jews.'

'Well, I just hate the way they strut around in uniforms so much of the time. We're not at war any longer.'

'No, but Hitler would like us to be.'

They then sat back in their seats to enjoy the operetta, which for Anton began to evoke happy memories of another glorious evening almost a quarter of a century previously when *The Merry Widow* had first been performed in Vienna.

'My God,' Anton exclaimed to Emilie as the interval began. 'You know, I think this as good as *The Merry Widow*. It's going to be another triumph for him, I'm sure it is. How does he keep on creating so much wonderful music after all these years?'

'I don't know, but for me, this is superior to *The Merry Widow*. I mean the story's so much better.'

'Well, that's thanks to Fritz Löhner-Beda. He's such a good librettist. I really must go and offer my congratulations to Franz. Will you come with me?'

'No, I don't think so. Surely, there'll be plenty of time for that once the performance is over. I'd rather like a drink, wouldn't you?'

'Yes, of course. Look, just give me five minutes...'

'Oh, all right, but I expect you'll be even longer.'

'I'll try not to be, I promise.'

Anton then made his way as quickly as he could to Franz's dressing room, which again evoked vivid memories of the première of *The Merry Widow* when he'd done just the same. He had to remember where it was after just one visit the previous year when he and Emilie had attended the première of *Frederica*. As a consequence he started to go in the wrong direction and ended up having to ask the way. He certainly didn't want Emilie to grow too impatient, but having come this far he pressed on.

When he entered the dressing room and offered his congratulations, Franz just gave him rather a bleak look.

'What on earth's wrong? I thought you'd be so pleased.'

'I've had an invitation from Adolf Hitler to visit his box. Honestly, it's the last thing I want to do.'

'Ignore it then.'

'I can't do that. It would be too, too impolite. Will you come with me? For moral support, I mean.'

'I said to Emilie I'd only be five minutes. Why not send him a message saying you'll be pleased to see him once the performance is over? Emilie and I will both come with you then.'

'Yes, that's a good idea. I'll do just that. Can you both meet me outside his box?'

'Yes, all right.'

When Anton then returned to his seat and told Emilie what had happened, she pulled a face. 'I don't want to be introduced to that horrible man.'

'It will only be for a few minutes. The theatre will be closing, after all. Franz isn't happy either, but doesn't feel he can refuse to see the man and would welcome our support.'

When the operetta ended there was a moment of silence and

then a few scattered claps before the auditorium broke into a torrent of applause. Glancing up at Hitler's box, Anton could see that he was standing up, as was Goebbels, and that they were applauding loudly.

There were several curtain calls with positively ecstatic applause for all the principal performers including especially Richard Tauber, who had performed the part of the Chinese Emperor. Then Franz came on stage, too, insisting that Fritz and Ludwig Hertzer should join him and once more the audience erupted in applause.

Once this had finally died down and people started to leave the theatre, Anton and Emilie made their way in the direction of Hitler's box. Upon their arrival, they found that Franz was waiting for them, looking distinctly ill at ease.

'This must be quick,' he said. 'We've a party to go to, after all.'

He then took a deep breath before opening the door to the box and stepping inside. 'Herr Hitler, it is a great pleasure to see you again. Thank you for waiting for me. I have my brother Anton with me and also his wife Emilie.'

'Maestro, it's such a pleasure for me, too, to see you again after all these years.' With a warm smile he then shook hands vigorously with Franz before doing the same with both Anton and Emilie. 'I heard about the première and asked my assistant to obtain tickets. It's a welcome chance to escape the hurly-burly of Berlin politics and the stupidities of my opponents and enjoy some culture. I so enjoyed tonight's performance. Now let me introduce you to my colleagues...' This was followed by another round of handshakes. 'I'm sure this operetta will be another triumph for you, maestro,' Hitler then added.

'You're very kind to say so. I mustn't take all the credit,

though. I owe so much to my librettists as well as the cast of the operetta, especially Richard Tauber. He played the part of the Emperor.'

'He's a Jew, of course,' Goebbels interjected in a somewhat sneering tone.

'But still a very talented one, you must admit,' Anton responded. '... As is the librettist Fritz Löhner-Beda. He's also a Jew,' he added with just a hint of defiance in his voice.

Goebbels, ignoring Anton, then looked straight at Franz. 'When our great movement comes to power as it surely will, both here and in Austria, you will need to keep better company, maestro.'

'Perhaps so, but you'll forgive me for saying that in the meantime I need a librettist of Fritz's talents. His skills fire my imagination and my musical soul.'

'I understand that but I'm sure there are plenty of excellent German writers whose work can form the basis for an opera.'

'I wouldn't suggest otherwise,' Franz responded, trying to be as diplomatic as possible whilst feeling increasingly uncomfortable as there was a slightly awkward silence that Hitler then broke:

'We all know that Jewish culture is so pervasive in Germany and Austria today that, at present, it is almost impossible to enjoy any cultural experience without some Jew being involved in the process of creation. However, I need to make it very clear to you, maestro, that this is not a situation which I, or any of my colleagues, enjoy or want to see perpetuated. If I have my way there'll be an expurgation of Jewish culture from the life of Germany and in time from the life of Austria, too. And maestro, when we knew each other in Austria all those years ago, I'm sure you never expected that I would become the leader of a great political movement.'

'No, indeed not. Of course, the letter you sent me after the war did tell me that you intended entering politics.'

'Ah, yes, but at the time I could not possibly have anticipated the path that would take me on. Who knows, as a naturalised German I may yet be Chancellor of Germany.'

Franz was almost left at a loss for words at this pronouncement. 'Hm... tell me, do you still paint? I mean, for pleasure.' The question struck Franz as rather inane in the circumstances but nothing better came to mind.

'No, no, I put my brushes to one side when I began my quest to save Germany from the abyss into which it has fallen.'

Franz was now feeling so uncomfortable that all he wanted to do was leave. 'You'll forgive me, but we have a party to attend.'

'Of course, maestro, I understand. It has been such a great pleasure to meet you again, it really has. I shall always be grateful to you for the great kindness you showed me.'

'Thank you, thank you.'

There was then another round of handshakes before they could withdraw, breathing a sigh of relief once they had done so.

'That man is a dangerous menace,' Anton exclaimed. 'I just pray he and his kind never come to power.'

At the subsequent party to celebrate the première, Franz couldn't wait to thank his librettists and leading cast members for their support.

'You've all been wonderful in helping us achieve what I believe will be a great success, the like of which I have not achieved since *The Merry Widow* was first performed.'

'And did I hear you say, Franz, that you'd been summoned

to an audience with Herr Hitler in his box this evening?' Fritz asked.

'Yes, that's right. As I've told you, we knew each other in Vienna before the war. He loved the operetta but I can't say that meeting him again was the most pleasurable of experiences...'

'He and his henchman Goebbels started spouting a lot of anti-Semitic nonsense, I'm afraid,' Anton added.

'Well, we all know what a threat he is to all Jews,' Fritz responded.

'At least he's no power to carry out his insane wishes,' Franz said.

'Not yet but that could well change. I fear for this country's future now that the German Chancellor Gustav Stresemann has died, so completely unexpectedly.'

In the event, much worse was to follow. Only twelve days later the Wall Street crash shook the world economy so badly that it sparked a terrible economic depression, putting millions out of work both in America and Europe with Germany being hit as badly as anywhere. Although it would take more than another three years for him to achieve his dream, for Hitler this disaster was like a gift from the gods.

23

Berlin, Monday evening, 1st August 1932

'Our worst nightmare is coming ever closer,' Anton said gloomily to Emilie. They had not long finished eaten dinner in their apartment and had been listening to a wireless broadcast confirming the results of the Federal election, which had taken place the previous day.

'Will Hitler be able to form a government, do you think?'

'I sincerely hope not, but even without an overall majority the Nazis are now by far the largest party. Imagine that over thirteen million people voted for their candidates. It just shows you the dire state into which this country is descending thanks to the financial crash and the huge rise in unemployment.'

'What I also don't understand is why so many people are attracted to Hitler the man. I just find his rants loathsome.'

'He promises to heal all their woes, restore the greatness of the nation. Worst of all, he offers them a scapegoat by which, of course, I mean the Jews.'

'The telephone's ringing.'

'Oh, so it is. I expect it'll be Franz. He said he'd call once the election results were known.' Anton then walked out into the hall and picked up the receiver. 'Hello, is that you, Franz?'

'Yes, it's me. I don't suppose you're happy at the news?'

'That, my dear brother, is an understatement. I'm appalled,

115

though I can't say too surprised.'

'But people are saying he won't be able to form a government...'

'And they may be right - this time. However, I don't see any weak coalition opposed to the Nazis lasting six months, in which case there'll just have to be another election...'

'When I expect you think Hitler will win an outright majority?'

'Unfortunately, yes. The writing's on the wall, I'm afraid, in which case next month's première will have to be the last held in Berlin.'

'At sixty-two, I'm not sure I have it in me to write any more operettas. I can tell you, my creative juices are not what they once were. Perhaps one more work, if I can find the energy for it, and then I'll be done.'

'Whatever the future holds, Franz, you've had an illustrious career.'

'That's kind of you, but I do hope you're wrong about Hitler. I can't imagine he really means half of what he says, so even if he were to come to power I don't suppose things would turn out as bad as you say.'

Anton sighed. 'I tell you he lusts for another war and doesn't give a damn for the consequences.'

'And you also know that the thought of another war as terrible as the last one horrifies me as I'm sure it does millions of others.'

'Including me, I assure you, but once Hitler is in power that's surely the direction in which he'll take Germany as fast as he possibly can. In the meantime, of course, he'll also make life hell for anyone who tries to oppose him, and begin to persecute the Jews.'

'So you're determined to leave, I take it?'

'If Hitler comes to power, I firmly believe I'll have no choice.'

'Um, at least you can come home to Vienna.'

'That's what I'd like to do, as you know. What concerns me is that Chancellor Dollfuss has strong fascist tendencies and Austria's economy is in an even worse shape than Germany's. France's decision to veto any customs union with Germany could easily backfire.'

'Why do you think that?'

'If Austria's economy doesn't recover, it will just encourage more people to support the Austrian Nazi party, and you know what that could lead to.'

'You mean unification with Germany?'

'It's possible. You know ever since the war some people have been arguing that Austria isn't a viable nation state.'

'We'll they're surely wrong. I think it's a dreadful idea. In fact, it really doesn't bear contemplating. But, look, I didn't just make this call to talk politics...'

So, they abruptly changed the subject, and after about ten minutes Franz rang off.

'I fear Franz is in a state of denial,' Anton told Emilie.

'In what way?'

'Like too many others, he doesn't appreciate the threat Hitler poses to not only this country and Austria but the whole of Europe.'

'At least Hindenburg is still our President. Hitler's party may also be the largest but it still lacks an overall majority,' she reminded him.

He sighed in frustration. 'It's only a question of time, I tell you. And surely you agree with me that Hitler's a menace, don't you?'

'Of course, I do. I think Hitler's odious, you know that. Has the time come then to plan our departure?'

'Yes, we need to be ready for that eventuality. I imagine it'll be easy enough for me to resign my directorship here in Berlin.'

'But what will you do once we arrive in Vienna?'

'I'd like to set up my own publishing company. We have some capital, after all.'

'True, though not nearly as much as before the financial crash.'

'Well, hopefully Franz would be willing to invest in what I have in mind, or I could approach a bank for a loan.'

Emilie made a face. 'I expect banks have little money to lend these days and when they do their rates of interest can be expensive.'

'I would only see that as a last resort. Hopefully, it won't be necessary.'

The following day, Anton was at his desk on the first floor of the office in which he worked, when he heard the sound of a brass band playing the military march *Königgrätzer*. It was coming closer so he went to the window, from which he had a view of the street below in both directions. Looking to his left, he could see a march by the Sturmabteilung (SA) approaching.

Several flags were being held aloft displaying the black swastika, while the men taking part in the march were all wearing the brown shirt uniforms of the paramilitary wing of Hitler's Nazi Party. It was obvious to him that this was a display of strength being staged in celebration of the Nazis' success in Sunday's General Election. Although as a former soldier he appreciated the fact that the men were well turned out and disciplined, what they were doing still made him shudder.

'Excuse me, sir.'

He turned round and smiled at his secretary Lily Bronovitch, who had worked for him for the previous four years. In her mid-forties, she was married with two sons, extremely efficient, good-natured, and also a Jew.

'I'm sorry about that din outside,' he said to her. 'They'll be gone soon enough, I hope.'

'I like to hear a brass band play, sir.'

'In normal circumstances, so do I, but not by these pretend soldiers. They're no more than thugs in uniform.'

Tactfully, she made no comment on this remark. 'Here are the letters you dictated ready for signing, sir.'

'But you agree with me, I hope?'

'I don't like them, sir, but I've never been one for politics. I just want to be allowed to get on with my life in peace.'

'Of course you do. I just fear that if Hitler comes to power life will be made very hard for anyone with Jewish blood. You and your husband should think seriously about emigrating, perhaps even to Palestine.'

Lily shook her head vigorously. 'Oh no, sir, I don't want to live in a hot climate and Germany's my home. Victor fought in the war, too, and was wounded, like yourself, sir. We're both loyal to this country.'

'Quite so, but the Nazis hate all Jews, I'm afraid. If Palestine is out of the question there are alternatives here in Europe; England, for example, is still a strong, liberal democracy with a constitutional monarchy.'

'I'll certainly talk to my husband about your advice, sir.'

'Please do. Now let me sign these letters.'

By now the march had passed by, but he could still clearly hear that its band had struck up another marching tune, which he only vaguely recognised and couldn't put a name to. However, in the years ahead he would come to know it better as *Badonviller*, which was played on cinema newsreels whenever Hitler appeared.

Half an hour later, he left the office to walk home. The leg which he had so nearly lost in the war and which caused him to limp was feeling painfully stiff but he did his best to ignore this. He knew the day would come when he would only be able to walk with the aid of a stick, but he was determined to avoid this for as long as possible.

He'd not gone all that far when he passed a shop whose window had been smashed in. It was a tailor's by the name of Treydel, which he assumed was Jewish. Then he saw the words, *Death to all Jews,* had been scrawled on the wall of the shop. In that moment his foreboding about the Nazis deepened, making him more convinced than ever that they were evil and would bring nothing but harm to Germany. More worrying still was what harm they might bring to Austria.

24

Monday 30th January 1933

On this fateful day, Hitler went to the Presidential Palace to shake hands with President Hindenburg on his being appointed Chancellor of Germany. At that moment it truly felt to him that he was fulfilling his God-given destiny as the saviour of his country.

A few hours later, he stood in the window of the Reich Chancellery to receive an ovation from a crowd of enthusiastic supporters whom he then proceeded to address.

'More than fourteen years have passed since the unhappy day when the German people, blinded by promises from foes at home and abroad, lost touch with honour and freedom, thereby losing all. Since that day of treachery, the Almighty has withheld his blessing from our people. Dissension and hatred descended upon us. With profound distress millions of the best German men and women from all walks of life have seen the unity of the nation vanishing away, dissolving in a confusion of political and personal opinions, economic interests, and ideological differences. Since that day, as so often in the past, Germany has presented a picture of heartbreaking disunity. We never received the equality and fraternity we had been promised, and we lost our liberty to boot. For when our nation lost its place in the world, it soon lost its unity of spirit and will.'

In response the crowd began to give the Nazi salute and shout as one:

'*Heil Hitler! Heil Hitler! Heil Hitler!*'

A fortnight later, not wishing to live under Nazi rule and knowing that he would be likely to be looked on with suspicion given his history of support for the Habsburg Monarchy in Hungary, Anton returned to Austria to live, with Emilie by his side.

They already had Franz's assurance that they could stay with him and Sophie at their apartment in Vienna and over their first dinner together following their arrival, they naturally discussed Hitler's coming to power in Germany.

'I've long feared this would happen,' Anton said.

'I just kept hoping the German people would have the sense not to allow it,' Franz responded.

'The sad irony is that Hitler's party didn't receive a majority of the votes in the election, although they're the largest party in the Reichstag. I fear that von Hindenburg, along with the former chancellor von Papen, who's now Hitler's vice-chancellor, have made a grave miscalculation if they think Hitler will respect democracy now he's in power. I'm sure he'll do everything it takes to become a dictator in furtherance of his aims.'

'I just pray that Austria can remain independent.'

'So do I. There's no immediate threat to that, but in the longer term…' He shrugged. 'I wouldn't be too confident.'

25

June 1934

Nearly seventeen months after becoming Chancellor of Germany, having succeeded in consolidating his hold on power, Hitler decided to give a press conference in the Reich Chancellery to foreign journalists. Dozens of them assembled in the palatial press room, and when Hitler appeared he was accompanied by Josef Goebbels along with an interpreter.

Norman Ebbutt, the *London Times* correspondent, was one of the first to ask a question. 'Herr Hitler, do you believe the National Socialist movement will endure as a permanent political force in Germany?'

'Of course. At the risk of appearing to talk nonsense, I tell you that the National Socialist movement will go on for a thousand years!'

'That's certainly an ambitious prediction, Herr Hitler.'

'Of course it is, but don't forget that my career has seen an endless procession of my ambitious predictions coming true! Don't forget, either, how people laughed at me fifteen years ago when I declared that one day I would govern Germany. They laugh now, just as foolishly, when I declare that I shall remain in power for the rest of my life!'

Dorothy Thompson, a journalist with *The New York Post*, then had a question. 'Herr Hitler, what are your ambitions so far as Austria is concerned? It's true, isn't it, that you would like to incorporate Austria into a greater Germany?'

'I have no immediate plans to do anything of the kind, but clearly, I see Austria as a natural ally of Germany, especially as it is a country where most people speak German and Germany is, of course, a community of German-speakers.'

'You envisage your plans changing at some point in the future, then?'

'As you know, any union between Germany and Austria was forbidden by the totally unjust Treaty of Versailles that was imposed on Germany at the end of the Great War. However, if it should one day be the common will of the German and Austrian peoples that they should unite, then no treaty should be allowed to prevent that.'

Alexander Dembitz, a journalist with the Viennese news-paper, *Wiener Zeitung*, then raised a hand and Hitler also took his question. 'Chancellor, you say that Germany is the community of German-speakers. Does that then also include the Sudetenland in Czechoslovakia, for example?'

Hitler smiled but with a decidedly steely look in his eyes. 'As I said, Germany includes all those who speak German. And yes, that must include the Sudetenland, as well as Austria. At this time, that's all I have to say on this subject.'

'Thank you, chancellor,' Dembitz responded.

Five days later, Franz and Anton were having coffee together in the Café Central in Vienna. Anton had a copy of the *Wiener Zeitung* in front of him and tossed it down on the table in front of Franz. 'You should read this.'

'What does it say?'

'It's a report by a fellow called Alexander Dembitz from a press conference with Hitler a few days ago. Hitler has called Austria a natural ally of Germany and has not ruled out the possibility of Austria uniting with Germany at some point in the future. You know, if that was ever to happen it would be very bad news for all of Austria's Jews, and, for that matter, anyone else who's opposed to the Nazis.'

'So friends and colleagues like Fritz…'

'Your wife Sophie, too.'

'Quite. Yet I tend to think that all Hitler's diatribes about the Jews were simply rabble-rousing to win himself votes. Now he's in power it's surely likely he'll adopt a different policy. Can he really have forgotten his friendships with men like Sammy Morgenstern?'

Anton shook his head. 'But remember what he said about the Jews when we met him five years ago or what he wrote in *My Struggle*. With respect, Franz, I think it would be naive to imagine that he isn't deadly serious about attacking the rights of Jewish people.'

26

Vienna, early May 1937

'Happy birthday, Franz.'

'Thank you, Anton. So pleased that you and Emilie have been able to join us for this little celebration.'

Anton smiled at his brother and they embraced. It was their first meeting since Christmas the previous year, a long enough gap for Anton to notice how much Franz looked every one of his sixty-seven years and perhaps a few more besides. In the last three years it seemed to him that he aged more like ten, and not just in appearance. He now walked with a noticeably slow gait and seemed to have completely lost his former vigour.

'I hope you're still enjoying life as a gentleman farmer,' he added.

'Tolerably well, thank you, Franz. It's certainly a change from publishing.'

He eyed him quizzically. 'Do I detect a note of doubt in that answer?'

'No, not really. It can be hard work at times but I've never shied away from that, as you know.'

'Or lacked courage either. It's not something I'd have wanted to take on at our time of life.'

'But I'm barely sixty-one, still in good health, and have the services of a first-rate herdsman,' Anton protested.

'Even so...'

From the hallway they could hear the voices of the guests who'd already arrived and amongst them Anton recognised that of Richard Tauber's. As they then walked into the large lounge with its tall ceiling and beautiful chandelier, bathed in evening sunshine, the smoke from the many cigarettes which had been lit made him cough immediately. For all that there were times when he missed Vienna's café culture, one thing he most certainly didn't regret leaving behind was the smoke of the city. Where he and Emilie were now living might be a rural backwater, but he was still convinced that life as a gentleman farmer was decidedly healthier.

Richard Tauber's larger-than-life personality, ebullient with good humour and optimism, dominated the room, but even he was almost overshadowed by the most attractive woman standing next to him. Anton had never met her before but guessed from what he'd already been told by Franz that she must be Richard's new wife, the English actress Diana Napier. She had what he thought of as a strong face with kind, sensitive eyes, and being in her early thirties, was about thirteen years younger than Richard.

Anton quickly discovered that her German was minimal, but with her winning smile and Richard as her interpreter, this barely mattered. The conversation, too, was all about the films the two of them had starred in together in England and Richard wasn't slow to sing its praises.

'It's a great country to work in and the freedom people enjoy is like a breath of fresh air, compared with what we have here.'

'You intend to live there permanently then, I take it?' Anton asked him.

Richard glanced at his wife, who was smiling sweetly without probably having understood a word he'd just said. 'That depends on what happens here.'

'The way things are looking I doubt if it'll be long before Germany invades,' Anton declared. 'She's busy rearming, after all, and we certainly can't expect Mussolini to defend us any longer.'

'Oh, why's that?'

'From what I've read he and Hitler have climbed into bed together because Italy couldn't even defeat the poor Ethiopians without help from Germany.'

This time Richard's wife gave Anton an anxious look, suggesting she'd at least got the gist of what he was saying. At the same time he heard a snort of disapproval and, turning his head, saw that Fritz Löhner-Beda had arrived accompanied by Helene, whose beauty he thought was still a match for Richard's new wife. He was frowning at him through his spectacles, his bald pate lit up by the evening sunshine.

'Hello, everyone,' he said cheerfully. 'This is happy occasion, is it not? I suggest you save your pessimism for another day, Anton.'

The tone of his rebuke was gentle, as he was a kindly man, but it still irked him somewhat. 'I'm sorry if you think me that, but Fritz, surely you appreciate what danger you'll be in once the Nazis gain control of this country? You understand that, don't you, Richard?' he added, gesturing to him with his right hand.

'I certainly remember how Hitler's Brownshirts attacked me before I left Germany,' Richard replied. 'I tell you, Fritz, if the Nazis come here they'll make life hell for anyone with Jewish blood.'

Fritz looked at Richard. 'Perhaps so, I can't help that, but I'm not convinced they'll ever invade. Our chancellor's still committed to Austrian independence, after all.'

'I don't doubt that,' Anton responded. 'All the same, he's already allowed Nazis into his government so I don't see his commitment being worth a pfennig once German tanks cross the border.'

'Well, this country's my home. It's all I know and I don't intend to leave. Let the Nazis do their worst.'

'With the greatest of respect, Fritz, I can't believe you really mean that.'

'I just want to be allowed to live my life in peace. Is that too much to ask?'

'Of course not. I'm just afraid that we live in dangerous times so precautions are necessary.'

Fritz shook his head. 'Well, I'm not leaving Austria and that's final. You can accuse me of burying my head in the sand as much as you like.'

Meanwhile, the expression on the face of Richard's wife had turned to one of total puzzlement. Anton was convinced she had completely failed to understand what Fritz and he were saying to each other, which he thought rather symbolic. Certainly, he felt total puzzlement at how the events of the last quarter of a century had so completely unravelled the world in which he had grown up, and might well continue to do so in the years that lay ahead.

It was enough to make him want to shake his head in sheer disbelief. But then two maids appeared, one carrying a tray of champagne and the other of canapés, which brightened his mood a little, though not for long. Glancing around the room, he recognised amongst the other guests the opera singer Louis Treumann and the librettist Victor Léon, both of whom were also Jews. They were deep in conversation with each other and he imagined they must have overheard something of what he'd just been saying to Fritz. Had they made any plans to leave Austria before it was too late, he wondered, or, like Fritz, did they prefer to bury their heads in the sand and hope that nothing terrible would ever happen?

Anton knew that Léon was seventy-nine, though he didn't look it. It would therefore be expecting a great deal to argue that he should give up everything at such an advanced age by fleeing abroad; and even though Treumann was younger than Léon, it would still be extremely difficult for him to leave Austria and start a new life at the age of sixty-five. It was also possible that the Nazis might be more lenient towards more elderly Jews, although Anton somehow doubted it.

So if, like Fritz, both Léon and Treumann decided to remain in Austria, Anton felt it certainly wasn't his place to blame them. On the contrary, he just felt terribly sad that such great men were being placed in such an invidious position, having done so much for the world of music and their country for so many years.

It wasn't long before they all went into the dining room to take their seats for dinner. By now Anton was feeling decidedly hungry and as Franz employed an excellent cook the meal didn't disappoint. Indeed, the dumplings were simply delicious, and by the time they had drunk several glasses of wine in addition to the champagne, everyone was in a state of relaxed good humour.

'I have some good news for you,' Franz announced.

Anton's first thought was that he might be composing again but that didn't prove to be the case.

'As you will all know, for me the last three years have been blighted by this awful accusation of plagiarism. However, I have here a letter from my lawyer...' And with that Franz picked it up off the table in front of him and waved it up and down. 'It informs me that Wilhelm Kienzl has admitted to never having even read the amateurish score that he and sixteen others were prepared to accuse me of plagiarising. What's more, he's prepared to make a full apology...'

This announcement was met by exclamations of delight around the table as well as cries of 'About time, too.'

Franz continued: 'Even better than this, it's now been admitted that the sixteen others who supported this ridiculous accusation only did so at Kienzl's request, and that none of them have the read the score either. All of them will therefore be withdrawing their accusation...'

'This is wonderful, Franz,' Anton declared. 'You've been completely vindicated at last.'

'It's a great relief, I must say, but not quite the end of the matter as I still need to prove defamation through the courts. Nevertheless, my lawyer has also advised me that now Kienzl and his friends are prepared to withdraw their accusation, the case is so overwhelmingly in my favour, I'm bound to succeed.'

There were smiles all round at this excellent news followed by a lusty rendition of 'Happy Birthday to You' once Franz had blown out the seven candles on his cake to represent each decade of his life. The ladies then withdrew to the lounge while the men remained at the table to enjoy cigars and brandy. For the sake of being sociable, on special occasions, Franz's birthday being one of them, Anton was willing to indulge himself in this pastime even while otherwise remaining a non-smoker.

Conversation around the table soon touched on the fear of a possible German invasion. Once again Anton therefore found himself reiterating his view that this was inevitable.

'But even if you're right, it might be five years from now, by which time I may well have gone to meet my maker,' Victor Léon declared.

'I hope you'll live many more years than that,' Anton responded. 'However, I fear any invasion could come quite soon.'

'You're not suggesting it's imminent, are you?' Fritz asked him in a somewhat irritated tone of voice.

'... No, I wouldn't go that far, but if it hasn't happened within two years I'll be pleasantly surprised. By the way, Fritz, I didn't intend any criticism of you when I suggested earlier that you should consider leaving Austria. It's completely wrong that any Austrian with Jewish blood should be faced with the prospect of losing their rights of citizenship and even loss of liberty.'

'You seriously believe the Nazis would start imprisoning us?' Treumann asked.

'They've already opened camps in Germany and I expect there are more to come. From what I've read, artists, musicians and intellectuals who they disapprove of are particularly vulnerable, and especially when they've Jewish blood.'

'But I'm with Fritz here,' Treumann declared. 'I'm as Austrian as the next man so I'll be damned if I'll run away from my homeland.'

'Believe me, Louis, I fully respect that. Don't forget, though, that it won't necessarily just be you who might be made to suffer...'

'You think they might imprison wives as well?'

'In the fullness of time, I wouldn't discount the possibility.'

'So what about my wife Sophie, then?' Franz asked. 'Are you suggesting she could even end up being imprisoned in one of these dreadful camps?'

Looking his brother straight in the eyes, Anton gave him a very short answer. 'Yes, I fear so.'

He grunted at him. 'Well, on that less than happy note I suggest we rejoin the ladies.'

'I apologise if what I've said has in any way spoilt what has been a splendid evening...'

'Don't worry, Anton, you've simply given us your honest opinion and we should be grateful for that.'

'And I agree with everything Anton's said,' Richard Tauber added.

'Ah, but it's an easy call for you,' Fritz responded. 'You've got an international career, an English wife, and you speak her language. It's different for the rest of us.'

'I understand that, Fritz, really I do. I'm really not suggesting it's an easy call for any of you, and nor is Anton.'

27

Theresienfeld, 12th February 1938

'*C*hancellor Schuschnigg has met with the German Führer today in order to discuss the future relationship of Austria with Germany. Following this meeting a statement was released in which the German Führer reaffirmed his support for Austrian national sovereignty. It is further announced that Herr Arthur Seyss-Inquart is to take up the position of Minister of Public Security with full responsibility for police affairs...'*

This announcement on the wireless was enough to make Anton bang his fist on the table in front of him in disgust. He and Emilie were eating their evening meal together. 'This is the beginning of the end,' he declared angrily.

'But I don't understand,' she responded. 'The Führer has reaffirmed...'

'That's bullshit!' Emilie gave him an offended look at his use of such language but he was unrepentant. 'Don't you know who Seyss-Inquart is?'

'No. Should I?'

'He's a prominent member of the Austrian Nazi Party. Hitler's only promised support for Austrian independence in return for one of his henchmen being put in charge of our police. I tell you, it won't stop there. There'll just be more tightening of the screws until the Nazis have total control of the government. And once that happens unification is bound to follow.'

'You can't be certain of that.'

'Oh, Emilie, please. You sound like Franz when you talk this way. It's coming, I tell you.'

For all Anton's warnings, he had found Franz to be in an increasing state of denial of late. 'You're just a doom-monger,' Franz had told him at Christmas time, the last occasion on which he'd mentioned the subject to him. It had forced him to the conclusion that to speak of it further was almost bound to be counter-productive.

Anton ate a mouthful of bratwurst while contemplating a future living under Nazi rule. It would not be pleasant, of that he was absolutely certain.

'Assuming you're right, should we be thinking about leaving?' Emilie then asked him, intently. 'After all, you were determined to leave Germany once the Nazis came to power there.'

Anton shook his head. 'As I've said before, we've moved enough. Much as I detest the Nazis I'm not politically active and pose no threat to them. Hopefully, they'll leave us in peace.'

'So you can't blame others for not wanting to leave.'

He sighed. 'Haven't I made it clear enough already that I don't blame any of them? All the same, I still think Franz would be wise to think of Sophie's safety. If she was ever taken away, it would completely break him, I know it would.'

'But don't you exaggerate the risk of that ever happening?'

'Possibly, but if I thought there was the slightest risk to you, I'd want us to leave for Switzerland without delay.'

'Will you talk to him again then?'

He shrugged his shoulders. 'I might. Unfortunately, he can be very stubborn at times. The more I go on about it, the less I think he listens.'

Anton still contemplated picking up the phone but not with any enthusiasm. All too quickly the days slipped by until over breakfast he read in his copy of *Wiener Zeitung* an article describing a speech Hitler had made the previous day to the Reichstag. As soon as he read the words, *the German Reich is no longer willing to tolerate the suppression of ten million Germans outside its borders*, he sucked in his breath.

Emilie was still in bed with a bad chill and he didn't want to trouble her with more bad news. Instead, he resolved to telephone Franz in order to give him the benefit of his opinion that a German invasion was almost certainly now imminent. But then again he still hesitated, thinking that Franz would not appreciate such a call at such a time of day.

After some agonising it was to be eight o'clock in the evening before he finally picked up the phone. He had made up his mind, too, that he would come quickly to the point and he kept to that resolution.

'Franz, I particularly rang you because I thought you ought to know that I'm now as certain as I can be that a German invasion is about to take place.' This was met by silence. 'Hello, Franz, are you there?'

'... Why do you say that?' He could detect a note of irritation in the tone of this question.

'Hitler's clearly leant on Schuschnigg, otherwise he'd never have agreed to make Seyss-Inquart his Public Security Minister, but what's really convinced me is the speech Hitler made yesterday to the Reichstag. It's when he said that he'd no longer tolerate the suppression of ten million Germans living outside the Reich that I knew the game was up. It amounts to an implicit threat to invade not just Austria but probably Czechoslovakia, too.'

'Oh dear. I don't suppose the League of Nations would be very happy.'

Anton snorted. 'That organization has no teeth. He might think twice if either Britain or France threatened war, but I don't see that happening. Anyway, I see no chance of either of them coming to the aid of Austria, and we know Italy won't either. Look, I just thought I ought to warn you, just in case you're willing to reconsider your position.'

Franz sighed. 'Don't think I'm not grateful for your concern on my behalf, and Sophie's, too, of course; but we're just too old and set in our ways to pack up and leave the country. Anyway, despite what you think, I don't believe the Germans would do anything to hurt Sophie. It's not as if she's even a practising Jew.'

'Oh God, Franz, as I've said to you before, that won't protect her from losing all citizenship rights.'

'Well, maybe not, but I don't see that mattering very much, just so long as we're allowed to live in peace. That's all we ask.'

Anton sighed. It was clearly pointless trying to take this conversation any further. 'Well, at least I've warned you. I can't do more, if your mind's made up...'

'It is, Anton, it really is. You've always been too much of a pessimist, you know you have.'

Anton was inclined to retort that he had had every good reason for being so, but instead bit his tongue. 'Perhaps...'

Franz chuckled. 'Everything will turn out all wrong, you

know!' This was an ironic Viennese catchphrase with which they were both all too familiar.

Anton chuckled back. 'Well, you said it, Franz.'

'So how do you think the people will vote?' Emilie asked Anton. They were about to eat supper on what had been a cold and miserable day, a little more than two weeks since his conversation with Franz. It had just been announced on the wireless that, faced with insurrection by Austrian Nazis, Chancellor Schuschnigg had called a plebiscite on continued Austrian independence.

Anton shrugged his shoulders. 'You know how I'd like them to vote. My worry is that Hitler won't even allow the vote to proceed...'

'But it's only in four days' time.'

'In which case I wouldn't be surprised if German troops aren't already preparing to invade. If I were Hitler I wouldn't want to risk Austria voting no to unification, even if it's only by the tiniest of margins.'

The following day, news reports on the wireless merely announced the terms on which the plebiscite would be held. It particularly worried Anton that anyone under the age of twenty-four was to be excluded, as that would just add credence to any Nazi claim that the plebiscite was being rigged.

He also thought the motive behind such an exclusion was dubious as Schuschnigg clearly believed that the youngest voters were particularly pro-Nazi. Whether that was true or not he really didn't know, but that was hardly the point.

Then the next morning when he picked up his copy of the *Wiener Zeitung*, he read a report from Berlin. This made it clear that Hitler had already condemned the plebiscite as fraudulent and that as such he would never accept a vote in favour of continuing independence. Although Anton didn't know it at the time, even as he drove back to his farmhouse, Hitler was on the point of sending Schuschnigg an ultimatum. This informed him that he should either immediately resign in favour of Seyss-Inquart becoming chancellor, or face an invasion.

By the time Anton showed Emilie the newspaper report he was thinking the worst. 'I wouldn't be surprised if German troops haven't already crossed the border.'

'Then I suggest we keep listening to the wireless.'

Waiting for news made the day drag interminably. Every hour they listened to news bulletins but were left none the wiser about what might be happening.

'Surely, if German troops had invaded, something would have been said,' Emilie declared and Anton couldn't disagree.

'I just can't believe that Hitler isn't going to invade very soon, though.'

'Perhaps tomorrow...'

Finally, after they had eaten supper, it was announced that the chancellor would make a statement to the nation at eight o'clock. Speculating on what he might be about to say was hard, but Anton couldn't imagine it would be anything encouraging.

'I resign.' Once the chancellor uttered these words it was beyond all doubt that Austria was finished as an independent nation. Anton was almost overwhelmed by a sense of grief as if a loved one had died, and he kept shaking his head, not in disbelief, but rather in simple sadness.

'I yield to force. May God preserve Austria,' were the chancellor's closing words. Anton immediately stood up and switched the wireless off before turning to Emilie.

'May God preserve us, too, my love,' he said.

Five minutes later, the telephone rang. It was Franz. 'So your pessimism was well founded, it seems,' he immediately conceded.

'That gives me no pleasure, I assure you.'

'But I still don't believe that the Nazis will harm Sophie.'

'I sincerely hope they won't.'

'Um, and you have nothing to fear either, I trust?'

'I pray not.'

'Well, I'll telephone again in a few days. Goodnight to you, Anton.'

It had been a very brief conversation. Anton sensed, too, that behind his words, Franz was nervous about what would happen next. In this, he was most certainly not alone.

28

Monday 14th March 1938

Hitler arrived in Vienna to more acclaim than he had ever imagined possible, with huge crowds of enthusiastic supporters lining the streets as his cavalcade of cars passed by, all of whom were happy to give the Nazi salute and shout '*Heil Hitler!*'

As he alighted from his car in order to walk into the Hotel Imperial in the Ringstrasse, where he would be staying, some boys of about twelve ran up to him to ask for his signature. Hitler's personal bodyguard gently pushed them away, but he insisted on talking to one of the boys.

'And what's your name, my boy?' he asked in an amiable, avuncular voice.

'Ludwig Schmidt, Herr Chancellor Hitler.'

Hitler looked around at his entourage and smiled. 'Perhaps we have another Beethoven in waiting here in Vienna, a rival one day, perhaps, to our maestro Franz Lehár.'

'This is my copy of your book *My Struggle*, Herr Chancellor Hitler. May I beg of you, please, to sign it for me inside?'

'Of course. Willingly. Do you have a fountain pen, my boy?'

'I do, Herr Chancellor.'

Hitler was about to sign the book when he realised he needed something to rest it on. Obligingly, and to the amusement of all present, Ludwig immediately turned round and beckoned to Hitler to use his back for this particular purpose. To general applause, Hitler then signed the book with a flourishing signature before handing it back to him.

'Thank you, Herr Chancellor Hitler. May all your struggles now be over and may nothing but victories lie ahead for you.'

'Thank you, my boy. Are you coming to see me at the Heldenplatz this evening?'

'Yes, I'm coming with my family.'

'Well, I'm afraid I may not spot you in the crowd, but I hope you enjoy what I shall say.'

When Hitler arrived at the Heldenplatz, church bells could be heard ringing out, whilst the crowd that had gathered there was simply vast, greeting him with huge acclaim.

He then went to the podium, looking down on this veritable sea of humanity, to give an address, which gave him immense pride. The acclaim continued, but as he stood patiently, as was his habit, waiting for the crowd to fall silent, it gradually did so.

'My German comrades, ladies and gentlemen! The nation of Austria is now part of greater Germany! This is continuing to grow and bring within its folds all German-speaking people, for where German is spoken, there Germany is. I can hardly express my delight at the friendly annexation of Austria by Germany. While I am now a naturalised German citizen, I was, as you will know, born in Austria myself, so when I learnt our wonderful language I learnt the Austrian form of it.

'What you feel now, at being part of greater Germany, I myself have experienced deeply in these past few days. A great historic change has confronted our German people. What you experience at this moment, all Germans experience with you: not only the two million people in this city, but sixty-five million of our people in our empire! I am seized and moved most deeply by this historic change. and all of you should now live for this oath: whatever may come, no-one will shatter and tear asunder the German Empire as it stands today!'

29

For two more weeks Anton's life as a farmer went on as it had before. Of course, the wireless and editions of *Wiener Zeitung* kept him aware of momentous events occurring elsewhere, but they had no immediate impact on his rural existence. Only fifty kilometres away, Hitler had made a triumphal entry into Vienna to the acclaim of tens of thousands of cheering Austrians, Arthur Seyss-Inquart had become chancellor, and it was announced that a plebiscite would take place on 10th April. Anton was sure there could be no doubt as to its outcome.

Then in late March he drove into Theresienfeld and saw a Nazi swastika flag flying from the roof of the Town Hall for the first time. An hour later, too, on his way back to his farm he was passed by a small convoy of German Wehrmacht vehicles also displaying swastikas. In his mind's eye, he could imagine this most potent symbol of Nazi power on display in every city and town in Austria.

That evening he talked on the telephone to Franz for the first time since the German invasion.

'I've not been feeling too well,' Franz told him. 'A bad cold, I'm afraid, so Sophie and I have kept to our apartment as much as possible. We have ventured out once or twice and I can tell you the city's streets are bedecked with swastikas. We've also seen some things that trouble me.'

'Oh, what might they be?'

'The windows of some Jewish-owned shops have been broken.'

'I see.'

'Sophie was also told by a friend yesterday that Nazi Brownshirts have forced Jewish actresses at the Theater der Josefstadt to clean public toilets. It troubles me that they should be humiliated like that.'

'Yes, that's dreadful.' Anton was tempted to be sanctimonious and point out the warnings he'd so often expressed, but he refrained from doing so. Nonetheless, he feared that there was a lot worse to come for the Jewish community.

'I suppose you still think the Nazis will persecute all Jews?' Franz asked him.

'... Yes, I'm afraid so.'

'I'll do everything I possibly can to protect Sophie, you know.'

'Of course. If I was in your shoes I'd want to do the same.'

'If I have to, I'll make a personal appeal to our new chancellor. The fact I'm such a well-known composer ought to count for something.'

'It might very well do so, but let's still hope you don't have to go that far. As you've suggested before, perhaps I'm being too pessimistic.'

'The trouble with your damn pessimism, Anton, is that it too often proves to be well placed.'

'I don't take any pleasure in that, I assure you.'

'Not even a tiny bit? After all, there's always satisfaction in being proved right.'

'No, not really. I just think we're being taken in the terrible direction of another war and I derive no satisfaction at all from suggesting that.'

'Everything really will turn out all wrong then?'

'I pray to God it won't.'

The next morning, Anton was woken by a loud banging on the front door. He'd always been an early riser and even more so since becoming a farmer. All the same, it was barely even light and he'd still been in a deep sleep.

'What the hell?' he muttered.

'Who on earth can it be?' Emilie asked sleepily.

His stomach turned over in dread of who it might be. Then he heard a man shout, 'Open up or we'll enter by force.'

By now he was already out of bed, and as their bedroom was at the front of the house he went to the window and opened it. He could see a car parked near the front door, which looked like a brand-new Mercedes-Benz.

'What do you want with me at this early hour?'

A man, who looked about half his age, wearing a black uniform, stepped out of the half-light. 'Are you General Anton Lehár?'

'I was once but I'm a long time retired.'

'I'll give you five minutes to get dressed and come outside. My orders are to arrest you.'

'On what possible grounds?'

'On suspicion that you're an enemy of the Reich.'

'But that's absurd...'

He looked at his watch. 'You now have four minutes to come outside before your front door is broken open. Make any attempt to escape and you will be shot.'

'All right, I'm coming.'

Emilie, who was shaking, Anton assumed, with a mixture of fear and the fact that the house was icily cold, helped him to dress. Then, even as he finished tying his shoelaces in the hallway, pulled on his coat, and placed a hat on his head, she offered him a glass of water, which he downed in one gulp.

'You have thirty seconds...' he heard the man call out.

'I'm just coming!' Emilie threw her arms around him and they kissed. 'I expect they only want to intimidate me,' he told her. 'God willing I'll be released after just a few hours.'

'Go with God.'

He nodded. 'Make sure you telephone Franz to tell him what's happened.'

'I will.'

Then he opened the door. Three men were facing him including the one he'd been speaking to, who had pulled out a revolver, presumably with the intention of shooting the lock off the front door. He noted, too, that they were all wearing the same black uniform with peaked caps. They were smartly turned out but also distinctly sinister.

The man he'd been speaking to then stepped forward. 'I am Lieutenant Kurt Weber of the SS. Come with me.'

Anton was led to the car, and once he'd taken his seat in the back, they sped away. He just caught a glance of the front door where he could see Emilie standing there. He was sure she was close to tears as she raised a hand in farewell. For all his reassurance, he worried that it might be a long time, if ever, before they set eyes on each other again.

They reached Vienna in barely half an hour and, as they drove through the city centre, Anton was shocked by the sheer number of swastika flags on display. Ten minutes later, they arrived outside the still imposing façade of the old North West Vienna railway station. No trains had operated in or out of it for about fifteen years, but in that time its large concourse had still been used for exhibitions. Lieutenant Weber immediately told him to get out of the car before ushering him past four armed guards wearing uniforms of the German Wehrmacht into that concourse.

To Anton's amazement, it was packed with men as if it was the busiest of days in the station's heyday before the Great War. He only had to make one scan of everyone within his range of vision to appreciate that there were no women amongst the throng, even though he found it hard to credit that not a single member of their sex warranted arrest. He could only assume they'd been taken elsewhere.

'This is where you'll remain until you've been processed,' the lieutenant informed him. Then, before Anton could even begin to protest, he clicked his heels together, turned his back on him, and walked out of the station.

A lot of the men he could see were sitting on the ground but maybe more than half were on their feet in groups and most of them were smoking. Had it been a café, the atmosphere would have been suffocating. However, the sheer height of the concourse's ceiling enabled the smoke to quickly dissipate, which was something to be grateful for, he supposed. He tried to guess at how many men had been herded here and decided that it had to be counted in four figures. Of course, too, he wondered if there was anyone he recognised.

'Anton, Anton!' A man who was on his feet was waving his hand in his direction and he immediately saw that it was Richard Schmitz, no less than the Mayor of Vienna. He was nearly ten years younger than Anton but they had got to know each other since his return to Vienna from Germany, thanks to

Franz's sixty-fifth birthday nearly three years previously being officially celebrated in the city. They had also quickly discovered that they had much in common as, like Anton, Richard was both a monarchist and a Catholic. It therefore came as no surprise to Anton that he'd also been brought there.

'How long have you been held here?' Anton asked him once they had managed to reach each other and shake hands.

'Two days.' He looked tired and the stubble on his chin was fast turning into a beard.

'Christ. And has anyone questioned you during that time?'

'No.' As Anton had noted before, for a politician Richard could be unusually laconic.

'And you've just been left here without food or anywhere to sleep?'

'Bread and soup have been brought in but otherwise yes. There are some taps, too, we can drink from, and the toilets are still just about functioning. Mind you, if they try to squeeze many more of us into this space... It's the nights that are really grim. Some poor buggers haven't even got coats on.'

'I see.'

What Richard had just told Anton brought back strong memories of the war and the physical deprivation he'd had to endure even as a senior officer.

Richard clearly felt the same. 'I went through some tough times in the war. But I was a lot younger then, of course. I've still got a few cigarettes. If you'd like to share one?'

'That's kind of you, Richard, but I don't...'

'Well, if you change your mind.'

Anton nodded, all the while trying to adjust mentally to what he'd suddenly been brought to from the peace of the countryside. That it was a nightmarish experience was almost too much of a cliché. Nonetheless, he was comforted by the thought that humans were very adaptable creatures and that at least he wasn't having to endure shelling as well as the risk of being killed by sniper fire at any moment. And so, in increasingly unpleasant conditions, never feeling anything but cold and miserable, he was forced to wait.

After two nights, for all that he tried to be as stoical as possible, he was feeling close to desperation. No doubt, too, like everyone else around him, he was beginning to stink as well. It made him concerned that if they were left there much longer they would begin to succumb to some nasty disease like typhoid. However, by the end of the second day, when Richard was taken away to God knows where, first raising a hand and wishing Anton good luck, it was noticeable that their numbers had actually fallen quite significantly.

Then on the morning of his third day in confinement, he saw three SS officers enter the concourse, who he assumed were about to take another group of prisoners away. He quickly realised, too, that they were heading in his direction, and didn't know whether to feel resigned or fearful at the prospect of it being his turn next.

'General Lehár,' the tallest of the three officers called out.

'Yes,' he answered, raising a hand.

He beckoned to him. 'Come here.'

He immediately did as he was told, feeling somewhat self-conscious as if he was once again at school and had been found out for some misdemeanour. Once he was standing right in front of him, the officer gave him a cold stare.

'I have some news for you. Come with me.'

Anton followed him out of the concourse, up a broad flight of stairs, and into a small office with stacks of files piled on the floor. There were also no pictures on its grubby walls save one to which his eyes were immediately drawn. Naturally, it was Adolf Hitler. The officer then motioned him towards a chair before sitting opposite him behind a desk whereupon he picked up a piece of paper.

'I have here an order signed by the Reich Governor Seyss-Inquart himself. You're to be released on certain conditions...'

Anton sighed with relief.

'You're the brother of Franz Lehár, aren't you, the famous composer?'

'Yes, I am.'

For the first time the officer smiled at Anton, who judged that he was probably about forty years of age. 'I always find that in life it's not so much what you know as who you know that's most important.'

Then he looked again at the piece of paper in front of him. 'Your brother has vouched for you, it seems, so your conditions of release are that you're to reside here in Vienna, either at his apartment or at an address that he's able to validate. You're also to report to SS headquarters here in Vienna once a week and these conditions will be reviewed after a year. I also have a copy of the order here, which I'll give you.'

And with that he pushed another piece of paper across the desk in Anton's direction. 'Right, you're free to leave.'

'Thank you.'

'Oh, don't thank me, I just follow orders. Thank your brother.'

'I will.'

Anton made his way to Franz and Sophie's apartment on foot, more than happy to be free once more as well as to be able to breathe tolerably fresh air. It was cold and soon began to rain, but he just pulled the rim of his hat down to keep the rain off his face a little and walked faster.

Upon reaching Franz and Sophie's apartment he was also in for the most pleasant of surprises, as who should come to the door to greet him but Emilie? She cried out in delight, rushing straight into his arms. 'I've been so worried about you,' she declared.

Moments later, Franz and Sophie appeared and he embraced them both as well. He said, 'I'm so grateful to you, Franz. The SS officer who let me go said that I had your intervention to thank for it.'

'As soon as Emilie told me you'd been arrested, I knew I had to go to the highest level in order to get you released. In the space of a morning, I made a lot of telephone calls, asking if I could possibly have a meeting with our esteemed Reich Governor. I said that it was on a matter of importance and that I was none other than Franz Lehár, the famous composer of *The Merry Widow*. It worked and yesterday I was invited to the Chancellery. Seyss-Inquart was quite charming. When I suggested that your arrest must be a mistake as you hadn't been politically active in any way at all for nearly twenty years, he agreed to look into your case.'

'And I decided I had to come to Vienna in the hope of making my own appeal for your release,' Emilie added.

'Well, I know I'm the fortunate one,' Anton responded. 'I was held along with more than a thousand others in the concourse of the old North West Vienna railway station. I met the mayor there, Richard Schmitz, before he was taken away. Many others had gone, too, by the time I was released. I imagine they've all been taken to one of the Nazis' concentration camps. I tell you, Franz, they're utterly ruthless.'

Franz looked into Anton's eyes and slowly nodded. 'Yes, I suppose they are.'

30

1st April 1938

Since the German invasion, Fritz had been in an increasingly dark mood. He'd appreciated for a long time what a threat Hitler posed to all Jews, yet he now felt that a misplaced sense of stubborn defiance had prevented him from doing what was best for Helene and his two daughters by fleeing Austria before it was too late.

He didn't know whether he was in any immediate danger but worried that he'd been too outspoken in public in his criticism of Hitler and his Nazi regime, giving them cause to now take their revenge.

'If the worst happens to me and I'm flung into some wretched concentration camp, remember, darling, that I will always love you and the girls with all my heart,' he had told Helene within a couple of days of Hitler's army marching into Austria. 'Given how rich I've become, even if they seek to sequester all my funds here in Austria, remember that I have a Swiss bank account with a small fortune in it and that I have made arrangements for you to have full access to. You and the girls should therefore be able to still live comfortably without me.'

Helene had quietly sobbed and he'd done his best to console her but a very dark cloud still hung over them.

It was about six o'clock in the evening, and he and Helene,

and along with their daughters, Liselotte, who was now eleven years old, and Evamaria, who was now nine years old, were all having dinner together in their apartment in Vienna. Suddenly, there was a ring on the doorbell. Fritz flinched, sensing the worst, and glancing at Helene and the two girls in alarm.

'I'll answer it,' he said, rising from his chair.

As he opened the door, he was confronted by three uniformed Gestapo officers.

'Are you Fritz Löhner-Beda?' one of them asked in a commanding voice.

'Yes, I am.'

'I have orders to arrest you as an enemy of the Reich.' The officer then turned to his colleagues. 'Seize him.'

As Fritz instinctively stepped backwards into the hall, he found himself being manhandled. 'Please,' he cried out in desperation, 'might I not even be allowed a few minutes to say farewell to my wife and children and pack a suitcase?'

By now Helene had followed him into the hall, closely followed by Liselotte and Evamaria, who were both in tears.

'You may have ten minutes to say your farewells and pack any personal possessions you wish to bring with you,' the officer told him. 'Make any attempt to escape and you will be shot.'

'Where are you taking me?'

'That is none of your business, Jew. Now hurry. If you do not get your belongings together in ten minutes you will have to leave without them.'

Helene, doing her best to hold her emotions in check, told the girls to go back to the dining room, before rushing in the direction of Fritz's and her bedroom, where she began to pack a suitcase for him. He immediately followed her.

'I'll get everything I need from the bathroom,' he told her.

'All right.' She was now struggling to hold back her tears.

When they had completed their efforts as best they could, they then joined the girls in the dining room, where Fritz embraced them both tenderly.

'You must be brave girls and support your mother. You understand that, I'm sure. I love you both with all my heart and soul.' Then he quietly sang to them the final lines from *The Land of Smiles*:

> *'Darling little Mi*
> *Let's not troubled be,*
> *Though with anguish our fond hearts weep*
> *Look in my eyes,*
> *I keep them dry,*
> *Yet my heart brims with emotions so deep.*
> *Darling little Mi*
> *Let's not troubled be,*
> *And accept what destiny holds,*
> *Patiently bear our loss and despair,*
> *Let's pretend that we both feel bold.'*

Next he embraced Helene, who clung to him in sheer desperation.

'You must be strong, my darling, for our daughters' sake. You know you are the love of my life. I have always adored you and always will.'

'Will we ever see each other again?'

'I hope we will. I will pray constantly for that moment.'

'I love you so much.'

Their lips met in a lingering farewell kiss.

'You've a minute left before we take you away,' the officer with the commanding voice called out from the hall, whereupon they sprang apart before returning to the hall together, holding hands.

'I'm ready to depart,' Fritz told the officer. 'But tell me, have you never heard of *The Land of Smiles,* composed by Franz Lehár? It brought pleasure to many thousands of Viennese and is still a popular today. Perhaps you've even seen it and it has brought pleasure to you?'

'What of it?' the officer responded.

'Well, I was the librettist.'

'Yes, I'm aware of that, but don't imagine for a moment that that can protect you. Now come with me, Jew.'

Fritz then picked up his case and, with a final wave to his Helene and his daughters, followed the officers out of the apartment. Within a few days he was deported to Dachau concentration camp.

31

I t was a huge relief to Anton to be reunited with Emilie, to be able to take a bath, and once again eat a civilised meal. He was hugely conscious of how fortunate he'd been to escape from the jaws of imprisonment so he continued to thank Franz effusively for his intervention on his behalf. After Anton had been so seriously wounded in the war, Franz had helped to save his life as an amputation might well have proved fatal. Now, he couldn't help thinking that but for Franz's appeal on his behalf, he could have ended his days in a foul concentration camp, far away from Emilie and everything he held dear.

Of course, though, given the conditions of his release, he was anxious about both the future of his farm as well as having to impose on the hospitality of both Franz and Sophie for longer than was absolutely necessary. Both of them, however, strove to be reassuring, while Emilie urged him not to worry too much about the farm, either.

'For the time being our herdsman, Hans, can continue to manage the farm perfectly well without us. I also still have the right to come and go from Vienna, don't I?'

'Why, yes. You can see for yourself that the conditions of my release don't mention you.'

'Quite. So I can return to the farm from time to time to keep an eye on things and we should be able to continue to derive a living from it. If not, we can always try and sell it, can't we?'

Anton nodded in agreement.

Emilie continued: 'I'm also sure we can find a small apartment similar to the one we used to rent without too much difficulty so all should be well.'

He had always been grateful for Emilie's level-headed support in times of difficulty and was pleased to receive it now. He anticipated, too, that their own private existence as a happily married couple was likely to be little affected by *Anschluss* (annexation), as the unification of Germany and Austria quickly became known. Of course, it would be an inconvenience to have to report every week to SS Headquarters, but in time he could see even that condition being relaxed. Otherwise, he decided that they ought to be able to enjoy their retirement and plenty of coffee and cake, even at the price of putting on too much weight. For many others, though, the future would surely be extremely bleak.

On the morning of 2nd April the clock on Anton's bedside table told him that he had woken early as it was still only six-thirty. He dozed for a short while before deciding to start reading a novel he had bought a few days previously entitled *Radetzky March* by Joseph Roth, chronicling the decline and fall of the Austro-Hungarian Empire. He was so engrossed in this that time slipped by all too quickly while Emilie continued to sleep next to him.

At just after eight o'clock, he became aware of the telephone ringing in the hall. It was not, of course, his place to answer it so he let it ring until he heard the sound of footsteps passing their bedroom door.

'Yes, hello.' It was Franz's voice answering the call. It was quickly apparent that something was seriously amiss. 'Oh dear, that's dreadful. Oh, I'm so sorry. No, there's no need to apologise for ringing me so early. Yes, of course, I'll see what I can do.'

By the time the conversation ended, Anton had got out of bed and put on his dressing-gown. Next, he opened their bedroom door before making eye contact with Franz. The expression on his face was one of deep sadness.

'That was Fritz's wife Helene. He was arrested yesterday evening. Poor thing, she's absolutely distraught. Two young daughters, too.'

'How old are they?'

'Liselotte must be about eleven and Evamaria nine.'

It was now obvious to Anton that Franz was close to tears, so he went up to him and put a consoling hand on his shoulder.

Franz said, 'You know, he's the nicest of men, wouldn't hurt anyone, so how can they be doing this to him, of all people?'

'He's never minced words over his hatred of the Nazis, has he?'

'No, that's true, I suppose, but then nor have you.'

'Except that I'm not Jewish and I'm fortunate enough to have you for a brother. My thoughts have also remained between friends whereas Fritz may have been unwise enough to make them more public...'

'Really, are you sure of that?'

'I admit I'm guessing here, but you know the old expression, *the walls have ears*.'

Franz nodded. 'I'm afraid we live in very dangerous times. I must do something to try and help him. I've just promised Helene that I would.'

'Another visit to the Chancellery then?'

'Some telephone calls at the very least. But first I must get dressed and have breakfast... Oh dear, what terrible news this has been...' Once again he looked close to tears.

'I don't want to upset you further, Franz, but I think you should brace yourself for more bad news like this.'

Franz looked him in the eye. 'I'll try. It's some comfort to me, at least, that Richard Tauber is now in London with that pretty wife of his. I expect they'll love him at the Royal Opera House. Oh, and I've heard that Oscar Straus has escaped abroad. I'll miss him. We were rivals but still good friends. I'm beginning to think Sophie and I should have left as well.'

'It might still not be too late...'

'No, Oscar's a lot fitter than I am. We've made our bed...'

Later that morning, Franz picked up the telephone. It wasn't long before he was able to leave a message asking if it might be possible for him to meet again with Seyss-Inquart.

'I was only able to speak to a secretary. She sounded quite young. She said that someone would return my call later today.'

'You can't expect that to be Seyss-Inquart himself,' Sophie said.

'No, of course not. I just need to be able to secure another meeting with him, if I can.'

In the middle of the afternoon, after they had taken lunch in a sombre mood in which there had been little conversation between any of them, the telephone rang again and Franz answered it as quickly as he could. This time Anton heard him have much the same conversation as he had in the morning, though he assumed with a person in a more senior position. It did not last long.

'That was Seyss-Inquart's secretary,' Franz said. 'He's willing to see me again and I'd like you to come with me, Anton, in order to give me some moral support.'

'Do you think that a good idea, given my recent release from custody?'

'Yes, I don't see why not. It will give you an opportunity to thank the Governor for showing such leniency towards you.'

When Anton and Franz arrived at the Chancellery the following morning, they went straight to the reception desk.

'How can I help you?' the officer on duty there said.

'Yes, good morning I'm Franz Lehár and this is my brother, General Anton Lehár.'

'You're the composer, Franz Lehár?'

'Why yes. I have a meeting arranged with the Reich Governor.'

'Please wait here, gentlemen. I will inform his secretary.'

He pointed to an adequately comfortable-looking pair of sofas on the left side of the hallway, next to a table on which reposed various Nazi newspapers and journals, along with a copy of *My Struggle*. Inevitably, Anton reflected, there was also a photograph of Hitler in full uniform on the wall nearby.

They then heard the Nazi officer speak on the telephone. 'The Reich Governor will be available in about a quarter of an hour. His secretary will be with you shortly,' he told them.

Again they waited until after about five minutes another uniformed officer, who said he was the Reich Governor's personal secretary, appeared and proceeded to take them up a flight of stairs and then through a set of double doors into what was clearly another waiting area, where they were again shown seats and asked to wait.

'Would you like some refreshment?' the secretary asked. 'Tea or coffee?' They both asked for the latter and the secretary disappeared telling them that the Reich Governor would be with them very shortly.

He'd barely departed before an inner door opened and the Reich Governor, Seyss-Inquart, now in his mid-forties and wearing spectacles, appeared.

'A pleasure to see you again, Herr Lehár,' he said, coming up to Franz and shaking hands with him.

'I'd like to introduce my brother to you. He's most grateful for your arranging his release from custody.'

'Indeed I am, Reich Governor,' Anton said, and with that Seyss-Inquart also shook hands with him although his manner towards him was, he felt, decidedly frosty.

As Anton had anticipated, the Reich Governor's office was spacious and luxuriously furnished with easy chairs, a fine quality carpet, along with an imposing desk and the obligatory photograph of Hitler on the wall behind it. Seyss-Inquart then motioned them to sit down before reposing in the large, grand-looking chair behind his desk.

'Reich Governor, it's most kind of you to see us. We're here to humbly plead for Fritz Löhner-Beda. He was arrested last week and taken I know not where.'

'Well, I can tell you he's on his way to Dachau concentration camp.'

'I beg of you, as one who knows my work and my commitment to the people of Austria and to German culture, to release him. He's been an assiduous writer and librettist who has contributed greatly to both German and Austrian culture. As you know, the operetta *The Land of Smiles*, the libretto of which he wrote and which I composed, has won the hearts of many Germans and Austrians. I would like to…'

Seyss-Inquart interrupted him. 'He really should have left Austria when he had an opportunity to do so.'

'He's a proud Austrian. I also don't understand what he may have said or done to merit imprisonment but I cannot believe that he poses any threat to Germany. As I say, he's also done so much for German culture. Can he not be treated leniently?'

Seyss-Inquart hesitated over his reply, fiddling with an expensive ballpoint pen, which he moved around in his right-hand, at which moment there was a knock on the door and his secretary entered carrying a tray.

Once coffee had been served, Seyss-Inquart fiddled with his pen a little more before finally giving Franz an answer to his question.,

'I'm afraid I have to disagree with you when you say that Herr Löhner-Beda doesn't pose any threat. He has been arrested because he is considered an enemy of the Reich. He has been an outspoken critic of National Socialism and cannot be trusted to refrain from such behaviour. I'm afraid that I am therefore unable to show him any leniency even as a personal favour to you, Herr Lehár.'

'And that is your final word on the matter?'

'Yes, I'm sorry, but it is.'

Franz sighed. 'I see. Can I ask if Fritz will be able to send and receive letters?'

'That depends on the rules put in place by the Governor of Dachau concentration camp but as I understand it, correspondence is permitted subject to certain conditions.'

'Thank you, Reich Governor. I do have one further concern.'

'Oh yes?'

'Can I be assured that Fritz's life isn't in danger?'

'Most certainly. Our government is not uncivilised. Herr Löhner-Beda has merely been incarcerated because he poses a threat to the Reich…'

'But will he ever be released?' Anton asked.

'That I am unable to say.'

Franz quickly finished his coffee and then stood up, realising that there was nothing more to be said. 'Well, thank you for your time, Reich Governor.'

'Not at all. Tell me, are you still composing, Herr Lehár?'

'I'm afraid not. My health isn't what it once was.'

'I'm sorry to hear that.'

Seyss-Inquart then pushed a button on his desk and almost immediately his secretary reappeared to escort Franz and Anton out of the building.

'At least you tried,' Anton said, consolingly, as they walked away.

'Hm, but how on earth am I going to be able to protect Sophie when there's so much hatred of anyone who's the least bit Jewish? That's what worries me most of all.'

'Put your fame to good use. It helped to protect me.'

'But you're not a Jew.'

'I'm family, though, and so's Sophie.'

Franz shrugged. 'And then there's this plebiscite in a few days' time. You'll vote against unification, I assume?'

'Of course. But what about you?'

'I simply won't vote. I'm really not feeling too well, and nor's Sophie. You could always feign a cold.'

'No, I don't think so. For me, voting against is a matter of principle. Anyway, the Nazis already know my views. Even if they discovered I'd voted in favour they'd think I was just trying to hide my true opinion. Mind you, as Emilie and I are registered to vote in Theresienfeld it's possible that we may not be able to vote here in Vienna.'

'That's a way out for you then.'

'Except that I intend to enquire if it's not too late for us to be allowed to vote here.'

'Well, if you must. Personally, I wouldn't bother.'

'But tell me, you don't believe in unification, do you?'

'No, certainly not. I've no more time for the Nazis than you have, especially after what they've done to poor Fritz. All the same, it doesn't matter what either of us think, does it? There's clearly overwhelming support for Anschluss.'

Reluctantly, Anton agreed. 'This vote will be no more than a rubber stamp for what's already happened. Even if a majority did vote against, I expect the Nazis would still just forge the result in their favour.'

The following day Emilie and Anton and Emilie went to the Town Hall in order to enquire about their right to vote. Franz clearly thought it a pointless exercise but Anton was determined to oppose unification and Emilie felt much the same. Two hours later, they came away with pieces of paper showing that their registration had been altered.

'Just present these at the polling station and you'll be allowed to vote,' the official told them.

32

When Emilie and Anton set off to vote it was a bright spring morning. It was breezy, though, which kept the temperature down so they were grateful for the hats and winter coats they were wearing. When they had left the apartment, Franz was apparently still in bed. Sophie told them he was complaining of a headache and a sore throat, although Anton wasn't at all sure how true that was, as Franz hadn't seemed particularly unwell the previous evening. Even so, he'd already made it clear that on the grounds of ill-health he had no intention of voting and, Anton supposed, felt bound to justify this. For her part, Sophie informed them that as a Jew, she was sure she wouldn't be allowed to vote anyway.

'It's been well publicised that Jews are forbidden from doing so,' she insisted.

Emilie and Anton had also naturally discussed their voting intentions and Anton made it perfectly clear that he wouldn't take any offence if she chose to vote in favour of unification.

'After all, I don't suppose we'll be allowed to vote in secret, so it will not be easy to run the gauntlet of animosity we may well have to face.'

'I don't care about that. To vote for unification would be to endorse Hitler and all he stands for, and you know I would never do that.'

'Then we must both support each other and be brave.'

The streets they walked along were bedecked not just with swastika flags but also with posters urging people to vote for unification and a greater Germany. Of course, according to the Nazis' propaganda the future was bound to be bright and glorious. Worse than that, to think otherwise was to be disloyal. Anton had to stiffen his resolve to vote against, knowing it wouldn't be easy. All the same, he knew this would not be harder than facing machine gun fire, or crouching in a trench as shells whizzed over.

As they approached the polling station, they could see that a long queue had formed of people waiting to vote. Anton estimated that it stretched at least a hundred metres down the street, which made him sigh at the prospect of a long wait.

'We'll need to patient, I'm afraid,' Emilie said. 'I know how much you hate queueing.'

'On this occasion it can't be helped.'

Once they had joined the end of the queue, Anton was pleased to discover that it was moving forward quite quickly. This helped to curb his natural sense of frustration whenever forced to stand in line for too long. Within about fifteen minutes, they had nearly reached the entrance, which was guarded by two police officers.

Then they heard the unmistakable sound of a loudhailer. Anton looked up the street and saw a car approaching with one attached to its roof. A man's voice was urging people to vote to be a part of the glorious Third Reich as it fulfilled its destiny. Anton thought of poor Fritz and Richard Schmitz and all the other poor sods already languishing in concentration camps, and he shuddered.

Within a couple of minutes they stepped inside the building, a church hall. There were two men in suits facing them behind a table but, to Anton's discomfort, no voting booth. Worse, there were also three other men in the room wearing the Brownshirt uniforms of Hitler's paramilitary SA. The older of the two men in suits was, he judged, about fifty. Otherwise, he doubted if any of the other men in the room were more than half his age and he was determined not to be intimidated. He could also see a box in which to place his vote, but to his further concern this had been placed on the table next to the two men in suits.

They had been allowed in two at a time and Anton was now called forward ahead of Emilie by the older of the two men sitting behind the table. When he then asked Anton to confirm his name and address, Anton handed him the piece of paper he'd obtained from the Town Hall. After reading it, the man gave him a nod before handing him the ballot paper together with a pencil. He glanced at the former.

Do you agree with the reunification of Austria with the German Reich which was enacted on 13th March 1938?

'Wait a moment,' said the other official. 'I've just checked that your name is on our proscribed list. I'm afraid you're not permitted to vote.'

'What?'

'I said you're not permitted to vote so I must ask you to leave.'

'Can I wait until my wife has voted?'

'Very well.'

Emilie then went through the same process he had just been

through. He was half-expecting her name to also be on the proscribed list but in the event she was allowed to vote.

'I wish to be able to vote in private,' she said bravely.

'I'm sorry, that's not possible.'

'Of course it's not possible,' one of the Brownshirts added. 'You're not thinking of voting against, are you?'

'That's my business.'

The Brownshirt gave her an angry stare. 'You're not another snivelling traitor, are you?'

'No.' And with that she then marked her cross on the ballot paper before trying to place it in the ballot box. However, the Brownshirt seized hold of her wrist before she could do so.

'I want to see how you voted.'

He then twisted her wrist, making her cry out in pain, until the ballot paper fell out of her hand. In the same instant, Anton stepped forward in angry protest at such behaviour.

'How dare you. Leave my wife alone...'

Another of the Brownshirts responded by seizing hold of Anton while the one who had twisted Emilie's arm picked the ballot paper up off the floor.

'So you are a traitor,' he said, sneeringly, to Emilie.

'I'm a loyal Austrian, nothing more,' she retorted.

He snorted at her before tossing the ballot paper in the direction of the two men sitting behind the table. 'Make sure it's recorded that this traitor voted against.'

At the moment that he and Emilie turned to leave, Anton felt two hands being placed on his shoulders. He was then shoved forward so violently that he fell onto his knees. Before he could rise to his feet he received a vicious kick up his backside.

'Get out of here, you snivelling traitor,' the Brownshirt said, whereupon his two fellow Brownshirts sniggered with laughter at what they saw as Anton's humiliation. On the contrary, he just felt defiant and, despite his discomfort, simply got to his feet and left the building with a sense of pride.

'Are you in much pain?' Emilie asked.

'I've known much worse. I'm still proud of you for doing our duty.'

The following morning while the four of them were having breakfast together, the result of the plebiscite was announced on the wireless. It was so overwhelmingly in support of unification that Anton guffawed in disbelief.

'This is ridiculous. It really can't be true,' he declared.

'If our experience is anything to go by, I expect large numbers of people were intimidated into voting in favour of unification,' Emilie responded.

'Maybe they were. All the same, I still struggle to believe that a little less than eighteen thousand of us either voted against or spoilt our ballot papers in comparison with nearly four and half million who voted in favour.'

'What does it matter?' Franz insisted. 'There was always going to be a huge majority in favour, and like it or not the deed's done. For better or worse, we're all good Germans now.'

'I just fear for our future. Hitler won't just stop here, you know. It'll be Czechoslovakia next. I tell you, sooner or later, he's bound to drag us into another terrible war.'

'So you say, so you say,' Franz responded, irritably.

'Please, let's not talk of such a dreadful thing over breakfast,' Sophie added, appealingly.

Anton held up a hand. 'I'm sorry.'

What was also left completely unsaid was the possible fate of

Austrian Jews. Fritz might have invited his fate through his high profile and fearless criticism of the Nazis, but there was now an imminent prospect of all Austrian Jews being discriminated against. Above all, Anton knew only too well how anxious Franz continued to be about Sophie.

33

That same evening, both Emilie and Sophie retired to bed early, Emilie complaining of a headache and Sophie merely saying that she was feeling tired.

'I'll join you soon,' Anton told Emilie, while expecting Franz to follow Sophie to bed without delay.

Instead, on this occasion, Franz continued to sit back in his easy chair. Then he took one of the cheroots he liked to smoke occasionally out of a small silver case in which he kept them in his waistcoat pocket.

'Do you mind if I smoke?' he asked and Anton shook his head. 'You're welcome to join me, of course.' With that, he held out his case but again Anton declined.

'Thanks, but I'd rather not.'

'A small brandy then before bedtime?'

This offer tempted Anton. 'Yes, that would be very nice.'

Franz stood up and crossed the room to where the drinks cabinet was situated. 'There's something important I'd like to talk to you about.'

'Oh yes?'

'It's been on my mind now ever since I had that meeting with our Reich Governor. At first I was inclined to forget about it, but after what's happened to Fritz and I expect many others, I've had second thoughts.'

He proceeded to pour them two brandies and handed one

of these to Anton before resuming his seat. Then he looked around for his lighter, which was on a small table next to his chair, and lit his cheroot. Finally, he raised his glass.

'Your health.'

Anton echoed his words and in turn raised his glass to him. 'So, what's been on your mind then?'

'Well, we know that Hitler loves my music.'

'Um, at least he still has good taste,' Anton said, a shade sarcastically.

Franz smiled at him before drinking a little bit more of his brandy. 'More than that, I've noticed that it's Hitler's birthday on the twentieth of April and I've been thinking that he might like to receive a souvenir edition of the programme of the operetta's jubilee...'

'As a birthday present, you mean?'

Franz held up a hand. 'Before you get too angry with me, I need to explain that I have an ulterior motive. After what's happened to Fritz, I can appreciate more than ever that Sophie, too, may soon be in serious danger. I can't allow that to happen and it seems to me that the best way of protecting her would be to have her declassified as any kind of Jew. Wouldn't you agree?'

'Yes... Assuming that's possible.'

'It must be possible, if Hitler himself was prepared to sanction it!'

'So, you're suggesting sending this present to Hitler and at the same time asking him to declassify Sophie?'

'I'm not sure... That might be presumptuous of me. I'm thinking that it might be better to send the present first and then... if, when the situation does get harder for anyone who's Jewish...'

'You mean, as a kind of insurance policy?'

'Yes, you could say that. So, what do you think?'

'I'm not sure. You know my opinion of the Führer and everything he stands for...'

'And I've no time for him either, I promise you. All the same, he has the power to protect Sophie. Sometimes in life you have to be prepared to sup with the devil. Call it a means to an end, if you like.'

'The twentieth of April is no more than a week away...'

'I don't imagine it would matter too much if the present arrived a little late.'

'No, I suppose not...'

'You still think it a bad idea, I can tell. But look, we have to live in the world as it is, not as we'd wish it to be. Hitler's all powerful and likely to remain so.'

'If he takes Germany to war as I believe he will, then it could end in a terrible defeat. I seem to remember the Kaiser was once all powerful.'

'You're suggesting I might be judged badly for appearing to be a Nazi supporter?'

'It's possible, one day.'

'But all I'm trying to do is protect Sophie. Anyway, who knows what the future has in store for us? We have to make the best of things as they are now, not as they might be many years ahead. I could well be dead by then, don't forget. I'm nearly sixty-eight, after all, and often feel a lot older.'

'Well, whatever you decide to do, you know you'll always have my full support.'

'Yes, Anton, I know that and am always grateful for it, I assure you. What I need at this moment is your honest opinion.

Have I still not persuaded you that this is worth doing?'

'So long as you have your eyes open as to how it might rebound on you, then all right, I'm persuaded.'

'Good. Now time for bed, I think. I'll sleep on what we've discussed and make a final decision in the morning.'

'By the way, do you think you still have a programme of the original operetta? After all, we're looking at more than thirty years ago now.'

'Oh yes, I'm sure I still have one.'

Throughout their conversation, it had been at the back of Anton's mind that, perhaps despite himself, it must have been flattering for Franz to know that his music continued to be loved by the man who was now one of the most powerful men in the world. Nonetheless, he was still prepared to accept at face value his stated reason for wanting to send Hitler a birthday present, while wondering if at least a small part of his motivation was a desire to express gratitude for being so well thought of.

'I've decided that I will send the present to Hitler,' Franz told Anton over breakfast the following morning. 'If it helps me to curry favour with him then it will be all to the good, whereas any harm it may do me must lie years in the future and is entirely beyond my control. I'll have to act quickly, of course. Fortunately, I know a good bookbinder who should be able to do the job for me as quickly as possible. I must also let Seyss-Inquart know what my intention is. Hopefully, he can help ensure the present reaches Hitler in person without delay. First, though, I must find that suitable programme amongst my papers. There should be one in my study. Sophie, will you help me look for it once we've finished breakfast?'

'I have to go out, my love. I told you, I'm meeting Helene at ten.'

'Oh, yes, that slipped my mind, I'm afraid.'

'I'll help you, Franz,' Anton volunteered.

'And so will I,' Emilie added.

Half an hour later, the three of them were in his study; a dusty, over-crowded place, with a distinctly musty, if not unpleasant, smell. There were not just shelves of books from floor to ceiling, but also piles of sheet music and also a good six boxes, too, stacked in one corner of the room.

'The programme we're looking for will be in one of these,' Franz said, pointing to the boxes. 'I'm not as organised as I should be, though, so I really can't remember in which one.'

'Well, if we divide them between us, it shouldn't take us very long to find it,' Anton responded.

In the event, they looked through the best part of a box each without finding what they were looking for. It also didn't help that for Franz it was a journey down memory lane, taking him back through a journey of nearly forty years of his creativity. Emilie, however, was far less distracted. Indeed, she hadn't long begun looking through her second box when she let out an exclamation.

'Aha, I've found it!'

She then handed it to Franz, who immediately smiled in delight. 'Yes, this is absolutely perfect. See, Anton, it's a souvenir programme of the fiftieth performance and still in good condition, too.'

As Anton looked at it appreciatively, one thing in particular caught his eye. On the front cover was a photograph of the youthful looking stars of the operetta, Mitzi Günther and Louis Treumann.

'Will Hitler appreciate the fact that Louis is Jewish?' he asked.

Franz shrugged. 'That can't be helped. I'm not going to ruin it by tearing off its front cover, and so long as he recalls their performances together with affection, he's hardly likely to care. Now, I need to telephone the bookbinders followed by the Reich Governor's office.'

His determination to get on with the task in hand had, Anton thought, given Franz a spark of youthful energy he now seldom displayed. Further, Anton couldn't help but smile to himself at the irony of what he had just done. After all, in assisting Franz in providing Hitler with a suitable birthday present, he had just been a party to the most outwardly sycophantic of actions at the same time as professing to positively detest the man. Did this make him an arch-hypocrite? he wondered. He could only hope not. The fact of the matter was that he owed his brother many favours, but never in his wildest dreams had he ever imagined that he'd be repaying him in such a fashion. Certainly, he decided they were entering strange times, which would perhaps make hypocrites of them all if they were to survive.

Within twenty minutes Franz had established that the bookbinders would be pleased to provide him with what he needed. 'They tell me that if I can bring them the souvenir copy before close of business, they can then have everything ready for me in no more than two days.'

He then rang the Reich Governor's office, which soon led to an entirely positive outcome once he explained his reason for doing so.

'I have good news,' he told Anton. 'I have an assurance that as soon as I can deliver the present to the Chancellery it will then be dispatched by special courier to Berlin. It should therefore be in Hitler's hands in plenty of time for his birthday.'

The bookbinders were true to their word in having everything ready in two days and even went to the trouble of delivering the finished article to Franz's apartment. When he then showed Anton what they'd created, he was partly impressed, partly repelled.

The programme had been bound in red Morocco leather and in the top right-hand corner this bore a small silver swastika. Further, in the centre was a silver badge bearing the words *To Mein Führer, on the occasion of his forty-ninth birthday, with warm regards.*

'I could hardly send it to him with anything less than *warm regards*, now could I?' Franz said, sensing Anton's discomfort. 'I need to sign it, of course.'

'I just hope it fulfils its purpose, is all I can say.'

'For Sophie's sake, if no one else's. Now, I'm going to take it to the Chancellery in person. Will you come with me?'

'Yes, of course.'

About ten days later, Franz received a letter thanking him profusely for his most kind gift. It was signed with best wishes by Hitler himself.

'A means to an end,' Franz said with a wry smile as he showed this to Anton. He could only pray that he was right.

34

In early May, Anton and Emilie were able to move into a small, furnished apartment in the Wieden district of the city. This was not far from the Karlskirche, an over-large Baroque church, which dominated the surrounding area. Life with Franz and Sophie had begun to get on all their nerves, so this gave them a welcome sense of freedom. At about the same time the Nuremberg Laws, which deprived Jews of their rights as citizens, were brought into effect in Austria. Almost immediately, Anton noticed more attacks on Jewish shops. Invariably, their windows were smashed and their doors daubed with the word *Juden*.

Anton wanted to remain close to his brother so he and Emilie continued to dine with him and Sophie at their apartment once a week on either a Friday or Saturday evening. In addition, they still met regularly at one of their favourite cafés, while, of course, there was always the telephone.

One evening in early June, Franz rang Anton in a tense frame of mind.

'I can't put this off any longer. Sophie's being growing more anxious by the day with all these attacks taking place. And then, to make matters worse, this morning when we went to the Café Central, this stranger approached us. He said, "I know who you are. You're Franz Lehár, the composer and well-known Jewish sympathiser, and this must be your

Jewish wife. Why haven't you left the country along with so many of your Jewish friends? You know you're no longer welcome here, either of you." He glared at us both, made a rude gesture, and then stalked off. I tell you, we were both really upset. It's made me decide I must try and have Sophie declassified.'

'Will you go straight to the top then?'

'If you agree it's a good idea.'

'Well, it's why you sent Hitler that birthday present, isn't it?'

'Yes, but I'm nervous about exactly how I go about it. I can't just write a letter to Hitler personally.'

'Why not? I expect lots of people do. But look, you could always consult your lawyers. They may well be familiar with an official channel of communication for the sort of thing you have in mind.'

'But I don't want this to get tied up in a lot of bureaucracy. If that were to happen I could see the whole process taking months or even years.'

'Then why not approach Seyss-Inquart first of all?'

'That did me no good when I was so worried about Fritz.'

'But this is different. If he was prepared to treat me leniently in response to your appeal, he'll surely be willing to be helpful when it comes to Sophie.'

'Yes, you're right, of course. I'll go to him first.'

Three days later, the four of them met for coffee and cake at the Café Frauenhuber in the Himmelfortgasse, the oldest of Vienna's many cafés; the Kaisermarren, a type of sweet pancake which they served there, being especially delicious. Franz and Sophie arrived a little late, and not for the first time Anton was struck by how slowly and stiffly Franz walked. All the same, when he raised his hand in greeting, there was a cheerful smile on his face.

'I did as you suggested and I'm pleased to say Seyss-Inquart has been most helpful.'

'You've been able to speak to him personally then?'

'Yes, on the telephone. He said he would be pleased to approach Hitler on my behalf, or at least his office. He also promised to come back to me as soon as possible.'

'Did he seem hopeful?' Emilie asked.

'I'm not sure I'd go that far. He just said he'd be pleased to take the matter up on my behalf. I suppose if he'd thought my request was hopeless he would have said so.'

'All we can do for now is wait,' Sophie added.

In the event, that wait lasted a month, by which time Franz was becoming anxious, even going so far as to make a fresh enquiry with Seyss-Inquart.

'I've been informed an assurance has been given that the request would receive due consideration so I need to be patient,' Franz told Anton. 'Mind you, this is becoming less easy with every day that passes and more attacks take place on Jews. Sophie's more nervous than ever, which is perfectly understandable.'

Anton, whilst sympathetic, couldn't help wondering if Franz was beginning to envy Richard Tauber for having escaped to England along with many other prominent Jews who'd done the same. Perhaps, if his request to have Sophie declassified failed, he might be prepared to try and follow them. He feared, though, that he'd now left it far too late, as Austria's borders were now surely closed to the outside world. Had he and Sophie been many years younger this might not have prevented a crossing of the border into Switzerland via some mountain track. However, such an option was now very obviously out of the question.

Anton and Emilie could still have managed such a feat without undue difficulty. Anton, though, was not about to desert Franz, and considered the restriction on his right of movement little more than a minor inconvenience. True, he thoroughly disliked having to step into SS Headquarters once a week, but he was never there for more than thirty minutes, and the officer he invariably reported to was always polite, if distant. He could readily believe that he had a cruel streak in him, but had no intention of doing anything to test that out.

Life in Vienna was basically comfortable, if sometimes boring, as Anton and Emilie adopted a routine, which included daily walks, reading a good deal and enjoying both films and concerts. Certainly in comparison with poor Fritz and others like him, they appreciated that they were the lucky ones, and Anton thought that provided Sophie's position could be safeguarded, there was no reason why they couldn't all continue to live out their lives in comparative peace.

Then came good news.

'Anton, dear brother,' Franz said with a beaming smile, the moment they met, this time at the Café Central in the Herrengasse, 'I had a telephone call from Seyss-Inquart's office just an hour ago. The man said that they'd heard from Berlin that the Führer is minded to accept my request. Sophie is now to be regarded as an Aryan by right of marriage.'

'That's excellent news, I must say. You were clearly right to send Hitler that birthday present.'

'Yes, wasn't I just? This calls for a celebration, don't you think?'

Anton nodded, and Franz proceeded to order an expensive bottle of champagne, reminiscent of the days when they had drunk to the success of his latest operetta.

Franz continued: 'I was also told we can expect to receive written confirmation in a few days' time, which will put an end to our worries, won't it, my love?'

With that Franz put his hand on Sophie's, and they smiled at each other with deep love and relief in their eyes. To Anton, they looked as if they had both just been exonerated from death sentences. When it arrived, the bottle also stretched to providing the four of them with three glasses each, enjoyed with some delightful cake, so by the time they came to leave they were all in a very good humour.

The late afternoon sunshine was also pleasantly warm as Anton and Emilie strolled home, and, helped by the champagne he had drunk, Anton was feeling relaxed. Then he reflected sombrely that it was all too easy to see the world at its best and forget the dark side of what had brought about their celebration.

By the time the four of them met again for their weekly evening meal, the promised letter had already arrived together with an accompanying certificate that designated Sophie an Honorary Aryan, signed by Hitler himself, which surely put her status beyond question.

Both Franz and Sophie were now noticeably less tense than they had been of late. As the evening progressed the conversation also became increasingly nostalgic for the lost world of their youths before the war changed everything. Franz then declared that he'd not given up all hope of being able to compose again.

'My last operetta *Giuditta* was a great disappointment, I must say, but at least that wretched allegation of plagiarism is now behind me. I still have a few musical ideas, you know, but the loss of the likes of Richard and Fritz makes it hard for me to see how I could ever create a complete work again. Perhaps a reworking of one of my earlier works might still be possible. What irks me most of all is that with the exception of *The Merry Widow* my work has really fallen out of favour. I fear it's considered far too frivolous. Indeed, but for Hitler's personal support I think even *The Merry Widow* would struggle to be performed.'

'But isn't it still popular around the world?' Anton pointed out.

'Yes, that's quite true. In fact it still brings me some handsome royalties, you know, even after all these years.'

'From which I expect the government benefits?'

'I pay my taxes, if that's what you mean?'

Anton smiled. 'I don't doubt Hitler's love of your music is perfectly genuine, but the money helps, too, I'm sure.'

35

Looking back, it struck Anton that the warm, dry summer of 1938 was just a lull before yet another terrible storm. For a few short weeks after Sophie was granted the status of an Honorary Aryan, Franz was happier than he had been for some time and talked more of trying to compose again, if only for his own amusement. All too quickly, however, the clouds darkened again.

As an avid newspaper reader, Anton was aware from May onwards that tensions were growing in Czechoslovakia between its government and the Sudeten German Party, which was closely affiliated to Hitler's Nazi Party. By August there were ever more frequent articles in the press condemning the Czech government for unprovoked attacks on innocent Germans. These, though, he found hard to take seriously and said as much to Emilie.

'All these reports of atrocities against German people in Czechoslovakia just aren't credible to me. I really can't believe the Czech government would be so stupid as to provoke Hitler. It just suits his purposes to make it all up.'

Then on 12th September matters started to come to a head when a speech Hitler had just made to a party rally at Nuremberg was widely reported. In this he launched an attack on Czechoslovakia, accusing it of being a fraudulent state and persecuting its German minority.

'I tell you, Emilie, this sounds just like a repeat of the speech he made before we were invaded.'

'But if he attacks Czechoslovakia couldn't that lead to war with France and England all over again?'

'Very possibly, I'm afraid. In fact he's even accused France of being behind the Czech government and wanting to drop bombs on Germany. Pure fantasy, I think, but still bound to increase tensions with France.'

Hitler's speech also very clearly alarmed the British, as three days later they heard that the British Prime Minister Neville Chamberlain had flown to Germany for a personal meeting with Hitler. After a few hours he'd then returned home and appeared to have achieved absolutely nothing. Indeed, in the ensuing days the crisis just appeared to deepen, with reports both in the press and the wireless that the 'evil' Czech government was continuing its campaign of persecution, which could no longer be tolerated.

'I hate all this talk of war,' Franz said when they next dined with him and Sophie. 'If the Czechs are really treating the Sudeten Germans so badly, surely the British and French governments will see how wrong that is.'

'But I doubt there's any truth in these accusations.'

'What, none at all?'

'No. Why should the Czechs really be so foolish? I tell you, Hitler just wants to try and place all the blame for this crisis on their shoulders.'

'But even so it's surely reasonable for the Sudeten Germans to have a right to self-determination, and isn't that basically all

Hitler's insisting upon?'

'If that's really all he wants... I just believe his real aim is the occupation of the entire country.'

'I just pray some compromise can be reached before it's too late,' Emilie said.

'I agree, my dear,' Franz responded. 'I can't believe it's in anyone's interests to start another war over this issue.'

'Except that another sovereign nation will have to pay the price for it,' Anton added. 'And you know my view that Hitler will never be satisfied. After Czechoslovakia I expect he'll want to absorb Hungary or Poland into the Reich.'

'Still as pessimistic as ever, Anton,' Franz declared with a shake of the head.

'Yes, Franz, everything really will turn out all wrong, you know.' And with that he raised a glass of wine to him and they smiled ruefully at each other.

On 22nd September they heard that Chamberlain had returned to Germany for further talks with Hitler, raising hopes that a solution to the crisis would soon be found. Yet two days later, the situation looked worse than ever when it was announced over the wireless that Hitler had given the Czech government an ultimatum to cede the Sudetenland within four days or face invasion. By then Chamberlain had also returned home again without apparently achieving anything.

'Now I think there really is a serious risk of war, at least with Czechoslovakia,' Anton told Franz when they met at the Café Frauenhuber. 'Whether France and Britain will retaliate by declaring war on Germany, I really don't know.'

'It's all too depressing, is all I can say. Frankly, in fact I'd rather not talk about it. After all, we're mere observers, nothing more.'

'But millions of people will still suffer the consequences if this all goes wrong, and to no good purpose. It's just Hitler's vanity project.'

These last words had barely left his mouth when Emilie kicked him under the table. 'It isn't sensible to be so critical of the Führer in public,' she hissed into his ear.

This thoroughly irritated him, for all that he could appreciate that her concern was probably well founded. 'All right, all right,' he said grumpily.

As it happened, Anton's expectation of war when the ultimatum ran out wasn't realised. Instead, an urgent four-powers conference was convened between Germany, Italy, France and Britain, and on the morning of 30th September it was announced that an agreement had been signed.

'So, Hitler's got what he wanted,' Anton said to Emilie. 'Czechoslovakia has effectively ceased to exist and he's free to occupy the Sudetenland.'

'But at least there won't be any war.'

'Not for the time being, anyway.'

Emilie gave him an exasperated look. 'Franz is right, you know. You're always far too gloomy about everything. It can be very depressing to have to live with.'

'I'm sorry, my dear, perhaps I am. Unfortunately, I just don't believe that Hitler will be satisfied with what he's achieved. On the contrary, it's likely to embolden him still further.'

'Yes, I know, Poland or Hungary will be next...'

'I'm afraid they will.'

'But do promise me one thing.'

'Oh, what's that?'

'Don't go on about it to Franz when we next meet. He'll just be happy there isn't going to be any war.'

'Yes, and he'll say that for once I was being too pessimistic.'

'Well, if he does, just humour him for a change. Otherwise, the argument will just go round in circles and I don't see the point.'

Anton nodded his head. 'Yes, that's true enough. I'll bite my tongue, I promise.'

Anton was true to his word and in the event Franz merely expressed pleasure at an agreement having been reached without trying to make too much of it. German troops duly entered the Sudetenland, according to all reports, to great acclaim and rejoicing. There was even talk of a new golden age with Hitler being compared favourably to Otto von Bismarck, the Iron Chancellor, who had united Germany in the 1870s. He'd also needed some successful wars to achieve this feat, whereas Hitler had managed to unite Germany with Austria and effectively Czechoslovakia, too, without having to fire a shot in anger. Much like a Holy Roman Emperor in the Middle Ages, he now held sway over all of Central Europe, but Anton still very much feared that he was greedy for yet more territory.

It was also becoming clearer by the day, with more unsolicited attacks on Jews and their property, that he had no intention of stopping his war on the Jews. Indeed that particular war was about to get even nastier. As so often with terrible events, there was also a catalyst for what was about to happen. It was the morning of 8th November and Anton was reading his copy of the *Wiener Zeitung*.

'I see a German diplomat has been shot and seriously wounded by a young Jew in Paris,' he said to Emilie. 'This report says that Reichsführer Heinrich Himmler has condemned it as a dreadful, politically motivated attack, on a perfectly innocent man. He's stated that any Jew found in possession of any weapon can expect to be sent to a concentration camp. What's more, he's ordered that all Jewish newspapers and magazines be closed down, all Jewish cultural activities be suspended indefinitely, and all Jewish children be barred from attending state elementary schools.'

'That's surely going much too far.'

'Yes, I quite agree. It's a very convenient excuse, don't you think?'

'You're not suggesting it's a hoax?'

'I'm not sure I'd go that far, but this didn't even happen on German soil and who knows why he really shot him? Anyway, one shooting doesn't justify this sort of response. Life is just going to get much harder for the Jews, I'm afraid.'

'As if it's not difficult enough already.'

Only the following day, after they learnt that the German diplomat had died of his wounds, what then took place exceeded anything Anton had previously thought possible. As it happened, they were due to meet Franz and Sophie at the Café Schwarzenberg in mid-afternoon, and strolled arm-in-arm on what was a cold and cloudy day, which seemed to herald the onset of winter although at least it remained dry. Emilie wanted to do some shopping on the way so they had given themselves enough time to walk into the city centre. It very quickly became apparent to them that there were a lot of Hitler's brown-shirted SA on the streets.

'Something's up,' Anton said quietly.

After a while they reached Seitenstettengasse approaching the

Stadttempel, one of Vienna's finest synagogues. Anton could see its doors were open and that these brown-shirted paramilitaries were busy coming and going through them.

'Look,' he said. 'They're looting the place. See? They're making a pile of what they've taken.'

'And do you think this could be happening at other synagogues as well?'

'Quite probably. I expect it's why we're seeing so many Brownshirts on the streets.'

They hurried by the synagogue on the other side of the street, and hadn't gone much further before discovering that the Brownshirts' activities weren't confined to attacking synagogues. The windows of yet more Jewish shops had been smashed, while, as with the synagogue, they saw the shops' contents being looted. What then shocked them most of all was seeing a middle-aged man being abused by half a dozen Brownshirts. They were calling him a Jewish pig and swearing obscenities at him.

Anton thought their behaviour so appalling, he was tempted to intervene on his behalf, but sensing what was on his mind, Emilie pulled him away.

'No, Anton, don't even think about it. They could easily turn on you and then report you, too. You don't want to end up in a concentration camp!'

'Oh, very well.'

They walked on in gloomy silence until they reached the department store where Emilie wanted to make a purchase, only to discover that this, too, was under attack.

'I never realised this was Jewish owned,' Anton exclaimed, shaking his head in disbelief at what was happening.

'Let's just go straight to the café. I can shop for what I need elsewhere another day.'

Arriving at their destination ahead of Franz and Sophie, it was a relief for them to be able to take their ease in familiar surroundings, which felt safe and secure, whatever desecrations might be taking place nearby. Then Anton noticed a familiar face sitting at a table on the other side of the café. It was that of the elderly librettist Victor Léon, who looked every one of his eighty years. Their eyes met and Anton put up a hand to him in greeting to which he responded in kind. Anton was tempted to go over to him and his wife, Ottilie, who was sitting beside him, for a chat. Then, out of the corner of his eye, he noticed that Franz and Sophie were just walking through the café's front door.

After Emilie and Anton had greeted them both, Franz also recognised Victor and Ottilie and walked over to them. There was obvious affection between the two men, which was hardly surprising after their many years of collaboration.

'Why not join us?' Anton heard Franz say.

'That's kind of you, but we're just on the point of leaving,' Victor responded. 'We need to get home, I think. I really don't like what seems to be happening on the streets.'

'No, I really don't know what's going on. I've never seen so many of these paramilitaries marching around. They're up to no good, I expect.'

Victor merely nodded, and as he and his wife stood up to leave, Franz returned to his table.

'We've seen Brownshirts looting the Stadttempel,' Anton told him. 'And they're assaulting Jews.'

'Oh dear, how awful,' Franz responded as he also waved

farewell to the Léons. 'Take care,' he called out to them and they waved back in return, just a frail, old couple, both vulnerable and harmless.

'Well, it appears the Nazis are seeking retribution for the murder of that diplomat in Paris,' Franz said, once the Léons had left the café.

'But only in the most disproportionate way imaginable,' Anton replied. 'For all we know the murder wasn't even politically motivated, and anyway the actions of one man can't possibly justify what's now happening. It's no more than an excuse to make life intolerable for anyone who's Jewish. I just hope the Léons will be left in peace.'

'Surely they will, at their age?'

Anton shrugged. In truth, when it came to the Jews he doubted the Nazis had any respect at all for civilised values. They were intent, he feared, on only ruthless persecution of their race, regardless of either age or sex.

'I'm just grateful Hitler gave you the status of an Aryan,' Franz said to Sophie, placing a hand on hers.

'But what's happening is still shameful,' Anton insisted.

'Oh yes, I didn't say it wasn't.'

When Anton and Emilie left the café they were able to take a more direct route back to their apartment. However, if anything, the situation appeared to have worsened. They hadn't gone far when they noticed smoke rising ahead of them. Shortly afterwards, they were able to see that the source of this was a burning synagogue.

'I wouldn't be surprised if they aren't trying to destroy every last one in Vienna,' Anton exclaimed.

They hurried on, anxious to get home as soon as they could,

only to pass a large private house that appeared to have been looted. The word *Juden* had been painted on it, windows had been smashed, and the door stood open.

Anton shook his head in dismay. 'My God, this is awful.'

The mayhem continued long after it grew dark. From the windows of their apartment they were able to make out fires raging and hear the sound of glass being smashed, as well as that of voices raised in anger. It really seemed to Anton as if the forces of hell had been unleashed against Vienna's unfortunate Jews, leaving him with an overwhelming sense of disgust at such conduct.

In the days following what came to be called *Kristallnacht* (night of broken glass), it became clear that virtually all of Vienna's synagogues had been destroyed. Furthermore, many Jewish shops, businesses, schools and houses were also ransacked.

When Anton read a report in the *Wiener Zeitung* of how the Reich Minister for Public Enlightenment and Propaganda, Joseph Goebbels, had responded to what had happened, he spluttered in anger.

'See this,' he said to Emilie, 'Goebbels has the nerve to suggest that the Jews are nothing more than parasites and that Germany has every right to be anti-Semitic. I tell you, the Nazis have no shame whatsoever for what they've done.'

Worse than this, it was also announced that the Jewish community were to be fined as much as one billion Reichsmarks as a punishment for the so-called 'assassination' of the German diplomat in Paris.

This fine was to be met by the seizure of twenty percent of Jewish property as well as insurance payments that Jews would have been entitled to for the damage to their property on *Kristallnacht* being taken by the state. When they next visited Franz and Sophie for an evening meal, Anton was full of indignation at what had occurred while Franz just seemed resigned.

'Yes, of course it's wrong and very sad, too, but what can we possibly do about it?'

'I'd like to protest, I really would.'

'But to what purpose? You've said yourself the Nazis don't tolerate any dissent. What's more, if you do anything they disapprove of, instead of confining you to Vienna, they could confine you to a concentration camp. I tell you, Anton, we just have to accept that we're powerless.'

Reluctantly, he had to agree that Franz was right, which only added to his sense of frustration. 'I just think it's terrible the Nazis are dragging us all down to their level. If only there was some way of escaping their vice-like grip on every aspect of our lives.'

'Well, I expect many more Jews will now emigrate, which I know is exactly what the Nazis want them to do.'

36

December 1938

A harsh regime of forced labour was imposed on all inmates of Dachau concentration camp, the first to be opened by the Nazis in March 1933, and when Fritz was transferred from there to Buchenwald concentration camp in September 1938 he found that conditions were much the same.

He had endured hardship before as a serving officer in the Great War so drew on that experience in order to cope with his confinement. It was some comfort to him that he was not in the physical danger that he had been in while fighting on the front line but that was not to say that he was in none at all.

Some of the guards were nothing less than brutal sadists, especially towards anyone they identified as Jewish. Who suffered at their hands was really down to luck, depending on which hours they were working and what mood they happened to be in. So far Fritz had been comparatively fortunate in suffering no more than the odd kick, or, on one occasion, vitriolic abuse, but he was conscious of the fact that sooner or later he was likely to be badly beaten.

The worst part of the whole experience, he decided, aside from the denial of liberty and deep sense of sadness at being separated from Helene and his girls, was the total loss of personal dignity. He'd experienced an element of that in the war along with some hardship, too, but as an officer had still enjoyed - and, he liked to think, earned - a measure of respect.

Here in Buchenwald he was acutely conscious of being regarded by the guards as nothing but a lowly turd. It was both humiliating and deeply degrading, making him reflect sadly on the capacity of human beings to derive satisfaction and even acute pleasure from inflicting physical and mental pain on their fellow beings.

He began to witness some of his fellow prisoners becoming shadows of their former selves, broken by a vicious combination of hard labour, monotonously poor food, and degrading, even violent treatment, on a daily basis. He feared that it might only be a question of time before he joined their ranks.

He didn't like to think how much weight he had lost since becoming a prisoner and in his darker moments feared that disease would carry him off long before there was any chance of achieving freedom. Fatalistically, he had reconciled himself to the prospect of many years of confinement, but his hope that this might be counted in single figures actually rose when war broke out.

He was as certain as he dared be that sooner or later Germany would lose and with Hitler's downfall would come freedom. He could also count himself fortunate in being blessed with a naturally cheerful and positive disposition, and this, along with the friendships he formed with fellow prisoners, helped to sustain him.

Above all else, what he believed gave him the will to stay alive were the letters he was able to send to and receive from Helene and his daughters twice a month. He was required to keep his short so could never properly express his emotions nor describe the true extent of the harsh reality he was having to endure. Equally, Helene's letters to him were heavily censored but nonetheless they gave him life-sustaining comfort.

His closest friend, because they had so much in common, was the Austrian composer and cabaret star, Hermann Leopoldi, who had been a casual acquaintance of his in Vienna for some years. Sheer chance brought them together in the same hut and they often worked side by side, dressed in their vertical-striped camp uniforms.

After a long day's hard labour using sledgehammers to break large stones that were then carved into smaller stones to provide building material for some Nazi building project, Fritz and his fellow inmates would assemble for the evening roll call where, exhausted though they were, they were subjected to a form of musical torture by the deputy camp commandant, Arthur Rödl.

At his insistence, they were forced to sing in unison, loudly and in tune; an almost impossible task for ten thousand men spread out across a huge parade ground. Arbitrary beatings were then inflicted on men deemed to be failing to obey Rödl's orders.

The irony that he and his fellow inmates should have singing of all things used as a means of inflicting pain certainly wasn't lost on Fritz. This also never failed to bring to mind bittersweet memories of much happier days working with Franz.

As winter approached and the weather became colder, Fritz was not alone in wondering if he would survive to see another spring. Then one evening Rödl had an announcement to make.

'I have decided that there should be a competition to select the best camp song. You may have a week to make your submissions. The selected winner will receive a prize…'

Rödl failed, though, to say what the prize would be, making Fritz suspicious that this was nothing more than a tempter. Nonetheless, when he and Hermann spoke to each before going to sleep that night, they agreed that they would work together on a suitable song.

'I'm sure I can write some suitable words, if you'll compose the music, Hermann.'

'All right, let's see what we can come up with.'

A mere three days later, enthused by the challenge as if he was once again writing a libretto, Fritz had created some lyrics that really pleased him.

'So, this is what I've written,' he said to Hermann, handing him the piece of paper on which he had scribbled the words to a song to which he'd decided to give the title 'Song of Buchenwald':

When the day awakes,
Before the sun laughs,
The crews embark for the toils of the day,
Into the dawn.
And the forest is black and the sky red,
We carry a small piece of bread in our bags,
And in our hearts, our hearts of sorrow.
Oh Buchenwald, I cannot forget you,
Because you are my fate.
Only he who leaves you can appreciate
How wonderful freedom is!
Oh Buchenwald, we don't try and complain;
And whatever our destiny may be,

We nevertheless shall say 'yes' to life:
For once the day comes, we shall be free!

Our blood runs hot and the girl is far,
And the wind sings softly and I love her dearly,
If she's true, remains true to me!
The stones are hard, but our steps determined,
And we carry the picks and spades with us.
And in our hearts, our hearts love,
Oh Buchenwald…

The night is so short and the day so long
But if a song from our homeland is heard
We do not let it rob us of our courage.
Keep pace, comrade, and do not lose courage
For we carry the will to live in our blood
And in our hearts, our hearts faith.
Oh Buchenwald….

'This is very good, I must say,' Hermann told him, approvingly.

'I'm glad you think so. I worry that Rödl might not be so keen….'

'Why, because it talks about freedom?'

'Of course.'

'Well, I think all prisoners are entitled to dream of freedom. I've got an idea in my head for a marching tune that will complement these words very well. Let's submit it anyway and hope for the best.'

As it happened, Rödl greeted the piece with enthusiasm and duly selected it, though as Fritz had suspected no prize was ever forthcoming. Instead, gruelling hours lay ahead in which Rödl forced the inmates of the camp to rehearse the song.

Yet they sang it with pride, feeling that it felt like an act of resistance. As one survivor of the camp put it, 'We put all our hatred into the song.'

It wasn't long before Hermann became one of the few men lucky enough to be released from a concentration camp but this was only because his wife possessed enough US dollars to pay the Nazi regime a large monetary bribe.

The two men embraced before Hermann's departure. 'I know I'm a lucky sod,' Hermann admitted. 'Good luck to you, Fritz.'

He managed a smile, trying not to feel too envious of his friend. 'God willing, I'll survive to enjoy my day of freedom, too.'

37

12th January 1939

'Hello, Anton, it's me, Franz. Sorry to ring you before ten o'clock in the morning but I've just received a letter in this morning's post from Hitler's personal secretary. It invites me to Berlin in four weeks' time. He wants to meet me in order to present me with an award for my services to music. What should I do?'

'After everything that's happened since Anschluss, I'd like to tell you to refuse but I know it's not as easy as that.'

'No, it definitely isn't. God knows, after what happened across the country in November, not to mention poor Fritz, I'd like to refuse, really I would. The trouble is Hitler's the head of state, the most powerful man in Europe, and adores my music.'

'So naturally you're flattered.'

'I can well detect that note of sarcasm in your voice when you say that. Yes, all right, I am, a little.'

'But you could still very easily claim ill health.'

'Except all that would do is lead to a postponement. I can't keep doing it; otherwise it would become obvious that it's just an excuse and all I'm really doing is snubbing the head of state.'

'True enough.'

'And there's another consideration, too. If I upset the great man he could turn vindictive.'

'You mean Sophie?'

'Of course. What he's been pleased to bestow he could just as easily take away. I can't take that risk.'

'So you'll go then?'

'I think I must. Suck up to him, too, if I that's what's required, and just get it over with.'

'Very reluctantly, I think I have to agree.'

'I also need to tell you that I had some really upsetting news yesterday. Sophie told me she's heard through a friend that poor Victor Léon has had his home seized so he and his wife Ottilie are now homeless. How the Nazis can single out a man in his eighties like this, I really don't know.'

'It's totally obnoxious but I can't say I'm too surprised. The Nazis want their pound of flesh after the death of their diplomat. Do you know what's happened to Victor?'

'Sophie was told that he and his wife have been taken in by friends. Beyond that I've no idea. Sadly, you might remember that Victor's only child Lizzi died years ago.'

'Yes, I vaguely recall that. You know if you do go to Berlin you could speak up for the likes of Fritz and Victor. Who knows? Hitler might even be sympathetic.'

'Do you really think that? I might just make him very angry.'

'I think it would be a risk worth taking. You owe it to them both to try.'

'I'll certainly consider it. And one more thing...'

'Oh yes?'

'The letter says I may take one guest with me to the ceremony. Sophie has said categorically she doesn't want to go so I wondered if you'd like to come instead?'

'But I'm not even free to leave Vienna.'

'I know but I could still make a request that you be allowed to accompany me. The letter gives me a telephone number I can ring to confirm that I'm able to attend and asks that I do so as soon as possible.'

'All right, if you can get permission, I'd be pleased to come, if only to give you the support you deserve. Otherwise, I imagine Emilie would be willing to come with you.'

'I'll bear that in mind and come back to you soon.'

For the remainder of the day, the abiding image in Anton's mind was of the elderly Léon and his wife making their way out of the Café Schwarzenberg. He could only pray that they were safe and well.

Meanwhile, Emilie had overheard his conversation with Franz. When he explained that there was an opportunity for her to be able to return to Berlin she made a face.

'I've no desire to be introduced to Hitler. He's a terrible man.'

'Nor have I but Franz needs to attend and it's not fair to expect him to travel that far on his own. If I'm not given permission to go with him he'd appreciate your support, I'm sure.'

'All right, if I have to.'

Anton really didn't imagine that Franz would be able to get the necessary permission. However, less than a week later, Franz told Anton that he had in fact been successful.

'You can expect to receive official clearance when you next report to SS headquarters. I've been given to understand that there'll be some conditions attached but nothing at all onerous.'

'I must say I'm pleasantly surprised. What on earth did you say to persuade them?'

'That you were totally loyal to me and would never to do anything to prejudice my reputation. I mentioned, too, that in

205

the Great War I'd helped to save your leg and done you some other favours down the years as well.'

The normally tight-lipped SS officer to whom Anton reported, seemed as surprised as he was to be able to hand him a pass allowing him to accompany Franz to Berlin in order to attend the ceremony at which he would receive his award.

'I need hardly add that if you step outside the terms of this permission, you will be arrested and imprisoned.'

'I understand.'

'I hope you do.'

Two days before the ceremony was due to take place, Franz and Anton undertook a familiar train journey through country-side which was covered in winter snow. Upon their punctual arrival in Berlin they were then taken by taxi to the prestigious Eden hotel, in which Franz had frequently stayed over the years, where he'd booked them two very comfortable en suite rooms. Franz especially was feeling tired after their day-long journey, so they both retired early to bed and enjoyed a good night's rest.

The following morning, after a leisurely breakfast, Anton was keen to stretch his legs with a stroll through the Tiergarten. Franz, though, complained that he'd not slept well and needed to rest so Anton was left to set off on his own. The weather was cold but dry and he found it a pleasure to be back in a city which he had always found attractive. All that marred his walk were the number of swastika flags everywhere but then it was the same in Vienna so this hardly shocked him.

He returned to the hotel in time for lunch and Franz joined him, but when he asked Franz if he'd like to go anywhere in the afternoon he once again declined.

'I'm feeling better than I was but I really don't want to go out. As you know the whole point of coming a day early was so that I could conduct this special performance of *The Merry Widow* at the Charlottenburger Opernhaus this evening and I need to prepare for that. I also keep worrying about what I say to Hitler tomorrow. It's not going to be easy to find the right words. He may not even hear me out. I could well lose my nerve, I'm afraid.'

'Just do your best, you can't do more,' Anton responded, trying to be encouraging.

'Of course, I might not even get the chance to try. I don't imagine he'll want to talk to me for long and it'll hardly be a private audience.'

'But there's a reception afterwards, don't forget. That will give you your best opportunity.'

'Yes, I suppose it might.'

'And he'll be at the theatre this evening, of course.'

'Yes, but I've been told there'll be no personal meeting until tomorrow.'

Anton decided that he wanted to go to the Neues Museum in order to revisit something really special. It was too far to consider walking there and as the day was slipping away fast, he rejected public transport in favour of the more expensive option of a taxi. This got him to the front door of the museum in barely twenty minutes, but in that length of time he still got a glimpse of several boarded-up shops with the word *Juden* painted on them as well as one burnt-out synagogue.

Once inside the museum he headed straight for what had brought him there: the head of Nefertiti, queen of the heretic pharaoh Akhenaten. He had seen it twice before while living in Berlin and been quite astonished by it. He thought it simply the most exquisitely beautiful piece of sculpture he had ever set eyes upon and marvelled at the genius of whoever had created it.

'It has an ethereal, timeless quality to it, don't you think?' Emilie had said to Anton when they'd visited it together and these words came back to him now as he gazed upon it in wonder. The civilization this Egyptian queen had lived in was long gone and if magically reincarnated he knew she would be astonished by the modern world with all its many inventions. Human nature, however, had surely not changed; there were still struggles for power, conflicting ideologies, and seemingly endless acts of cruelty. Her world had no doubt been a dangerous one while his was surely more dangerous still.

Franz, as he'd done for the first night of *The Merry Widow* all those years before, was able to get him a complimentary seat, though only at the back of the grand circle.

'I'm perfectly happy with that. I'd rather be lost in the crowd, I think.'

'You're not thinking of doing anything stupid, I hope?'

'Of course not, Franz. I'm only here at all on the basis that I would never let you down and I won't, I promise you.'

The theatre was almost full for the performance, bringing in its wake the usual buzz of conversation until suddenly an announcement was made over the theatre's loudspeaker system.

'Please rise and salute the Führer and Chancellor of Germany, Adolf Hitler.'

A great hush fell across the audience and seemingly as one, everyone around Anton thrust out an arm. Much as he would have liked to remain in his seat, he'd made a promise to Franz not to cause any trouble so duly stood up along with the rest. It was far harder to thrust out an arm in salute and he couldn't bring himself to do so, even half-heartedly.

From where he was sitting he also only had a restricted view of the box Hitler had entered, and had to crane his neck to get any view at all of the man himself, even as he stood holding up his right hand in response to the salute he'd received. Many around Anton were also crying '*Sieg Heil!*' but the very notion of doing any such thing stuck in his throat so he remained silent. Then the orchestra struck-up the national anthem '*Deutschland über alles*' which the audience sang with an exuberant enthusiasm, which he was again unable to share. He moved his lips but nothing more.

After a very short delay, the audience then began to applaud Franz's arrival in the orchestra pit and continued to do so for at least a minute. Anton was sure that Franz would be very gratified to receive such acclamation and he could look forward to even more once the evening's performance ended.

'I must say, it all went very well,' he said to Anton in the taxi on the way back to their hotel, 'but I am feeling very tired.'

The ceremony was to take place at the Reich Chancellery at noon so Franz and Anton had plenty of time to prepare themselves and enjoy a leisurely breakfast before catching their taxi. The weather also remained cold but dry and Anton had time to enjoy a brief walk to the zoological gardens and back before they needed to depart. Over breakfast, they had reflected on the previous evening's performance.

'You know, Anton, I feel revitalised when I'm in front of an orchestra, conducting. The years just fall away and I lose myself in the music. Now back to reality, I'm afraid.'

They both then lapsed into silence. It was clear that Franz

was feeling quite tense so Anton decided it was best to let him keep his thoughts to himself. What will be, will be, he decided, and it was only when they were about to get out of their taxi upon their arrival at the Chancellery that he offered him any encouragement.

'Good luck, Franz. I'm sure it will go well, whatever you're able to say to our leader, not that he's really any leader of mine, of course.'

'And nor of mine, Anton, I assure you. But thank you anyway. I expect it will.'

They were met at the entrance of what had once been a palace, built in the Rococo style towards the end of the eighteenth century, by a uniformed officer who introduced himself as an aide and adjutant to the Führer. He was exceedingly polite, without being in the least unctuous, referring to Anton with a salute as General Lehár, which in the circumstances exercised his ego somewhat.

The adjutant then led them through a series of corridors to a large reception area, which from its design formed part of a modern extension to the original palace. Anton was immediately struck by how long it was, as well as by the height of its ceiling and of its windows, which were built from floor to ceiling.

At the far end of the room, a lectern had been set up and a number of the invited guests had already taken their seats, which were arranged in rows. Further, a door opposite the lectern was guarded by two soldiers with rifles so Anton assumed Hitler would make his entrance through this.

The adjutant showed them to their seats immediately in front of the lectern and said quietly that the Führer was due to arrive in about five minutes. He then disappeared through the guarded door and they waited. The guarded doors were then suddenly thrown open and in walked Hitler, wearing a plain grey uniform save that Anton's eyes were drawn to a swastika symbol on his right arm.

Everyone stood and albeit half-heartedly Franz and Anton joined other guests in saluting Hitler, having previously agreed that it was politic to do so. At the same time Anton saw nothing in the man that impressed him. He wasn't handsome, he wasn't more than average height for a man, his tiny moustache was, he thought, vaguely ridiculous, and he didn't begin to dominate the room with his personality in the way he knew someone like Richard Tauber could.

Only a couple of steps behind him, he also recognised the features of Hermann Göring, President of the Reichstag and Commander-in-Chief of the Luftwaffe. He was slightly shorter than Hitler, quite plump, and far more grandly attired in a uniform covered in medals, some of which he knew were well earned as an air ace in the Great War. Further, whereas Hitler was smiling, albeit somewhat limply, Göring was positively beaming and certainly seemed to Anton to have more presence.

A third man, somewhat younger than either Hitler or Göring, also followed them into the reception area. He was wearing a dark, well-tailored suit and holding a piece of paper. Once he reached the lectern he welcomed everyone before proceeding to give a brief summary of what he called Franz's illustrious career and the great contribution he had made to German music through his many operettas.

'The Führer has now been pleased to recognise his services by the award of a medal, which he will now bestow upon him.' He then took this medal along with a red sash off the lectern and handed it to Hitler. 'If you would care to step forward, Herr Lehár.'

Franz duly did so to enthusiastic applause before shaking hands with Hitler, who, with a friendly smile, placed the sash over his head. Franz then returned to his seat and Hitler immediately began to speak. Anton thoroughly disliked what he often called his ranting speeches on the wireless or newsreels. This, however, was quite different as he spoke appreciatively of his love of Franz's music and how, as a young student in Vienna before the Great War, it had given him great pleasure to attend performances of *The Merry Widow*.

'So, it has been a privilege today to be able to bestow on such a fine composer an award recognising his talents, what an asset he has been and continues to be to the great German Reich, and the enjoyment I know he has brought to millions of people around the world. I now look forward to speaking to him at the reception, which will immediately follow this ceremony.'

Waiters then appeared carrying trays with champagne glasses on them. It struck Anton that Hitler had spoken with both eloquence and charm, although he was slightly surprised that he'd made no mention of Franz's kindnesses towards him before the Great War. With his piercing blue eyes, he could believe, too, that for those who believed in his cause he had more than just presence. Rather, he had all the charisma of a prophet, albeit a very dangerous, false prophet of hatred and division.

Hitler then came towards Franz and Anton and shook hands with Franz a second time. 'Once again, my congratulations, maestro. It really is a great pleasure to meet you again. I still so love your music.'

'Thank you, thank you so much... It has been... a great honour, I must say.'

Anton immediately realised that Franz was failing to address Hitler as *Mein Führer* as his adjutant had told them they should. Perhaps, though, he was just losing his way a little out of nervousness, and Hitler certainly didn't appear to mind at all.

'And General Lehár, I understand you're here to support your brother as you've always done.' He then looked Anton in the eyes, smiled and shook his hand with a firm grip.

'... Führer, I'm grateful to have been allowed to attend.' At the last moment, Anton simply couldn't bring himself to say *Mein*.

Hitler merely nodded, apparently completely indifferent to any rudeness on Anton's part, intentional or otherwise, before giving Franz his full attention. Now Anton wondered if his brother could find the courage at some point in their conversation to bring to Hitler's attention the fate of both Fritz and Victor. But, of course, it was never going to be easy.

A waiter then approached with a tray bearing glasses of champagne. This gave Hermann Göring, who had been hovering at Hitler's side, the chance to step forward and also offer his congratulations, which was followed by another round of handshakes.

Göring's face still wore a beaming, jovial smile, as if, Anton thought, butter wouldn't melt in his mouth. He also thought, too, that he had an exceedingly high opinion of himself, but then again, perhaps not without reason, for he now stood very high indeed in the echelons of power of the Third Reich. Indeed, he would soon become the designated successor of one of the most powerful men in the world.

Anton also noticed that Hitler hadn't picked up any glass of champagne. Instead, the waiter, who clearly understood his duties, offered him a glass of mineral water, which he took from him with thanks. He had also barely begun to tell Franz how much he'd enjoyed the previous night's performance when an attractive woman stepped forward, whom Göring introduced as his wife, Emmy, who was an actress. She had married Göring, then a widower, about three years previously, and only the previous summer had given birth to a daughter.

Yet another round of handshakes took up yet more time, whereupon more waiters arrived bearing plates of canapés. Meanwhile, Hitler and Franz talked on with Hitler starting to reminisce about the Vienna of his youth and Franz simply listening politely. This frustrated Anton as he wanted his brother to seize the moment for the sake of his working colleagues and friends of many years.

Amidst a babble of conversation all around him, all he could do, though, was sip his champagne, a waiter having kindly refilled his glass, and eat another delicious canapé. Then Franz, who had his back to him, coughed, as if he was about to come to the point, so Anton took a step closer to him in order to be able to hear what he said.

'*Mein Führer*, at the risk of displeasing you, I must say that I could not have achieved what I did without the skill of my librettists, of which two of the very finest were Fritz Löhner-Beda and Victor Léon, both of whom are from a Jewish background. Fritz is now in a concentration camp...'

'Enough, maestro,' Hitler interrupted him, sharply. 'This is meant to be a happy occasion, not one at which I wish to hear of such matters. If action has been taken against the men to whom you refer, I'm sure it's in the best interests of the Reich. I hope I make myself clear?'

'Of course, *Mein Führer*, please forgive my presumption.'

Hitler held up a hand. 'Do not worry. I can understand your desire to help men you have worked with in the past. Nevertheless, the interests of the state demand that firm action is taken to free this country of its Jewish cancer, once and for all. Now allow me to introduce you to someone who I know would very much like to meet you...'

For all Anton's profound sense of disappointment, he was still proud of Franz for having found the courage, when the moment was right, to at least try to intervene on his friends' behalf.

'You did your best,' he assured him once they were again ensconced inside their taxi on the way back to their hotel.

'But it still wasn't good enough, was it?'

He shook his head. 'There was nothing more you could have done once Hitler made it clear that he wasn't prepared to listen. Had you tried to argue with him he would have just become angry. That would have simply made matters worse, I'm sure.'

Throughout their journey home the following day, Anton kept reflecting on what an experience it had been to mingle with the highest echelons of the Nazi party. He had to confess to himself that it had exercised his ego a little and he imagined that the same applied to Franz. How easy it is, he thought, for power to take you in its warm embrace, even at the cost of your very soul. In the circumstances, a lesser man than Franz might not have found the courage to say anything about his Jewish friends so once again he sought to reassure him.

'I'm proud of you for having tried, dear brother.'

'Thank you, Anton, that's a comfort to me, it really is.'

38

29th August 1939

'Oh dear, this is bad,' Anton said to Emilie. The early evening news broadcast had just made it clear that the German government had demanded the restoration of Danzig to Germany. Worse, it had given the Polish government just twenty-four hours to send a representative to Berlin to begin negotiations.

'But the Poles will agree, surely?'

'Possibly, but I doubt Hitler would have ordered such an ultimatum to be sent if he wasn't ready to attack Poland.'

The so-called Danzig corridor was just another piece of the German Reich that had been lost as a consequence of the Great War so it was understandable that Hitler should be intent on recovering it. Nonetheless, Anton could hardly imagine that his ambitions would stop there and said as much to Franz on the telephone.

'If this does mean war, I suppose you'll accelerate your plan to live permanently in Ischl?'

'Somewhat, but everything's in hand anyway. I still pray for peace, of course.'

'As do I.'

Yet within forty-eight hours came the even grimmer news that Poland had rejected the ultimatum. Worse, that there were to be no further negotiations.

'This is it then,' Anton said to Emilie. 'The next thing we'll hear is that the invasion's begun.'

'Will the Poles put up much of a fight, do you think?'

'They might do but I doubt they'll be much of a match for our armed forces. It should all be over pretty quickly.'

'Except you've always said if Hitler goes too far the British and the French will declare war.'

'And I fear they will.'

The Polish invasion, which started the following day, began yet another world war. Meanwhile, the Poles fought on bravely for a month, the knock-out blow actually being delivered by the Russians, who invaded from the east. The wireless and newsreels proclaimed another stunning triumph and didn't hesitate to compare Hitler to the likes of Frederick the Great

'How cunning of Hitler to agree a carve-up of Poland with Russia before instigating any invasion,' Anton told Emilie. 'I must say it puts him up in my estimations, if only a little.'

By October, Franz and Sophie were also ready to effectively retire to Bad Ischl.

'We'll see you at Christmas, Anton, if not sooner,' he assured him.

'And we'll look forward to that. Life will not be the same without you.'

'Let's keep in regular contact by telephone. I suggest we agree to speak every week.'

They shook hands on that and life went on, although for Anton it was all the poorer for not being able to see Franz twice a week.

Ever since Anschluss, Anton had been aware of some Jews, like Fritz, being sent to concentration camps and no doubt the numbers suffering that fate had increased as a consequence of Kristallnacht. Now, not long after Franz and Sophie's departure, he became aware of yet more Jews being taken away.

He particularly knew of a Jewish family living nearby. The father ran a drapery business but it had been closed down in the summer. Now, suddenly, he and Emilie noticed that their house had been ransacked, the word *Juden* painted on one of its walls, while the family, of course, was gone. Through friends and acquaintances, they also heard very similar stories.

'If I was Jewish I know I would be very scared,' Anton said to Emilie. 'At any time it could be my turn next and as far as I can see, this is being done totally indiscriminately. It would make me want to hide.'

'I do hope poor Victor and his wife are all right.'

'Provided the friends who took them in aren't Jewish and have the means to support them, they should still be well, though living off the charity of others surely can't be easy. Victor always struck me as being a proud man, too.'

When Franz and Anton next spoke on the telephone, Anton naturally told him of the continuing disappearance of Jews, which most upset him. Like Emilie, Franz also expressed concern for the welfare of Victor and spoke of his fears for the wellbeing of other old Jewish colleagues. In doing so he particularly mentioned the likes of Louis Treumann.

'You know, Anton, what really brings home to me the terrible position Jews find themselves in is Sophie's recent experience.'

'Really? Why should she be affected any longer, given her special status?'

'Indeed, why should she? Unfortunately, some nasty official based in Vienna has got it into his head that her special Aryan status can't be genuine. I received a very unpleasant telephone call from him the other day. He scoffed when I told him who I was and he's demanding to see the original certificate. We're going to have to return to Vienna with it in the course of the next few days as I'm certainly not risking its loss in the post.'

'I'm afraid officious little bastards seem to thrive under the system of government we have now.'

'Oh yes, what a disaster that was, but at least he was polite. This man is thoroughly rude and threatening. It's quite put the fear of God into Sophie, I can tell you. Anyway, we must meet up.'

Five days later, the four of them were once again be able to enjoy coffee and cake together in the Café Central.

'Is everything now sorted?' Anton asked Franz and Sophie, once they were seated and had placed their order.

Franz frowned at him. 'I sincerely hope so but I can tell you it's not been without further difficulty. Two days ago we had a visit from an official.'

'What, the same one you spoke to on the telephone?'

'No, this was someone else. He just banged on the door of our house as if he wanted to wake the dead. It was only eight o'clock in the morning so neither of us were up and dressed. He really couldn't have been more unpleasant. Sophie was practically in tears, weren't you, my love?'

'Yes, he demanded to see both of our identity cards and even when Franz handed them over, still wasn't satisfied.'

'Yes, I produced Sophie's certificate as well, but he still asked a lot of unnecessary questions. It was as if he'd been told to make life as difficult for her as possible.'

'And you still had to bring the original here to Vienna?'

'Oh yes, I checked and that was insisted upon. It was as if the left hand didn't know what the right was doing. I've a good mind to complain to the Chancellor's office.'

'Don't do that, I don't want you making a fuss,' Sophie insisted. 'I really can't see it helping.'

'All right, I expect it's all behind us now and we'll be left in peace in future.'

Until Christmas, Anton was only in contact with Franz by telephone. Franz complained of a bad cold and feeling tired, and then, at the beginning of December, confessed that the same official who'd originally come to their door was continuing to make life difficult for them.

'Food rationing is the excuse,' he told Anton. 'You know Jews are entitled to less than the rest of us?'

'Yes, but why should that be a problem so long as Sophie is regarded as Aryan?'

'Oh, apparently there's an issue over whether her Aryan status is sufficient to exempt her under the wording of the regulations which brought in rationing.'

'That just sounds like an excuse to me.'

'Yes, I still think someone in Vienna hates Sophie's exemption and is determined to try and get round it if they can.'

'So have you complained?'

'No, no, I've been too poorly and Sophie still hasn't wanted me to.'

When Franz and Sophie returned to Vienna to celebrate Christmas with Anton and Emilie, Anton was frankly worried by how sickly Franz seemed and Sophie, too, looked tired and anxious.

Though the country had now been at war for almost four months, in Vienna at least, unless you were Jewish, life went on much as it had in peacetime. There were still plenty of goods in the shops as well as food. Furthermore, since the beginning of October there had been no fighting, just a stalemate as the French and British defended the so-called Maginot line on the border between France and Germany. What the New Year might bring was anyone's guess and Anton was reluctant to speculate. Meanwhile, over dinner, Franz's thoughts naturally turned to his forthcoming seventieth birthday.

'I'd be happy to celebrate it here in Vienna over dinner with family and a few friends. I don't seek any special attention and don't expect it,' he said modestly.

'And what about the harassment you've been getting at the hands of this official?' Anton asked.

'Oh, thankfully we've been left in peace for a few weeks.'

'I thought it might help if I had myself baptised,' Sophie added.

'You've actually done this?' Anton asked.

'Oh yes, a few weeks ago now.'

'Well, I hope it does make a difference.'

Anton didn't want to be discouraging so he tactfully said nothing more. However, he thought her action pointless, believing only Sophie's special status could protect her.

By the time they came to enjoy their dessert they'd all drunk more wine than was perhaps good for them and Anton thought Franz was looking particularly maudlin.

'Cheer up, Franz,' Anton said. 'It's Christmas, after all.'

'Oh, I'm sorry, Anton, I can't help thinking about poor Fritz and what sort of Christmas he'll be having. A pretty miserable one, I'd imagine.'

'Hard too for Helene and her daughters,' Sophie added. 'This will be their second Christmas without him and rationing won't be helping either.'

'Yes, I do hope Victor and his wife have enough to eat, wherever they are,' Franz responded.

'Well, I propose a toast,' Anton said. 'To absent friends.'

39

As it turned out, Franz's expectation that his seventieth birthday, 30th April 1940, would be a quiet affair, cele-brated merely by family and friends, couldn't have been more wrong. Only a few weeks into the New Year, when he spoke to Anton on the telephone, he had some important news for him.

'I am to be presented with the Goethe Medal of Arts and Science.'

'Many congratulations.'

'What's more, Hitler himself is going to come to Vienna to present it to me on my birthday.' At this news Anton was almost lost for words. 'Hello, Anton, are you still there?'

'Yes, of course, I'm sorry. A great honour for you, indeed. So much for no one important wanting to take an interest in your birthday!'

'You don't really approve, do you? I can tell.'

'It's not a question of that, Franz. I don't like Hitler, or anything he or his party stands for, you know I don't. Nor did I think you did either.'

'So you believe I should refuse in order to make some sort of statement of my disapproval?'

'That would require great courage.'

'And do Sophie no favours at all. I will protect her at all

costs, you know that.'

'Yes, of course, I do. If I were in your position I would wish to do the same.'

'We have to be realistic, too. Nothing I or any other individual can say, in protest at the way in which Hitler and his government are treating the Jews, will change anything.'

'Yes, I know. He's a very powerful man.'

'In fact, arguably the most powerful man on the planet at this moment in time, wouldn't you say?'

'I'm not sure I'd go that far but no doubt he'd like to be. If he can defeat the combined might of the British and French Empires then he might well be able to call himself that.'

'Well, be that as it may, I intend to accept the award with gratitude. After all, I fear that without Hitler's personal support, Sophie would be in great danger. Naturally, I'd like you and Emilie to attend the ceremony.'

'We'll be pleased to do so, Franz. You know, you've always been able to rely upon my support.'

'And, as you'll also be aware, I've always been grateful for it.'

This honouring of Franz did not, however, stop there, as only a couple of weeks or so later he had more news.

'The city of Vienna is now going to award me its Ring of Honour of the City of Vienna. It will be awarded at the same time as the Goethe Medal. I must say such recognition from my own city really pleases me. And even better, the City Opera House is now going to perform *The Land of Smiles*. It's in honour of my birthday, of course, which I expect I have Hitler's support to thank for.'

'Yes, I imagine so.'

'Oh come off it, Anton, we both know the truth of the

matter. *Mein Führer* has to be sucked up to, after all.'

'That's unusually caustic for you, Franz, if you don't mind me saying so.'

'Yes, well, it's because it's not all good news, I'm afraid.'

'Oh dear.'

'Yes, Sophie had a telephone call from a friend in Vienna yesterday. Victor's dead, I'm sad to say.'

'Oh, I'm so sorry to hear that. How old was he now, eighty-two?'

'Yes, his birthday would have been the beginning of January.'

'So not a bad age.'

'No, I suppose not. What really saddens me is that he seems to have died of malnutrition.'

'Starved to death? Are you serious?'

'It's what Sophie was told. The friends who were looking after him and Ottilie were Jews themselves. The food rations for them are so meagre, they could barely manage to feed themselves, never mind two elderly guests.'

'How is Ottilie then?'

'All right, I think, but then with Victor's death there's one less mouth to feed.'

'But why didn't Victor and Ottilie register for their own food rations?'

'After what's happened to Fritz and so many other Jewish musicians and artists, Victor preferred to go into hiding. I really don't know what's the worse fate, dying of starvation, or dying in some wretched concentration camp.'

'At least he avoided the humiliation of being taken away.'

'Yes, some consolation, I suppose. His age was against him, too. But really, what a tragic end for a man of such charm and ability. What is the world coming to?'

Anton was tempted to say, *hell and damnation for its many sins*, but checked himself. Instead, he merely said, 'I don't know, it's very sad.'

Meanwhile, the 'phony war', as it was beginning to be called, continued until early April, when German troops occupied Denmark in a single day and invaded Norway as well. The British and French responded by coming to Norway's aid, so by the time of Franz's birthday it was by no means certain that the country would be successfully overrun, although German propaganda never allowed for the possibility of defeat. Otherwise, in pleasant spring weather, Anton thought it all too easy to forget that the nation had embarked upon its second major conflict in a mere twenty-five years.

Understandably, Franz was preoccupied with arrangements for his 'big day'. To help ensure that everything went smoothly he and Sophie arrived in Vienna on 28th April, staying once again at the König von Ungarn hotel, where Anton and Emilie joined them both for dinner the following evening. They were also joined by their younger sister Emmy and her husband Stefan Papahazay. They had travelled from Budapest to be with Franz for both this occasion and the award ceremony the following day.

Like Anton, Stefan had managed to reach the rank of major-general. Although Anton had seen little of either him or Emmy down the years, he still knew them well enough to be confident that they were of a like mind when it came to political issues. After a quiet word with them both upon their arrival, it was, however, agreed that out of respect for Franz they would endeavour to keep their conversation as light-hearted as possible.

'Unless he wants to talk politics,' Stefan suggested.

'I doubt that. Anything but, I'd have thought. How's life in Hungary these days?'

'All right, provided you're not Jewish. It's in Hitler's pocket, of course.'

'So likely to join Germany in the war effort?'

'I'd imagine so, provided Germany keeps winning.'

'We'll have to see what happens this summer then.'

'You're looking well, if I may say so, Anton.'

'Yes, not too bad for my years, I hope. You're looking fit, too.'

'Reasonably so. A few aches and pains, but nothing to grumble about.'

'And Emmy's still looking quite youthful, I'm pleased to say.'

'Yes, she's fifty this year, but you wouldn't know it.'

The hotel prided itself on an excellent, if expensive menu, but as generous as ever, Franz made it clear that he would meet the bill for all six of them. When Anton looked the choice of food, he found it hard to believe that any rationing had come into force. He was also pleased to see that both Franz and Sophie were looking quite well, whilst he had by now grown used to his rather laboured gait.

Conversation was also for the most part confined to the following day's arrangements as well as reminiscences about family. That is until Stefan, perhaps a little tactlessly in the circumstances, said how sad it was that Franz's Jewish colleagues would be unable to celebrate his birthday with him. Franz lowered his eyes and for a moment Anton thought he was about to burst into tears.

'I think of poor Fritz every day, you know. I did try to get Hitler to listen to my appeal on his behalf but he just swept it aside.'

'And I hear that Victor Léon has died,' Emmy said.

'Yes. In the most tragic of circumstances.'

'Really?'

While Franz began to explain, Anton glanced at Sophie and had the distinct impression that she wanted to say something quite important. At the first opportunity she duly did so.

'I've also heard, through an old friend I went to see today, that the librettist Bela Jenbach has gone into hiding. What worries me is that he may suffer the same fate as Victor.'

'Though his wife isn't Jewish, as I recall,' Franz added. 'What's more, I don't think their property's been seized. She should still able to support him. Even so, it's just awful that he should feel the need to take such a drastic step.'

They all nodded in agreement and the whole tone of the evening now took on a far more sombre note as they all became lost in their own thoughts. Fortunately, however, within minutes a birthday cake with seven lit candles arrived at their table, which lifted everyone's mood considerably. Franz duly blew them out and they all happily burst into song, singing 'Happy Birthday to You'. The evening did not, however, end without Franz being frank with them all as to how he was feeling about the forthcoming ceremony.

'I want to make it clear to everyone that while I will gratefully accept the honours which are to be bestowed upon me tomorrow, I will not do so without feelings of great regret concerning this country's treatment of its Jewish citizens. Having tried once before, totally unsuccessfully, to raise the fate of colleagues like Fritz with Hitler, I'm afraid I see nothing to be gained from trying again. Indeed, if I were to do so, it might not just turn him against me, but also at the same time threaten Sophie's very vulnerable position. By remaining silent I do not, however, in any way condone what is happening to so many old colleagues and friends.'

It was clear to Anton that Franz was still struggling with his conscience and, in so doing, was looking to his family to support him.

'Don't worry, Franz, Emmy and I are a hundred percent behind you on this,' Stefan said reassuringly,

'As are Emilie and I,' Anton added, looking Emilie in the eye as he spoke and she nodded in agreement.

Franz smiled. 'I'm very grateful for that. Let's just hope then that tomorrow goes well.'

As Anton and Emilie arrived at the City Hall the next day, it was cloudy and overcast with a hint of rain in the air. Erected as a piece of Gothic fantasy in the previous century, it had never much appealed to Anton's taste. Nonetheless, the interior of the hall into which they were directed to enter was vast, like the nave of a cathedral, and certainly impressive. It was also already filling up with a large number of invited guests and Anton anticipated a ceremony not dissimilar to the one he had sat through the previous year in Berlin. What immediately struck him, though, was that a full-sized orchestra was present. He noted, too, from the programme they had been handed upon entry, that they were to be entertained by a selection of music from Franz's operettas including, of course, *The Merry Widow*.

'Franz will be delighted when they play his music,' Emilie whispered in Anton's ear after they had taken their allotted seats near the front. He nodded in agreement.

Glancing around he thought what might please Franz less

was that many of the men present were wearing uniforms of one sort or another. Given that the country was at war this was to be expected, he supposed. For sure, if one thing had changed on the streets of Vienna since last September, it was the sight of so many men in uniform.

After a brief wait the buzz of conversation was brought to a sudden halt by an announcement inviting everyone to rise and salute the entry into the hall of the Führer and other dignitaries. As one they did so and Anton was struck by the enthusiasm with which people around him thrust out an arm. He felt obliged to raise his arm as well, but it was no more than a token gesture. Certainly, he couldn't bring himself to chant 'Sieg Heil' as Hitler advanced up the hall in full-dress uniform, holding up his hand like some Roman emperor acknowledging the acclaim of his grateful subjects.

Franz had been given the honour of being one of the official party that had greeted Hitler upon his arrival at the City Hall so was only a few steps behind him, walking next to the city's current mayor. It was a sight which immediately brought to mind the fate of the former mayor Richard Schmitz. For his sins, Anton assumed that, like Fritz, he was still suffering in Dachau or Buchenwald.

Amongst those following Hitler, he also recognised Josef Bürckel, whose face was becoming familiar as the most powerful Nazi in Austria following Seyss-Inquart's departure to take up a post in newly conquered Poland. Bavarian by birth and a teacher by profession, he had been a member of the Nazi Party since its early days.

As in Berlin, the ceremony of awarding Franz both the Goethe Medal and the Ring of Honour was carried out with military precision, and his brain must have been awash with the inevitable plaudits he received. Most touching was when the orchestra struck up 'Happy Birthday to You' and everyone sang along to it. He could just see Franz's face and could tell that he was very emotional, which was completely understandable.

Of course, at the end of the ceremony the national anthem was played, and once again this was an excuse for everyone to not only sing along but also salute the Führer as the almighty, all-conquering hero. Anton shuddered at the patriotic fervour around him, recalling all too well how such displays of emotion had done nothing to help Germany and Austria achieve victory in the last great conflict.

Having warmly shaken Franz's hand, Hitler then presented him with his medal. However, he then departed as soon as the ceremony ended, as did Kaltenbrunner.

'They've a war to fight, after all,' Anton whispered in Emilie's ear.

They could not know it at the time, but within weeks Hitler was set to sweep all before him. Some no doubt likened him to a god of war descending from the heavens, but Anton preferred to think of him as a devil ascending from hell.

The rest of the invited guests were left to enjoy a generous buffet lunch along with an equally generous quantity of champagne and wine. Of course, notable by their absence, Anton reflected, were all the many distinguished Jewish librettists and musicians, without whom Franz would have never been able to achieve such success.

Meanwhile, Franz looked tired but happy. But then after such a proud day, when his praises had been sung to the very rafters of the Festival Hall, that was to be expected. It was a very bittersweet experience for him, too, though only those who knew him well were privy to that. After it was all over there was also no opportunity for a private word until he had returned to Ischl, whereupon he telephoned Anton.

'I hope it wasn't too emotionally draining for you, Franz?'

'I was a little overwhelmed at times. Of course, I've grown used to the sound of applause over the years, but I must confess that some of it rang a little hollow to my ears. I just couldn't get out of my mind the faces of those who deserved to be there in the front row sharing my happy day. Not *Mein Führer* and those who serve him, but Fritz and Victor and Louis, as well as so many more. You know it's a cruel irony that I should enjoy such praise from the very man most responsible for ruining their lives.'

'Yes, Franz, indeed it is.'

40

Within two months of Franz's seventieth birthday, Hitler was master of Europe. Even in his most ambitious dreams, he would surely not have believed that he could accomplish so much in such a short space of time, thanks to the weaknesses of his opponents and the power of the Blitzkrieg tactics employed by the Wehrmacht and Luftwaffe. The world must have seemed to be almost literally at his feet, so it was hardly surprising if such dizzying success gave him a sense of invincibility. Mussolini, too, whom Franz had met in 1939 whilst holidaying in Italy, decided which side his bread was buttered on, while Hungary didn't take all that long in following his example.

Had anyone dared to voice the suggestion that within five years everything would come crashing down completely, they'd have been laughed at before being promptly dispatched to a concentration camp. Certainly, Anton never imagined it possible, and was resigned as he could be to a Nazi victory, which might well endure for decades to come.

A year later, so by the summer of 1941, that still seemed to be the grim reality, for all that England remained unconquered and defiant. After all, the United States remained neutral, the Balkan States, including Greece, were now in German hands, while the Afrika Korps was in the ascendancy in North Africa. But then

233

Hitler made the ultimately fatal error of invading Russia.

Meanwhile, Franz's music was now receiving more attention, and with it an increasing opportunity for him to conduct performances of his music both at concerts and on wireless broadcasts. Blessedly, too, Sophie was being left in peace. However, all the while a terrible darkness was closing in as slowly but surely the Nazis continued their relentless persecution of Europe's Jews.

It was evening time and Anton had not long eaten supper. He was dozing in a chair when the telephone rang.

'Hello, Anton, it's me, Franz. I need to come to Vienna soon so I was hoping we could meet.'

'Why, of course, Franz. Is something wrong?'

'Not with me, though I find it a struggle getting out of bed in the morning. No, it's Louis Treumann. A mutual friend has been in touch to say that he's been arrested. I need to try and get him released, if I can. Another old friend on my conscience would be too much.'

'None of this is your fault, Franz.'

'I know it isn't, but that's not the point. I need to do something to try and help, otherwise I just couldn't live with myself any longer.'

'So what will you do?'

'Now Seyss-Inquart's gone, I'm going to ask for a meeting with his successor.'

'Baldur von Shirach, you mean?'

'Yes, that's his name. I'm not going to be specific; just that it's a matter of some delicacy on which I'd appreciate a few minutes of his valuable time. I'm hoping that might be sufficient to get me through his door.'

'Um, maybe.'

'You think I'll need to be more specific then?'

'I'd rather imagine so.'

'In that case I will be. If necessary, I'll have to resort to just writing a letter. The trouble is they're too easily ignored. I want to be able to look the man in the eye, if I can. Admittedly, I know nothing about him, but if he'll listen to me, I'm hoping I might be able to win him round.'

'He could easily fob you off with someone of no importance.'

'I'll just have to take that risk. I'll make enquiries by telephone tomorrow morning in the hope he'll agree to see me in a couple of days or less. I'll ring again to let you know exactly what's happening and we can arrange a time and place to meet.'

'All right, I'll look forward to that. Will Sophie come with you, do you think?'

'Oh yes. She can do some shopping, I expect, while I'm busy.'

'In which event Emilie might want to join her.'

'I'm sure Sophie would be happy for her to do so. Of course, I can see us having to stay a night or two at the König von Ungarn hotel. Anyway, I've also had one more piece of bad news, I'm afraid. We only found out a few days ago that the librettist Julius Wilhelm is dead. Apparently, it happened several months ago and he went the same way as poor Victor.'

'Starved to death, you mean?'

'Sadly, yes. I believe he'd gone into hiding, too, and just couldn't get enough food to eat. He'd have been nearly seventy, I think. I tell you, apart from Louis, every Jewish colleague and friend I ever had is now either dead, in hiding somewhere, already in a concentration camp, or has fled abroad. It just

235

makes me more determined than ever to do what I can to protect him.'

Franz rang Anton again the following day. It was late afternoon and he sounded frustrated.

'I'm worried I'm going to be fobbed off. It took me practically all morning to speak to von Shirach's personal secretary, only for her to tell me he was extremely busy all day with meetings, and that she'd be unable to disturb him. All she could promise was that she'd put my request on his desk and let me know his decision as soon as possible. She also warned me that his diary's very full for the next few days. Look, Sophie and I will come to Vienna first thing tomorrow morning. As soon as we arrive, I'm going to go straight to von Shirach's office. Once he knows I'm actually in the building, I hope he'll find the time to see me.'

'How frank were you with his secretary about your reason for wanting a personal interview?'

'After giving it some thought, I decided to be completely frank.'

'So he'll know this is about Louis?'

'Yes.'

'Um, in that case what you're proposing is probably the right thing to do. Emilie and I can also be at the station to meet you. Then I could accompany you to von Shirach's headquarters while Sophie and Emilie do some shopping. What time do you expect to arrive?'

It was nearly one o'clock in the afternoon before Franz and Sophie arrived in Vienna. Not surprisingly, both of them were in need of refreshment so their first priority was to make for the Café Central for lunch. It was crowded and smoky too, but fortunately they didn't have to wait long for a table. Franz looked tired and his breath was laboured, but he was in a determined frame of mind.

'We haven't come all this way for me to be put off,' he told Anton and Emilie. 'I'll camp outside von Shirach's office for the remainder of the day, if I have to. As needs must, I'll return tomorrow to do the same.'

It wasn't all that far to the Chancellery building, where von Shirach's headquarters were situated. However, having said farewell to Emilie and Sophie, because of Franz's laboured gait it took them all of twenty minutes to cover a distance Anton would normally have managed in ten.

By the time they arrived in the Ballhausplatz, where the Chancellery building was to be found, Franz was breathing heavily, making Anton worry he might be about to be taken ill.

'I'll be all right,' he insisted. 'Let's just pause a few moments so I can catch my breath.'

The Chancellery was a comparatively modest building dating from the eighteenth century, blackened by age and bedecked with swastika flags. At its entrance Anton could see just one uniformed guard, carrying a rifle over his arm. Franz pulled himself upright and managed to put a little spring into his step as he and Anton approached the guard, who gave them a cold glare and demanded, 'Who goes there?'

'I am Franz Lehár, the composer - I expect you've heard of me - and this is my brother General Anton Lehár. We have an appointment with Gauleiter Baldur von Shirach.'

Anton had no idea if the guard actually recognised Franz, but in any event without argument he simply stood to attention to allow them entry.

'The bigger the lie, the better said with confidence,' Franz said to Anton quietly as they approached a large reception desk, just as they had three years previously when they were about to meet von Shirach's predecessor Arthur Seyss-Inquart, behind which stood a fresh-faced young woman, who couldn't have been more than twenty-five. She was soberly dressed and diminutive in stature but perfectly pretty.

'How can I help you, gentlemen?' she asked them with a smile.

Again Franz announced who he and Anton were. 'I've been speaking on the telephone this week with the Reich Governor's personal secretary about my need to speak to him on a matter of some urgency. I know he must be very busy but I was hoping he might be able to give me a few minutes of his valuable time.'

'Please take a seat, Herr Lehár, and I will see if I can speak to her.'

They did as she'd asked and then watched her pick up the telephone. After not very long it became clear that she wasn't having any success.

'Continue to bear with me, gentlemen, there's another number I can try.'

This time she got through rapidly to someone and asked if they could locate von Shirach's secretary. 'If she could return my call as soon as possible, I'd be grateful.'

They then continued to wait for what must have been the best part of twenty minutes, watching people come and go. All the men, bar one or two who looked as if they would never see fifty again, were in uniforms of one sort or another. There were three or four women, too, all of them young and very plainly dressed with their hair worn short. It was noticeable to Anton that when they had met with Seyss-Inquart even his personal secretary had been male. The cost of war, he reasoned.

Finally, the receptionist received a very brief call and then smiled in their direction. 'Herr Lehár, that was the Reich Governor's secretary. She'll be down shortly.'

Another five minutes elapsed before a smartly dressed woman who looked to be in her mid-thirties came down a flight of stairs and walked towards them. She was wearing spectacles and had an air of efficiency about her.

'Herr Lehár, a pleasure to meet you,' she said to Franz, holding out her hand to shake his. 'And you must be General Lehár,' she added, looking Anton in the eye before shaking his hand as well. 'A pleasure to meet you, too. I tried telephoning you this morning, Herr Lehár, but now I realise why I couldn't get any answer. I'm afraid the Reich Governor is presently engaged.'

'Will he be free at all today? I'm quite prepared to wait.'

'He may be free at four o'clock. I can ask him then if he's able to see you. I can't disturb him in the meantime, I'm afraid.'

Anton glanced at his watch and saw that it was still barely three o'clock. Franz also looked at his, but the prospect of having to remain where he was for another hour at least didn't deter him. 'Yes, I'll wait, thank you.' He then turned to Anton. 'There's no need for you to do so.'

'No, no, I'm happy to keep you company. It's as well we told Emilie and Sophie we'd probably be all afternoon.'

'I can take you to a room with easy chairs,' the secretary said. 'And would you like tea or coffee?'

She was clearly used to situations like this, Anton thought,

239

and unflustered by the unexpected; no doubt, just one of the reasons she was good at her job. Fifteen minutes later, they were ensconced in a fairly large lounge on the first floor of the building, which exuded elegant good taste, with pictures on the walls of long-dead city dignitaries, as well as a view out of its windows of the Hofburg Palace. With its tall ceiling, it had felt cold when they first entered it, but the secretary had immediately lit a gas fire, which was now providing a welcome amount of heat. It had also not then taken her long to provide them with the refreshment they had asked for along with some biscuits for good measure.

'I will leave you for now, but as soon as I have any news for you, I will return.'

Anton feared that time might begin to drag on. Franz, though, was soon dozing in front of the fire, while he found some well-illustrated magazines to browse through, before turning his attention to looking out of the window so he could take in both the view and the sight of people walking by. Finally, he joined Franz by the fire and also began to doze, until the sound of a door opening startled him awake and he turned round to see the secretary walking towards them.

'Reich Governor von Shirach will see you now, if you'd both care to follow me. He regrets to say that he can only give you twenty minutes as he has another meeting to attend.'

Franz struggled a little to get out of his chair, but once he'd done so the secretary led them out of the room and then back the same way she'd brought them until they reached the same door they'd walked through to see Seyss-Inquart, which she promptly knocked on.

'Come in.'

'Herr Lehár, the composer, and his brother, General Lehár, to see you, sir,' she said upon opening the door, before standing to one side to let them enter.

As they walked in it was apparent that nothing had noticeably changed. The man who came towards them, holding out his hand in greeting, also struck Anton as being ridiculously young and fresh-faced for the most powerful individual in Austria. But then he was easily half Franz's age and until the previous year had been head of Hitler's youth movement.

'A great pleasure to meet you, Herr Lehár,' he said with a friendly smile to Franz, which seemed perfectly genuine, before shaking hands with him. 'And a pleasure to meet you as well, general,' he added. Anton was immediately struck by the firmness of his handshake as well as his relaxed manner, which lacked any hint of the arrogance he'd been expecting to find in someone who had risen so far while still so relatively young. Having invited them to both sit down he then did the same and leant back in his chair.

'So, Herr Lehár, my understanding is that you're here to intercede with me on behalf of an old friend, the Jew, Louis Treumann, who's been arrested. That's correct, I assume?'

'Yes, Reich Governor, it is. I've known Louis for the best part of forty years. He starred in the very first production of my operetta, *The Merry Widow*, which as you may know is a favourite of the Führer's. I'm sure, indeed, he will have seen him perform and will appreciate what a fine singer he is. I've come here today to plead with you to have him released from custody. I'd ask you, too, to take into account his age as he's certainly not much younger than I am, as well as his distinguished career. Might I also add that you'd struggle to find a nicer or more gentle human being? Indeed, I've never heard him utter a cross word against anyone.'

Anton thought it hopeful that von Shirach had let Franz speak without interruption, and once he'd finished there was a pregnant pause. From the expression on von Shirach's face, it seemed to Anton that he hadn't quite made up his mind how best to respond. He then cleared his throat.

'I hear what you say, Herr Lehár, and I can understand your concern. I've had my secretary make some enquiries as to Herr Treumann's present whereabouts. You're fortunate he's not yet been transported to the concentration camp at Mauthausen. Had he been, then it would have really been too late for me to consider your request. You must also understand that I do not normally have the power to interfere in such matters. Nonetheless, what I'm prepared to do on this occasion is speak on the telephone to the officer in charge of Jewish deportations and see if he might be willing to agree to Herr Treumann's release. Please bear with me...' And with that he picked up the telephone on his desk and asked to be put through to the officer concerned. 'Let's hope he's available...' he then told them.

After a short delay someone answered his call but it was quickly apparent that this wasn't the person he wanted. 'Please ask him to kindly return my call as soon as possible. Tell him I'd appreciate it if it could be within the next ten minutes.' Von Shirach then replaced the receiver and smiled at Franz.

'Are you still composing, Herr Lehár?'

Franz shook his head. 'Oh no, I'm afraid those days are behind me. I and my wife retired to Ischl two years ago although I still do a little guest conducting from time to time.'

'So you've travelled by train from there to try and see

me today?'

'Yes, I wanted to do all I could to help Louis. I thought it was the least I could do.'

'I expect you don't approve of the government's treatment of Jews?'

What had begun as a piece of small talk had now suddenly taken a dangerous course and Anton found himself willing the telephone to ring. Franz, however, was unflustered.

'Reich Governor, I'm not a politician. I simply see it as my duty to try and assist a valued colleague who as far as I'm concerned has done nothing wrong.'

Von Shirach then looked at Anton. 'And you, general? I assume you're merely here to support your brother?'

'Quite so, Reich Governor. Franz asked me if I'd be good enough to accompany him.'

'But you're no friend of the National Socialist Party, I think.'

Anton felt a twinge of fear. Clearly, he'd checked his file. 'Like my brother, I'm no politician, I assure you.'

'But you once sought to restore the monarchy in Hungary, did you not?'

'I did, but that was twenty years ago.'

To his relief, the telephone began to ring and von Shirach answered it. 'Ah, thank you for returning my call. You're holding a Louis Treumann, I believe... I've received an appeal from no less than the composer Franz Lehár that we should show leniency and I hope that you would agree. Yes, I know it's against party policy, but I thought on this occasion we could make an exception... It's your decision to make, of course, but I actually have Lehár here in my office. The Führer has a high regard for his music, especially *The Merry Widow*, and

Treumann was the star of the first production, all of thirty-five years ago and more... All right, I'd appreciate it if you would make the order as a personal favour to me. Otherwise, I can put Herr Lehár onto the line and you can explain to him yourself why his request cannot be granted... Good, I appreciate that, I really do. When will he be released? Tomorrow? Excellent. Thank you.'

'Reich Governor, on behalf of Louis, I am extremely grateful to you for your intervention,' Franz said, the moment von Shirach put down the telephone.

'On this occasion I am pleased to have been able to be of service to a composer of your distinction, Herr Lehár. I should warn you, though, that it will be next to impossible for me to obtain such a reprieve again. As you'll gather I had to beg a personal favour, so my capital is fully spent. You follow my meaning, I'm sure.'

'Of course, I just sincerely hope there'll be no next time.'

Von Shirach made no comment. Instead, he picked up the phone again to speak to his secretary who promptly returned to escort them from the building.

'I wish you good day, gentlemen,' von Shirach said, shaking both their hands. Anton thought he might be about to say '*Heil Hitler*' and offer them a Nazi salute but was thankful he spared them this.

'A decent fellow, I think,' Franz said once they'd stepped outside. 'I'm so pleased to have been able to secure Louis's release.'

'You did very well, I must say. I really thought he'd fob you off. He could easily have done so, had he been so inclined.'

'Perhaps he wanted to demonstrate that the Nazis have some

humanity in them.'

'Or at least wished to give the impression they have when a famous composer, who's favoured by the Führer himself, makes the approach. You made all the difference, I'm sure.'

'Whatever, the important thing is that Louis is to be freed.'

'So, will you and Sophie return to Ischl this evening?'

'No, I'm much too tired. We'll book into the König von Ungarn hotel for the night. And anyway I'd rather not leave the city until I can be certain they've let Louis go.'

They made a tentative arrangement to meet the following afternoon for coffee and cake at the Café Central.

'I intend to visit Louis's house at around midday,' Franz told Anton. 'He should be home by then, in which case meeting up should not be a problem. If for any reason I'm delayed, I will telephone you.'

In the event, he didn't receive any such call so assumed everything had gone to plan. Happily, Franz's smiling face was enough to confirm that this had been the case, when they greeted each other upon their arrival at the café.

'Louis couldn't have been more grateful. He was convinced that he was on his way to a concentration camp so suddenly being released came as a huge relief, as you can imagine. His dear wife Stefanie wept tears of joy. It was an emotional occasion, I can tell you. I just wish I could have helped others in Louis situation, especially poor Fritz.'

'He was a marked man from the moment the Nazis came to power.'

'But what about Victor?'

'It was his decision to hide. Of course, I can understand why he did it, but you mustn't blame yourself for his fate.'

'Had I had any idea that Victor didn't even have enough to eat, I would have helped him.'

'Well, you didn't know. Just take pride in the fact that you've been able to help Louis.'

'I still can't help thinking that I was very lucky yesterday.'

'Maybe you were, but isn't it true that fortune favours the bold? I think you deserved your luck.'

41

By the third summer of the war, life in Vienna for non-Jews was still quite good. All the same, there had been a failure to achieve a quick victory over Russia and Germany was now at war with the richest nation on the planet, namely the United States of America.

'But haven't they got their work cut out fighting the Japanese?' Emilie asked Anton when he expressed the view that Germany might ultimately be defeated.

'To an extent, but I expect it has the resources to fight a long war on two fronts, whereas I doubt if the same can be said of Germany.'

Meanwhile, following his success in having Louis released, Franz continued to work occasionally as a conductor. At least twice in the early months of the New Year he came to Vienna for that purpose, bringing Sophie with him. The high point came when radio Vienna made a live broadcast of his operetta *Paganini* with Franz conducting the orchestra.

'I know I'm an old man,' he told Anton, 'but the conducting helps to keep my brain active and I enjoy it.'

Then in late July everything suddenly went downhill again. Since the previous autumn Jews had been forced by law to self-identify when going outside their homes by wearing a Star of David on their clothing.

'It's the pettiest, meanest thing they've done yet,' Anton said vehemently to Emilie when they first saw it happening.

Already, Vienna's once large and prosperous Jewish population had been decimated and those who remained were struggling to survive on the meanest of rations. Now came the *coup de grace*. It was a warm, sunny morning with barely a cloud in the sky as Anton and Emilie went for one of their regular morning strolls. These would invariably end in their enjoying coffee and cake in one of their favourite cafés; not that this was quite the experience it had been before the war as there was now far less choice.

'What's that group of people coming towards us?' Emilie asked. 'They're under guard, aren't they?'

She pointed as she spoke and Anton's eyes were drawn to a long line of men, women and children, being herded along by soldiers armed with rifles apart from their officer. He was holding a pistol in his hand, shouting 'Faster, you vermin!'

'Oh God,' Anton said, recognising the Star of David. 'They're all Jews!'

'What's happening to them all?'

'I dread to think, I really do.'

'How awful for them to be treated like this.'

He nodded. 'Best to say nothing more while we pass them.'

He noticed that the officer and his men were wearing Waffen-SS uniforms and his jaw dropped when he began to realise just how many people were being herded along so brutally. The line just seemed to go on and on.

'Have they rounded up every last Jew in Vienna?' Emilie asked.

'I fear so, I really do.'

'So that could include Louis and his wife, then?'

Again Anton merely nodded. Inwardly, though, he groaned at this suggestion, sensing it was almost inevitably true. As they continued to pass the long line of sad figures going in the opposite direction, he felt an almost overwhelming degree of sadness. Even more than this, that one of the supposedly most civilised Christian nations on the planet should behave so inhumanely towards people whose only crime was to have Jewish blood, filled him with a sense of disgust.

There was a part of him that wanted to scream out, 'This is wrong!' But instead he walked on, on the opposite side of the road, feeling the eyes of these sad, lost souls upon him. He had no doubt some were thinking, *You lucky sods, still free to stroll along in your expensive clothes, while we're being marched off at gunpoint to some hell-hole of a place.*

By the time they reached the Café Schwarzenberg he felt almost physically sick at the thought of what they'd just witnessed. 'I'm in need of a strong, black coffee to steady my nerves,' he said to Emilie, who gave him a concerned look. Then he headed very deliberately for the quietest corner of the café while resolving to keep his emotions in check and his voice down.

'Are you all right?' Emilie asked him once they'd sat down.

'Not really. What we've just seen was too shameful for any words to do my sense of horror and disgust any justice. If there is any God, which these days I rather doubt, he's a very vengeful one indeed.'

Emilie said nothing, but nodding just a little, she stretched out a hand to place it on Anton's, and gave him a look of seemingly infinite understanding.

'Oh shit!' he suddenly exclaimed. 'I've just thought of Helene and her daughters. They're bound to have been taken, too. This just gets worse and worse. When we get home, I'm going to telephone Franz and tell him what's happening. If Louis and his wife have been taken away it might not be too late for him to try and intervene on their behalf as he did last time.'

Even as he said this, however, Anton wondered if there would be any point. Von Shirach, as he recalled, had said something about using up all his capital to get Louis released the last time and that was probably still true. He also couldn't say that the black coffee had done much for him; it was too tasteless and probably adulterated in some way. However, the sugary cake at least gave him an energy boost and as they stepped outside the sun was still shining.

They walked home hand in hand. As ever Anton was grateful for Emilie's support. He was dreading having to pick up the telephone to Franz and tell him that all his brave work of the previous autumn had probably been in vain. Still, as a young man he'd found the courage from somewhere to lead his men against machine-gun fire so he told himself he could surely find the courage to pick up a telephone in order to be the bearer of bad news. When he did so it was Sophie who answered. He could tell instantly that her voice was trembling and that something was badly wrong.

'Thank God you've telephoned, Anton. Something dreadful's happened. I'm sure that horrid official is trying to have me taken away again. There was a terrible banging on the door at some ungodly hour this morning. Franz went to it in his dress-ing-gown and this man in uniform said he was under orders to take all Jews away and that there were to be no exceptions...

Ah, Franz is just here now. He'll tell you the rest of it himself. I'll pass the phone to him...'

'Hello, Anton, hope you're well. I think I've got the situation under control but, of course, the more times this happens the more it frightens Sophie half-to-death.'

'Was it the same man as before who turned up on your doorstep?'

'No, someone different, claiming to have no knowledge at all of Sophie's special status. I managed to shove the certificate under his nose before he could barge his way into the house. Fortunately, I've made a point of keeping it safe in a small bureau in the hall just in case this sort of thing happened again. He huffed at it a bit but I pointed out the Führer's own signature and that shut him up. Of course, he didn't apologise, just said he had his orders and would report back to his headquarters. I'm hoping he won't trouble us again. Anyway, what can I do for you?'

'It's bad news, I'm afraid. Emilie and I went out for a walk this morning and saw several hundred Jews being marched away under armed guard. There were men and women of all ages, and children, too. It's obvious the Nazis are purging the city of what's left of its Jewish population. I'm worried that Louis could be in danger again and then there's his wife as well, of course. What's more, Helene and her daughters must also be in serious danger, too.'

'Oh no, that's dreadful. I suppose I'd better come to Vienna again although I certainly can't do it today.'

'I wouldn't suggest that for a moment. In fact, why not see if you can get hold of von Shirach's secretary and ask if she'll speak to him in order to find out if there's anything he can possibly do. You'll recall what he said last autumn about using

251

up his capital, and that because of that he wouldn't be able to help again. I've got a feeling, too, that this mass rounding up of Jews could be part of something bigger...'

'You mean Hitler himself has ordered it?'

'Yes, or at least given his approval. In any event, if I'm right, it could override any discretion someone like von Shirach might otherwise have.'

'So you're saying my coming to Vienna again could be pointless?'

'Yes, I fear so. Just see if you can speak to von Shirach's secretary. Who knows? He might even be prepared to speak to you himself over the phone.'

'All right, I'll get onto it this afternoon and let you know how I get on.'

'Hello, Anton, it's me.' A day had gone by since they'd spoken and Anton could immediately sense from the tone of Franz's voice that he didn't have any good news for him. 'Von Shirach actually had the decency to return my call about half-an-hour ago. I'm afraid it's as you thought. This is a mass deportation ordered from on high, not just here but across the Reich. He was apologetic but there's nothing more he can do. Poor, poor Louis, he really didn't deserve this, and nor does his wife. It also breaks my heart to think of Helene and her daughters being taken away, too.'

To say to Franz that he'd already done his best to help his friends, seemed too trite to Anton. Instead, he just railed against the Nazis. 'Hitler and his cronies are just behaving monstrously. When it comes to the Jews, they haven't got an atom of humanity in them.'

'I just know that what's happened is terrible. You know, Louis was the last of all my Jewish friends and colleagues that hadn't already fled the country, been sent to a concentration camp, or gone into hiding.'

'Yes, you've mentioned that before.'

'Have I? Well, I'm sorry, but it's hard to believe it could have come to this. All your pessimism has been proved correct in the end.'

'But as I've said before when we've had this sort of conversation, don't imagine for an instant, Franz, that I derive any satisfaction from that, because I really don't.'

He snorted ruefully. 'No, but things really have turned out all wrong, I'm afraid.'

42

I t was barely nine o'clock the following morning when the phone rang again. As an early riser, Anton had been up some while but he and Emilie were still eating breakfast.

'Who can that be?' he asked rhetorically as he stood up to answer it.

'Yes, hello.'

'Sorry to bother you again so early, Anton, but then, knowing you, I expect you were out of bed two hours ago.'

'More or less. Anyway, Franz, what can I do for you?'

'I've had an awful night. I just couldn't sleep, thinking of poor Louis. But look, I've made up my mind, I need to go to Berlin and beg for a personal audience with Hitler... Hello, are you still there?'

Anton drew in his breath. 'That's a tall ask, Franz.'

'But I'm the Führer's favourite living composer. Why shouldn't he grant me one?'

'To reminisce about Vienna before the last war, or chat about the wonders of your music, maybe, but to hear you out on what's happened to Louis... Well, I'm not so sure.'

'Even so, it's got to be worth a try. I owe it not just to Louis but also to Fritz, as well as their families.'

'You tried before, of course, and it got you nowhere.'

'Everything's got even worse since then and anyway it was a feeble attempt. This time I'll go down on my knees, if I have to.'

'If you're allowed to get that far. Anyway, with your knees, Franz, you'd struggle to stand up again.'

'Hum, I didn't expect such levity from you, Anton, though you may well be right.'

'And how are you to get anywhere near Hitler in the middle of a war, which, I fear, is turning nastier by the day? You can't just turn up at the Chancellery and expect to be seen at the drop of a hat. And for all we know, he might be at that mountain retreat of his in Bavaria, or with his generals somewhere in Russia.'

'I'm quite prepared to go to Bavaria, if I have to.'

'But hardly Russia.'

'No, of course not, but he's bound to return to Berlin, sooner or later. I'll wait if I have to. I expect the Eden hotel is still perfectly comfortable. I'd also like you to come with me, of course.'

'But I don't see how. It was all very well that I was allowed to accompany you to that award ceremony. This is totally different. You know, this simply isn't going to happen at all without help from someone with a lot of influence.'

'Then what about von Shirach? He seems a decent enough young man to me.'

'Yes, I agree, and probably close enough to Hitler, too. In fact I think he's your only option.'

'I'll get in touch with him again then and ask for his help. If he says no at least I'll have tried. He'll have the authority to allow you to come with me, I'm sure.'

'No doubt.'

'Right, I'll get onto it then. Hopefully, he'll be happy to speak to me again in the next few days. I'll let you know how I get on, of course.'

'Good luck, is all I can say.'

'Thank you, dear brother, I realise I'll need it.'

It was to be another four days before he heard anything further from Franz, in which space of time he'd been able to make one of his regular returns to the farm in Theresienfeld that he was now permitted to undertake.

Inevitably, he was beginning to wonder if it was a case of no news is good news, or whether Franz had been totally rebuffed and felt too upset to tell him.

Finally, in the late afternoon of the fourth day, the telephone rang again.

'It's on!' Franz declared excitedly.

'Really?'

'Yes, really. It took me two days to speak to von Shirach but when I did he was sympathetic and said he'd see what he could do. Of course, he didn't make any promises, but this afternoon I had another call from him. I don't know how on earth he wangled it, but I can expect an invitation within the next couple of days to visit Hitler, not in Berlin but at his retreat at Berchtesgaden in Bavaria. What's more, you'll be allowed to accompany me and we'll be taken there and back in a chauffeur-driven car from Hitler's own fleet. You'll have to get yourself here first, of course.'

'Well done. I must say, I'm rather surprised.'

'That's your typical scepticism at work. But no, I simply made the request. It's von Shirach you have most to thank for this opportunity.'

'But tell me, did he actually say to Hitler why you wanted to see him so much?'

'He told me that he did.'

'Well, that's hopeful, I must say. I mean it would have been so easy for Hitler to refuse to see you, rather than invite us both to his private retreat. I imagined it was strictly reserved for only his inner circle.'

'I think it may have been because I mentioned to von Shirach that my health wasn't what it was and that the journey to Berlin would tax me. Berchtesgaden also isn't all that far from Ischl, less than two hours' drive in fact, and Hitler's apparently due to stay there soon for ten days in order to enjoy the summer weather.'

'So, we can expect to see Hitler within a couple of weeks?'

'Yes, I believe so. Von Shirach didn't suggest there was any doubt about it.'

It was mid-morning on a beautiful high summer day, when they set off from Ischl in the magnificent black Mercedes that had arrived to collect them. As a major-general, Anton had grown used to being driven around for a while, but that was now a long time ago. The smartly uniformed chauffeur was also suitably polite although there was to be no 'small talk' with him during the course of a journey that took a little less than two hours. Instead, they had the hills and then the increasingly Alpine terrain to enjoy, bathed for the most part in bright sunshine.

Anton reflected that it was all too easy on such a journey to think that all was well with the world, and terrible conflict, with all its accompanying misery, was completely remote from his still relatively comfortable existence. The realisation that men were probably being killed or maimed in their thousands in various locations across the globe even as he enjoyed the sunshine was never, though, too far from his mind. Likewise, he was apprehensive about what lay ahead of them and although Franz said nothing of any consequence during most of their journey, he expected he felt much the same.

'We shouldn't be more than another fifteen minutes,' the chauffeur told them once they'd passed through the old border post between Austria and Germany.

Franz spluttered a little as the man's voice woke him. It had been apparent to Anton for at least half an hour that Franz had fallen asleep, while he preferred to keep awake by looking out of the window and pondering what lay in store for them both.

'So, we're agreed we'll offer Hitler the Nazi salute,' Franz whispered to Anton.

'Yes, all right, though I won't find it easy.'

'Oh well, when in Rome...'

'More like the lion's den, I fear.'

As the road they were travelling on became ever steeper as it climbed into the mountains, and the village of Berchtesgaden was reached, Anton also couldn't help thinking not of lions but of Count Dracula's castle. Of course, once it came into view above the village round a rather alarming hairpin bend, Hitler's Eagle's Nest looked nothing like a Medieval Gothic fortress. Rather, it was no more than a substantial villa, albeit in a most spectacular setting, built in the style of so many other Bavarian houses. All the same, the image of Hitler as a blood-sucking vampire was still a powerful one in Anton's mind and almost made him shudder.

As they drew up outside the residence, a uniformed SS officer, who must have seen them coming, emerged from the house to greet them. As the chauffeur helped Franz alight from the car, for even a journey of barely two hours had made him very stiff, the officer greeted them both with a Nazi salute. I suppose it was second nature to him, however inappropriate, taking Anton back again to his wartime years when he was forever exchanging salutes with fellow soldiers.

'Herr Lehár, general, welcome to the Eagle's Nest. If you would care to follow me.'

The officer reminded Anton of the one who had greeted them when Franz had attended the award ceremony at the Chancellery in Berlin; tall, good-looking, very Aryan and blond-haired in appearance, to the point of being stereotypical. Also respectful, very well spoken and, he imagined, proud to serve his Führer with a measure of loyalty that bordered on the fanatical.

They were led into an impressively large reception area with the most glorious of views of the mountains all around them. It was furnished with lots of easy chairs as well as a large round table. In the centre of this had been placed a vase full of tulips and Anton noted that it been laid-up with cutlery as well as glasses for four people. What most drew his attention, though, was a large red-marble fireplace that really dominated the room.

'Do sit down, the Führer will be with you shortly,' the officer told them. 'Coffee and tea will also be provided and as you can see there is water on the sideboard, if you would like some.'

He then withdrew. Franz, meanwhile, had been happy to take his ease but Anton preferred to remain standing, fixing his eyes on the mountains. He felt tense, and whilst this was to be a private audience, it was apparent that there would be more than just the three of them in the room. Since he had last met Hitler, Anton was particularly conscious that he'd conquered

259

most of Europe and that his armies had advanced deep into both North Africa and Russia. He was all powerful with control over life and death at the snap of his fingers... Anton's mouth felt very dry.

'Would you like some water, Franz?'

'Yes, that would be nice. Thank you.'

Anton poured him a glass and handed it to him before pouring one for himself and drinking it greedily. 'God, I'm feeling tense,' he confessed. 'This isn't going to be easy.'

'I know, but this is my appeal to make, not yours, and Hitler already knows why we're here. You'll help me down onto my knees if necessary, I hope?'

Anton laughed nervously. 'If you really want me to...'

Seconds later, they heard a sound behind them. They turned and saw the officer who had greeted them walk back into the room, accompanied by a waiter carrying a large tray with pots and cups on it.

'The Führer is just on his way. If you wouldn't mind standing for him, Herr Lehár. I can assist you, if necessary.'

'No, no, I can manage, thank you.'

'It is customary to salute the Führer but you are personal guests so he has said we can dispense with any such formality.'

Anton breathed a sigh of relief at that piece of news before tensing again as Hitler walked quietly into the room accompanied by none other than Baldur von Shirach, who smiled faintly at him with his eyes. Like Hitler, he was wearing a suit rather than a uniform, emphasising the informality of the occasion.

'Good morning, maestro, it's a great pleasure to meet you again,' Hitler said before shaking hands with Franz and giving him a warm smile. 'You know, I still love your music so much,

I play it often on my gramophone. I find it relaxes me after the toils of war.'

'Thank you, *Mein Führer*. I am greatly honoured,' Franz replied with due deference.

Then Hitler fixed his piercingly blue eyes on Anton and they also shook hands. 'Good morning, general, also a pleasure to meet you again. You know I do admire the support you've always given your brother.'

Anton nodded his head slightly. 'Thank you, *Mein Führer*.'

As on the last occasion they'd met, his grasp of Anton's hand was firm. His voice, too, was gentle, his manner relaxed as well as perfectly friendly, denoting the fact that they had been acquainted with one another for more than thirty-five years. Of course, Anton could see the lines of age beginning to creep up on Hitler, but he was now fifty-three so that was to be expected. To compare him to Count Dracula suddenly seemed inappropriate. Dr Jekyll and Mr Hyde was far closer to the mark, he decided.

Von Shirach now stepped forward to shake hands with them as well while Hitler walked over to the corner of the room where a gramophone player was standing. He proceeded to select a record from its cabinet, place it on the machine and switch this on. Moments later, they were being regaled with the sweet tones of the music from none other than *The Merry Widow*, although Hitler was quick to adjust the sound so this was not so loud as to impede conversation.

Once more he then smiled at Franz. 'Of course, I know perfectly well why you are here, maestro. Baldur here has explained. We will talk about that later, I promise you. For now, though, let us enjoy your music. The waiter here will also

261

serve us tea or coffee, as you prefer, and let me take you onto the terrace. The view is really very impressive, as you've no doubt already realised. Soon luncheon will be provided: soup followed by a fish pie. It's Friday, after all.'

'I'm really most grateful for your kind hospitality, *Mein Führer*,' Franz said.

'Not at all, maestro. I'm delighted to be able to entertain my favourite composer, I do assure you. Perhaps I should add the prefix "living" but for all that I allow the world to believe I adore Wagner's music above anyone's else's, we both know that isn't really true, don't we?' And with that Hitler chuckled.

For the best part of the next hour, rather than going down on his knees, begging Hitler to show mercy to Louis and Fritz and their families, Franz was given no choice but to reminisce about Vienna before the Great War and talk about his music. Hitler simply wouldn't allow it to be otherwise, leading the conversation at all times, whilst displaying as he did so a considerable knowledge of several of Franz's operettas.

It was increasingly obvious to Anton that for Hitler this particular meeting with Franz as an opportunity to indulge in pure escapism, allowing him for a while at least to forget about the war as well as the burdens of leadership. All the while, he was little more than an observer, indulging in no more than polite small-talk with von Shirach and otherwise being totally ignored by Hitler. For all that the excellent hock served with lunch relaxed him a little, he also remained not just tense but also increasingly frustrated as Hitler talked on and on to Franz about his music. Finally, when they had finished their meal and more coffee had been served, Hitler came to the point.

'I must say, maestro, our meeting today has been a delight

to me but do not imagine that I have forgotten why you came. I understand your loyalty to your friends and colleagues, as well as your concern for their families, and do not hold this against you. Do not forget, though, that I have already been especially generous to you when I allowed your wife Honorary Aryan status.'

'I would never do so, *Mein Führer*. I will always be grateful to you for having taken that action.'

'And so you should.'

'It's just that I owe so much of my success to men like Fritz Löhner-Beda and Louis Treumann...'

'Let me assure you, maestro, that you owe it to your own great talent. I must also make it clear that ridding this great nation of ours of its Jewish cancer has been central to my destiny ever since the Great War. I have never forgotten your kindnesses to me as a struggling artist in Vienna, but I must tell you by the time I left there in 1913 I had begun to appreciate what exploitation the Jews are capable of; only lending money, even to those who could least afford to repay them, at exorbitant rates of interest. I did not, I assure you, start out by disliking the Jews! No, I reached that conclusion simply by observing their rapacious behaviour. When the war came they tried to undermine the Reich by shamelessly profiteering at its expense. Such a betrayal was utterly unforgivable, I say again, utterly unforgivable!'

He paused, just for a moment, clenching his right fist, the expression on his face one of warped rapture as his piercing blue eyes looked upwards. It was an image that Anton thought would remain with him for the rest of his days. *The anti-Christ has come to earth*, he thought.

'What's more,' Hitler added, 'it did not end there as they continued to conspire against the interests of our nation for their own selfish financial gain. I don't deny their talent, but nor do I excuse either the way they exploit others less fortunate than themselves, or their greed. As a race, they declared war on our nation, and for that crime they *all* deserve their just punishment...'

He was now in full speech-making mode, once more the man Anton and Franz had come to know in countless newsreels. Indeed, in a matter of seconds, before their very eyes, he'd transformed himself into the ranting, evil proponent of hate whom Anton in particular had come to fear. That Hitler was possessed of an apparently sincere belief in ideas which Anton thought were either based on a gross exaggeration of the facts, or frankly preposterous, made Anton want to shout him down. Instead, he knew he had no choice but to just remain impassive.

'Even as we speak,' Hitler went on, 'I also carry in my heart the burden of all those fine young men fighting and dying for their Fatherland and the righteous cause which they serve... As they are making such a sacrifice, I simply will not intervene when the Jews have behaved so wickedly.'

'But Führer,' Anton boldly interjected, unable to contain himself any longer, 'Franz is only asking that you make an exception for a very few individuals who are themselves blameless.'

Hitler turned his gaze on him. 'I appreciate that, general, but at a time of great sacrifice for the greater good I have decided that there can be no exceptions... The cancer must be totally expunged. You may see that as a drastic step but I tell you that nothing less will protect our nation from the insidious threat that the Jews pose to its wellbeing.'

'But I beg you, *Mein Führer*,' Franz said, finding his voice. 'Please... It is surely no more than a small favour that I ask of you. I'm sure Louis Treumann's fine voice will have given you great pleasure when you were young. Likewise, it is clear to me that you admire *The Land of Smiles* and so much of the credit for that is owed to Fritz. He's such a truly talented librettist.'

Hitler shook his head. 'No, enough! It's true that I very much enjoy *The Land of Smiles* but that is because of the quality of your music. Whatever the talents of these men, I have not the least doubt that we have many fine Aryan singers and librettists who are their superiors. Let me also stress that as Führer, I must, above all other considerations, have regard for what is in our great nation's best interests. I am more than satisfied that there must be a total excision of the Jewish cancer once and for all, so I say again there can be no more exceptions when so many of our finest young men are sacrificing their lives for the sake of the Fatherland. Now, I must once more give my full attention to our struggle for total victory...'

'But these are old men, women, children...' Anton protested.

'Enough, general, enough! I will not, I cannot indulge your sentimentality, so do not try my patience any further. I have spoken!'

Anton lowered his eyes before glancing in Franz's direction. He thought for a moment that he really was about to try and go down on his knees, but then decided he had merely hung his head and was close to tears.

Hitler was now on his feet and, after coming round the table to where Franz was still sitting, placed a hand on his shoulder. A startled Franz tried to immediately stand up but Hitler restrained him. 'There is no need to get up. I hope we shall meet again when our great victory has been achieved and the Reich is once more at peace.'

And with that he strode out of the room, leaving Anton with a sense that their paths were very unlikely to cross again. Von Shirach, meanwhile, had an apologetic expression on his face. 'The officer will show you to your car shortly.' He then followed Hitler out of the room.

It was now Anton's turn to place a hand on Franz's shoulder. 'We tried, dearest brother, at least we tried.'

'But he was too clever for us, Franz. We were totally outflanked.'

'He's not clever!' Anton's tone was scathing. 'He's just a fanatic. You can't reason with a man like him, I'm afraid.'

'I really should have gone down on my knees.'

Anton shook his head. 'I can't believe it would have made any difference, though.'

'I just think it's so sad that he has so little empathy.'

'It's worse than that. He's lost his very soul.'

43

31st August 1942

Rebekkah Weiss, who had rejected Hitler all those years before, had gone on to fall in love with a fellow Jew, whom she married a few months before the outbreak of the Great War. Her husband had then gone away to fight, never to return, leaving her a widow without children, and she had never remarried.

She had led a simple, innocent, somewhat lonely life, compensated for by being a kindly aunt to several nieces and nephews. Now for no other reason than her Jewish blood, she had been taken from her home in a suburb of Vienna and made to line up in the street with twenty fellow Jewish neighbours. Fiercely independent and well read, she had feared this day for a long time and was feeling angry.

'What right have you to do this to us?' she berated an armed soldier standing in front of her. 'I've done nothing to justify this and nor I'm sure have my neighbours. Let us go back to our homes.'

'Shut up. You're all coming with us.'

'But where?'

'That's none of your business. I said shut up, Jew.'

An elderly Jewish man, a near neighbour of Rebekkah, then shouted out, 'We'll be taken to some camp somewhere in the east and never heard of again. It's what already happened to other Jewish people.'

Another German soldier immediately pointed his rifle at him. 'Be silent or you die!'

'I'm not going to let you, or anyone else, ship me to some death camp in the east until I die of starvation or get shot. I'm going home,' Rebekkah said.

'Stay where you are or you'll die.'

'If I'm going to die I would rather die here, in the city I love where I was brought up, and where I was once courted by Adolf Hitler himself.'

'What, are you mad?'

'I tell you I once walked out with him when he was living here in Vienna before the Great War.'

One of the soldiers went up to Rebekkah and slapped her across the face. She swayed, but didn't fall to the ground. 'You lying Jew! Our Führer would not even touch a filthy Jewish bitch like you!'

'Well, I tell you he did.'

'If you don't shut up, Jew, I will shoot you, do you understand that?'

'Very well, I'll shut up, but I'm not going to some death camp.'

Rebekkah knew she was dicing with death but tried to look unafraid. Still, there was fear in her eyes as she met the gaze of three soldiers who were now levelling their guns at her.

'I'll give you one more chance, Jew,' said the soldier who had slapped her. 'Stay where you are and you will be allowed to live. If you try leave these ranks, you die.'

'Very well.'

At first Rebekkah didn't move but suddenly, with surprising speed and agility, she started running away from the soldiers. They all fired at her, but missed, as she was weaving, and one of them deliberately aimed high.

However, she had run into the road, and a black van coming round a bend at speed hit her, killing her outright. Her mangled body lay still.

'Good riddance to the Jewish bitch!' exclaimed the soldier who had slapped her.

44

4th September 1942

I n early September, Anton and Emilie received a very nasty
shock. Vienna was about two and a half thousand kilometres
from the then eastern front with Russia. According to Nazi
propaganda the Luftwaffe also enjoyed total air superiority
over that of the Soviet Air Force. Yet, in the early hours, Anton
was shaken awake by Emilie and became aware of the wailing
sound of an air raid siren.

'Get up, Anton, we haven't long to get to the shelter!'

'All right, all right,' he responded as he sleepily climbed out
of bed before beginning to dress as quickly as he could.

'This wasn't meant to be happening, you know,' Emilie
complained. 'We've been told that Vienna is out of range of
any British or American bombers.'

Anton laughed scornfully. 'Well, we know how little trust
we can have in anything Hitler's government tells us. It could
just as easily be a raid by Russian bombers.'

Emilie gave him an anxious stare. 'I just can't bear the
thought of our home being destroyed.'

'Unless there are literally hundreds of bombers, I don't believe
that's very likely. This is a big city, after all, and I imagine they'd
want to attack industrial targets as a first priority.'

They then hurried to get out of their apartment as fast as

they could before descending the stairs and heading in the direction of the shelter, the cold night air coming as quite a shock. As they hurried along amongst a growing number of other people heading in the same direction, Emilie took up their conversation again.

'The bombers could come again, I mean night after night, couldn't they?'

'I doubt that's very likely, but I tell you, this is just another sign that the war is beginning to turn against Germany. Hitler's bitten off more than he can chew by invading Russia and now we've America to contend with as well.'

'But haven't they still got their hands full fighting the Japanese?'

'I think they're proving to be more of a threat to the interests of the British Empire. Anyway, America's a rich country. As I've previously suggested, it's much more able to fight the war on two fronts than Germany. This could just be the beginning of the end, I'm afraid.'

Emilie responded by seizing hold of his left hand and squeezing it. 'I'm frightened...'

'Try not to be, my love. Once we're in the shelter we should be perfectly safe.'

In the event, they didn't even have to remain in the confines of the shelter for what remained of the night, as within the hour the siren sounded that the air raid had ended. Further, to their relief, when they walked out into the street once more, they could see no sign of any bomb damage. All the same, it had been a serious wake-up was call, and everyone they passed seemed to have an anxious expression on their face.

Even for those who didn't have children serving in the armed forces, the war was now no longer merely something to read about, or hear about on the wireless, or watch on newsreels. It was very real and Anton knew it had the capacity to kill indiscriminately. While it was to be another two years before the city experienced any more raids, the mood in the city had changed for the worse, and everyone watched the skies more, fearing the possibility of more bombs raining down.

45

Mid-September 1942

Treated like worthless cattle, rather than human beings, Helene and her daughters were nearing the end of a journey of about seven hundred and fifty miles from Vienna to a road near Minsk in German-occupied Russia.

They were travelling inside a lorry with an open tender compartment crowded with about another twenty Jewish prisoners of both sexes and all ages. The lorry then halted close to a sinister-looking grey van, about twenty feet long, with no windows in the back, a driver compartment at the front, and a ramp at the rear.

Three armed guards emerged from the driver compartment and, once the lorry's driver had opened the back of the tender, shouted at the prisoners to climb down.

'Hurry up!'

Once they had done so they were chivvied along with rifle butts in the direction of the grey van before being ordered to enter it at the point of the guards' guns.

Helene, Liselotte and Evamaria ascended the ramp into the back of van in some trepidation, wondering what on earth this was about, only for the back door of the van to be slammed shut behind them once they and all the other prisoners were inside.

The interior of the van was dimly lit by an overhead electric bulb but otherwise the van was empty, save for a wide pipe at the front protruding a foot or so into the back of the van. Suddenly, the van's petrol engine started up, evacuating the carbon monoxide exhaust into the back of the van which started to choke all the prisoners.

Helene desperately banged on the wall of the truck but, unable to breathe properly, was barely able to embrace Liselotte and Evamaria before they all collapsed, choking to death as the fumes overwhelmed them.

Helene's last thought was of Fritz, as she offered a prayer that they might one day be reunited.

46

At the end of October came the admission that Rommel's Afrika Korps had suffered what was euphemistically called a setback at a place called El Alamein in North Africa. Furthermore, there was also still no decisive victory on the eastern front. It was now evident to Anton that for all Hitler's early successes, he'd embroiled Germany in a struggle which had become just as bitter and prolonged as the Great War.

Fortunately for Franz and Sophie there had as yet been no repetition of the attempt to take her away. Nevertheless, after they visited Anton and Emilie in Vienna in early November, it became clear that Sophie was still very fearful of that possibility.

'What Sophie told me today while we were shopping together really shocked me,' Emilie said as she and Anton were getting ready for bed.

'Oh what was that?'

'She's so frightened that the Nazis will finally succeed in arresting her that she's got a vial of poison, arsenic I think she said it was, that she keeps in her handbag. She was adamant that she'd rather commit suicide than be taken away to one of these terrible camps.'

'Thinking of those poor sods we saw being marched away back in the summer, I must say I can sympathise with her fear. All the same, I think the honorary status Franz obtained for her should continue to protect her.'

'There's another thing she told me, too.'

'Oh yes?'

'She's worried about Franz becoming more frail so has undertaken a nursing course in case she has to care for him more.'

'I see. Well, he is rather slow on his feet, but he's been like that for some years now.'

'And he falls asleep a lot, apparently, and has become rather forgetful.'

'Well, he is seventy-two now and none of us are getting any younger. Still, I can see that what she's done is a sensible precaution.'

It was on the same visit that Franz announced that he'd received an invitation to go to Budapest to conduct the Budapest Orchestra in a revised version of his operetta *Gypsy Love*.

'It's to be performed at the Royal Opera House and is to be entitled *Garaboncias (The wandering scholar)*. It'll run for a couple of weeks at least, maybe longer, if it's successful enough.'

'And you'll conduct every night?' Anton asked.

'So long as my health permits me to, yes.'

'I'm concerned that it could be too much for him,' Sophie said anxiously.

'Oh, I'll be all right. In fact I'm rather looking forward to seeing Budapest again after all these years. There's more, too. This revised version is to be based on the novel by Erno Vincze set during the 1848 war for Hungarian independence. It'll be a ballet rather than an operetta. I've even been asked if I might like to compose a new piece of music for it. I must say it'll be quite a challenge, but I'm flattered to have been asked, so I'm certainly going to give it a try.'

'Will it need to be very long?' Emilie asked.

'Oh no, it's just for one ballet sequence so I should be able to manage it. Of course, I can't just turn up for the first night. There'll need to be rehearsals. I've been asked if I could have the piece ready for these before the end of January.'

'And when exactly in February is the first performance?' Anton asked.

'Um, the twentieth, as I recall.'

'So, you'll be in Budapest for a month then?'

'Longer in fact. You see, I've been asked to be involved in rehearsals from when they begin during the second week in January. Sophie will accompany me, won't you, my love? And we'll stay at one of the city's best hotels where I'm sure we'll be very comfortable.'

'Is Budapest at any risk of being bombed, do you think, Anton?' Sophie asked Anton.

'Well, we've been promised that last year's raid was a completely isolated incident that won't be allowed to happen again. Mind you, I don't know how much we can trust anything that Hermann Göring says. If his invincible Luftwaffe was that good, we'd have knocked England out of the war by now.'

'So you don't think we should go?'

'I didn't say that. I think the risk is probably pretty small, just so long as there aren't any more raids between now and the end of the year.'

'My heart's set on going, I must say,' Franz emphasised. 'I may never get a chance to see Budapest again, and I'm really looking forward to doing some creative work again.'

'Oh, I'm sure it'll be fine, Franz. I must say I rather envy you the opportunity.'

'Well, apart from anything else, it'll help to distract me from brooding on recent events.' He looked Anton in the eye as he said that and they both knew that he was alluding to the failure of their recent meeting with Hitler. 'I'd also very much like you and Emilie to be able to attend the first night.'

'Except I don't see how that could be possible. I'm still *persona non grata* in Hungary and I'd also need special permission from the German authorities here in Vienna. There's the cost as well to take into consideration. I doubt if we could afford it.'

'Don't worry about that. I'd happily cover your expenses and I could try and "pull a few strings" for you. I've been told that once I arrive in Budapest there's every chance I'll receive an invitation to meet the Hungarian leader Miklos Horthy. I could always ask him to waive the ban you're still under.'

'But the Germans would still have to agree as well.'

'Of course, but if I can secure Horthy's approval, I don't see why the Germans shouldn't go along with that, too. After all, you were allowed to accompany me to Berlin, and I'm quite prepared to try and speak to von Shirach. He's amenable enough, as we both know.'

'Well, if you could, that would be much appreciated, I must say. Not that I'll get my hopes up too much until it actually happens.'

'It would certainly be wonderful to see the city again where we were married all those years ago,' Emilie added. 'It's such a beautiful place, but, like Anton, I won't be too hopeful. Still, just a few days there would make a very nice change.'

'Yes, we all need something to look forward to in life,' Franz responded.

47

4th December 1942

On 17th October 1942 Fritz was taken from Buchenwald to Monowitz concentration camp near Auschwitz. He was now in an increasing state of anxiety. Even before he left Buchenwald, letters had stopped coming from Helene and his daughters and he couldn't understand why. He was now fifty-nine, and four years and more of imprisonment on a poor diet were also beginning to break his health whilst conditions in this new camp were even harsher than in Buchenwald. When he was told that Jews were not allowed to either send or receive letters he was devastated.

As the weeks went by and it grew colder, he increasingly struggled to keep up with the work he was expected to carry out, until on 4th December the door to the packing shed he had been assigned to opened and in walked an SS officer and three factory managers.

'Here, gentlemen, we see where the paints are packed that the inmates make in the factory we just inspected. The paints are made to a precise chemical specification, as you know, and fulfil a large order.'

'Who is that there doing the packing?' one of the managers asked, pointing at Fritz.

'A Jew who's too old and ill to work in the factory so we

employ him here in the packing-shed.'

'It's obvious to me he's not working fast enough.' Then he strode up to Fritz. 'How many boxes have you packed in the past hour?'

'About ten, sir.'

'You should be packing at least one every two minutes, you Jewish swine!'

'If Jews like him can't work fast enough they should be sent to the gas chamber,' one of his fellow managers remarked, sneeringly.

They then left the packing shed, leaving Fritz to continue with his work as best he could. Unfortunately, though, this encounter had not gone unnoticed by one of the so-called Kapos. These were prisoners themselves, turned guards, many of whom, though in some cases Jews themselves, had been members of violent criminal gangs.

Every Kapo also understood that in order to curry favour and not lose their favoured roles, they could not be seen to neglect their duty, which in practice meant being as harsh as possible.

When the day's work ended and Fritz and his fellow workers lined up to return to their huts, Fritz suddenly heard his name being called out by this Kapo guard.

'Come here, you!' the Kapo shouted. Nervously, Fritz did as he was told. 'You little shit, you're not working hard enough. How do you think that makes me look?' Then he hit Fritz in the face so hard he fell to the ground. 'We've hundreds of inmates here who would love to have the soft number you have in the packing-shed, you ungrateful little bastard!'

As Fritz continued to lie on the ground, the Kapo guard began kicking him, both in the body and in the head. As this assault continued it was also witnessed by more than one German guard, who did nothing to intervene. On the contrary, their presence merely encouraged the Kapo to hit Fritz even harder.

Fritz was so bloodied and battered by the time the Kapo had finished that he died in the arms of a fellow inmate.

48

By the end of the year it was clear, even from the heavily censored news Goebbels's Propaganda Ministry permitted, that the mother of all battles was being fought in the eastern part of Ukraine at a city named after the Russian leader Joseph Stalin. In North Africa, too, it was admitted that the Afrika Korps was on the defensive and that American troops were now fighting alongside the British.

'If the Russians defeat us at Stalingrad and we're driven out of Africa, too, the tide of war will definitely be against us,' Anton said to Emilie.

'But the war could still go on for years, couldn't it?'

'Quite possibly.'

It had been good of Franz to suggest that he might be able to 'pull a few strings' for them, but with the coming of the new year and some bitterly cold weather, neither Anton or Emilie were too expectant that he'd actually succeed. In mid-January, after he'd been in Budapest about a week, Franz then telephoned.

'The weather here is absolutely bitter, I can tell you. My hotel apartment's comfortable enough but because of this damn war there's a shortage of coal so it's hard to keep it warm.'

'How's the composing coming along?'

'I'm pleased to say that I'm making good progress. Thank goodness it's only a short piece. Apart from anything else my hands are getting too cold to hold a pen.'

'I'd stay in bed as much as possible, if I were you.'

'That's what I'm doing, I can assure you. Of course there are the rehearsals to attend.'

'And they're going well?'

'Oh yes. The orchestra has been very welcoming and it's extremely professional. Like me, they're also getting rather old but that's to be expected with so many young Hungarians now fighting on the eastern front. Apparently thousands of them are involved in this battle that's raging at...' He hesitated.

'Stalingrad.'

'Yes, that's the place. Anyhow, I've got some good news for you. As I anticipated, I've received an invitation to meet with Miklos Horthy. It'll be in ten days from now and I haven't forgotten my promise to you and Emilie.'

'I appreciate that, Franz. He'll be another string to your bow after Hitler and Mussolini,' he quipped.

'Um, rather a dubious trio, though, don't you think?'

'Yes, but that's hardly your fault.'

'No, I suppose not.'

It was eleven days later when Franz telephoned again with more good news.

'I met with Horthy yesterday and found him very approachable. I said that you were my brother and that you'd been exiled from the country of your birth for more than twenty years because of the role you'd played in trying to restore the monarchy. He said he was aware of that but certainly didn't hold it against me. "None of us get to choose our relations," were his precise words. Anyway, I said how supportive you'd always been of my career and how much you would have liked to be able to attend the first night of *Garaboncias*. And would you believe it? His immediate response was to say that you could. Of course, I then had to tell him you'd still need clearance from Vienna but that hopefully von Shirach would be amenable...'

'Very well done. Let's just hope he is.'

'Oh, he will be, I'm sure. You see Horthy even said he'd arrange for von Shirach to be contacted and asked to give his permission as a favour to the Hungarian government. I must say of the three leaders I've met, Horthy was the most normal. Mussolini's a show-off with the biggest ego I've ever come across and as for Hitler... Well, after what he's done to so many of my Jewish friends and colleagues, and the way he rebutted our appeal to him last summer, I just think he's no better than an evil fanatic.'

Little more than three weeks later, Anton and Emilie were free to board a train to Budapest. There was still plenty of snow around, but the daytime temperatures had risen a little since January, and their journey was completed on time. It was also such a pleasure to be able to embark on their first holiday in more than five years, even if it was still wintertime. Further, with their happy memories of Budapest, they were confident that it wouldn't disappoint, even if there was a shortage of coal to keep their hotel bedroom warm.

'I know the battle for Stalingrad's been lost, and probably the entire war as well, but for the moment we're free to enjoy ourselves while we can,' Anton declared as they approached their destination.

Franz had booked them a room for up to four nights in the Danubius hotel in the city centre and they met them in the hotel lobby. Anton thought he looked extremely tired, and Emilie agreed.

'I worry that he's taken on too much at his age,' she said to Anton as they unpacked in their room. 'I mean all these rehearsals, composing a new piece of music, and now the strain of a first night tomorrow.'

'But it's what he loves doing. He's in his element.'

They then dined with Franz and Sophie in the hotel restaurant. The quality of the meal was excellent, but Anton noticed that Franz rather scratched at his food and ate barely half of what he'd been served.

'My appetite's not what it was and I've been experiencing some pain that seems to be coming from my kidneys.'

'Are you sure you'll be able to conduct the orchestra tomorrow evening?' Anton asked him.

'Oh yes, I'll be able to manage. I haven't come all this way, and worked so hard on the rehearsals, to miss out on what should be a splendid evening.'

'And you're happy with what you've composed?'

'It's adequate. I've given it the title "Fairy Dance".'

'Well, here's to another success, Franz,' Anton said, raising his glass of wine. 'It'll be just like old times.'

'Except I can't help remembering old friends and wondering with sadness what's become of them. Fritz, Louis, and several more; for all we know, they may no longer even be alive.'

'And what about Hungary's Jews? You seemed to like Horthy but has he treated them in the same way the Germans have?' Anton asked.

'From what I understand, the Jews have been discriminated against and treated harshly, but there's been no mass deportation to concentration camps.'

'That's to Horthy's credit then, but I don't suppose the Germans are best pleased.'

Anton and Emilie spent a good deal of the following day sightseeing despite a cold wind and grey skies. They also made a point of enjoying themselves at the Széchenyi baths where they swam outdoors in the naturally heated waters even though it was beginning to sleet.

The performance of *Garaboncias* at the city's handsome Royal Opera House indeed evoked memories of previous such occasions. The war didn't prevent a sell-out of seats as the people of Budapest were as keen as people anywhere to indulge in the escapism that the ballet offered them. Franz, too, was enthusiastically applauded, and while Anton was anxious about his stamina, he appeared to cope with the performance perfectly well.

Afterwards, just as they had all those years before on the first night of *The Merry Widow*, they met in one of the city's cafés close to the opera house where members of the orchestra and the ballet company joined them. Conversation was mostly in Hungarian, a language Anton hadn't spoken for more than twenty years, but it soon came back to him.

'That was very successful,' he said to Franz. 'And I particularly enjoyed "Fairy Dance".'

'Yes, it wasn't too bad, but God I'm feeling tired. To be honest with you I don't know how long I can keep this up. A few more nights, maybe, and then I'll have to give up, I'm afraid. This has definitely been my last first night, but I mustn't complain. All good things have to come to an end eventually.'

'Here comes the champagne,' Emilie said, and a few minutes later they were all pleased to raise their glasses to Franz, who smiled benignly, even if he did look fit to drop.

'I must get back to the hotel,' he insisted after taking only a few sips from his glass. 'I really do need to sleep. You younger people can enjoy yourselves into the early hours if you want to.'

'Not much younger in my case, dear brother. Let me see to a taxi for you.'

The four of them shared this for the short journey and they'd barely set off when Franz groaned.

'Are you in pain, my love?' Sophie asked in some alarm.

'Yes,' he responded in a strangulated voice. 'I think it's my kidneys playing up again. Oh dear, the pain's quite sharp. Ah, it's easing off a little now. I expect I'll be better soon.'

The following morning, Franz wasn't well enough to come down for breakfast and Sophie said she was going to call a doctor.

'I'm very worried about him. I don't see how he'll possibly be able to conduct tonight.'

However, by the time a doctor arrived, Franz had got up, managed, with some difficulty, to dress himself, and joined the others for coffee in the hotel lounge.

'I'm feeling better,' he insisted. 'You two should continue with your sightseeing.'

It was a bright morning so Anton was keen to visit Buda Castle with the magnificent view it offered of the Danube and the city below.

'If you're sure you'll be all right?' he asked Franz.

'Yes, of course, I always have Sophie to look after me.'

By the time Anton and Emilie returned, it was late afternoon and they went straight to Franz's room where they found him resting in a chair.

'What was the doctor's advice?' Anton asked.

'That I should continue to rest and forget about conducting tonight.'

'And are you going to follow his advice?'

'Certainly not. A little more rest and I'll be okay, I know I will.'

Sophie tutted at him. 'You can be awfully stubborn at times. You really should follow the doctor's advice.' Then she turned to Anton. 'Can't you persuade him, Anton?'

'I doubt it. Once Franz makes up his mind about something, I'm afraid there's no budging him.'

Neither Anton nor Emilie had wanted to attend the second night's performance, but Sophie was so anxious about Franz that Anton agreed to change his mind.

'Will you come, too?' he asked Emilie.

'I'd rather not. I was hoping for an early night.'

So, they went without her, and more than once on the way Franz grimaced with pain.

'It's not too late to abandon this,' Anton appealed to him. 'I expect they can find someone else to take your place.'

He shook his head. 'I'll be all right, don't worry about me.'

Whether out of courage or sheer bloody-mindedness, Franz managed to get through the entire performance, at which point he was able to enjoy the audience's rapturous applause once more. Anton had a seat in the upper circle of the house, and once he'd reached the auditorium where they'd arranged to meet afterwards, Sophie was quick to join him. She was in tears.

'He's collapsed and is in terrible pain. An ambulance has been called for. Hopefully, it should be here very soon. Oh, why did he have to be so stubborn?'

'That's just him, I'm afraid.' Anton was tempted to add that it was part of the male condition: too much pride, which he knew so often had a tendency to come before a fall.

49

Franz was taken in an ambulance to a hospital in Vienna the following morning with Sophie by his side, leaving Anton and Emilie to follow on by train.

'No one has yet been able to tell me what exactly is wrong with him but he certainly has severe kidney pain,' Sophie told them both just before she and Franz left in the ambulance.

Anton felt rather sad to be leaving Budapest again after such a short visit. However, his overriding concern was for Franz's health, so as soon as they arrived back in Vienna they went as quickly as they could to the hospital to which Sophie had told them Franz was to be admitted. It was outside normal visiting hours, but Franz had his own room, and Sophie had been allowed to stay with him, so upon their arrival she was able to speak to them.

'A doctor here has said he might have kidney stones and is definitely anaemic. He's going to need a change of diet and a lot of rest.'

'If it is stones, will they operate on him?' Anton asked.

'The doctor didn't say but I suppose that's quite possible. Anyway, they're going to keep him under observation for a few more days at least. He's asleep at the moment so you can't disturb him.'

They then went back to their apartment, returning the following day during visiting hours, when they found Franz sitting up in bed. He looking somewhat better than he had but still very pale.

'I hope to be out of here soon so we can get back to Ischl.'

'So you're not in pain at the moment?'

'No, just very tired, but with a little more rest I expect I'll be well again.'

Fortunately, his condition did indeed continue to improve while it was also decided that he didn't in fact have kidney stones. Sophie, meanwhile, accepted Anton and Emilie's invitation to stay with them and also took the opportunity to visit various old friends in the city. It was after one of these, a couple of days later, that she arrived back with some very sad news.

'I've heard that both Bela Jenbach and his wife are dead.'

'But that's awful. How? When?' Anton asked.

'Apparently it was towards the end of last month. Bela was admitted to hospital with stomach cancer and died quickly. Then - would you believe it? - his wife followed him less than a week later with breast cancer. I'm reluctant to tell Franz in case it causes a relapse, but I suppose I've no choice but to break it to him as gently as I can.'

A couple of days later, Anton visited Franz in hospital, having first checked with Sophie that she had given him the sad news of the two deaths. He seemed to have more colour in his cheeks and said that physically he was feeling much better. However...

'This news about the Jenbachs' deaths is really upsetting. It's something I suppose that neither of them starved to death, but I don't suppose their circumstances can have helped their health. Think, first Victor, then Wilhelm, and now Bela; all dead. Look, lying here in bed has made me think that I need to know what's happened to Fritz and Louis. It would give me some peace of mind to discover they're both still alive. And their wives and Fritz's daughters, too, of course. Perhaps it might even be possible to correspond with them. You still have to report to the SS once a month, don't you?'

'Why yes.'

'And they're responsible for these concentration camps, aren't they?'

'Yes, I understand they run them.'

'So, I want you to do me the favour of making enquiries with the SS as to where Louis and his wife, as well as Helene and her daughters, were sent. I imagine Fritz is still in Buchenwald but I'd like to be sure. I realise this is an imposition but I really haven't got the strength to make such enquiries myself.'

'And are you asking me to make this enquiry on my own behalf? After all, none of these people were ever more than acquaintances of mine.'

'No, no, on mine of course. Tell the truth that I'm too old and sick to make these enquiries myself and otherwise dress it up in the best way you can. I know to the Nazis they're only Jews, but to me they're old friends and colleagues and I still care about them as well as their families.'

'Very well, I'll do what I can for you, Franz. I might not have any success, though.'

'Of course, I appreciate that. Just do your best, is all I ask.'

'I'm due to next report in a week's time. Are you happy for me to wait until then?'

'Yes, by all means, a few days aren't of any consequence. I hope to be back in Ischl by then. You can always let me know how you get on by telephoning.'

Fortunately for Franz he was discharged from hospital four

days later and taken straight to the station by taxi. Anton then received a telephone call from Sophie to say that they'd arrived home safely, but that Franz had been so tired out by the journey that he'd gone straight to bed and was sound asleep.

'Give him my best in the morning and I'll be in touch once I've visited SS Headquarters in a couple of days' time.'

Anton was somewhat apprehensive about the task he'd undertaken to fulfil for Franz. He feared that he might provoke suspicion, if not outright hostility, and achieve nothing. Nonetheless, he was not about to give up before he'd even begun. Furthermore, Lieutenant Veats, the officer he'd been reporting to for the last year, was young enough to be his son, and behind a mask of inscrutability was always respectful in his manner towards him, so he decided he really had little to lose by making an enquiry with him, as a first step. Before he'd even opened his mouth to begin, the officer also had some good news for him.

'It's been decided that in future you only need report here every three months. You're also now at liberty to visit your brother Franz Lehár in Ischl, for up to a week once a month.'

This further easing in Anton's conditions of residency was certainly something he welcomed. It had also come as a complete surprise so he was genuinely effusive in the gratitude he expressed. 'There is also a certain matter that I'd like to raise with you, if I may, on behalf of my brother. You may have heard that he was taken very ill in Hungary last month...'

'No, I'm afraid I was not aware of that. I trust he's now recovering?'

'Yes, he's much better now and has returned to Ischl to recuperate. The thing is, though, he's now almost seventy-three and I fear can only become more infirm. His peace of mind has also been affected by the fate of a number of old working colleagues. Some have died while alas others have been sent to concentration camps. He's therefore asked me to ask on his behalf to which concentration camps these individuals have been sent. Also, whether there is any possibility of his being able to write to them.'

'I take it these individuals are all Jews?' the officer asked sharply. It was an inevitable question, which Anton was ready for.

'Yes, until Anschluss it was a fact of life that most of the librettists in Vienna were Jews and many singers likewise. Franz's operettas would not have happened without them. Louis Treumann, who was sent to a concentration camp last year, was the male lead in *The Merry Widow* when it was first performed back in 1905.'

Anton looked the officer in the eye, hoping he'd gained his understanding, if not his sympathy.

'Very well, give me all their names and I'll see what I can do. I must warn you it may take some time.'

'Do you mean some months?'

'Possibly, your brother will have to be patient.'

'If I give you my telephone number, you could contact me as and when you have any news.'

The officer picked up his pen. 'Give it to me then.'

Anton did so and proceeded as well to give him the names he needed. 'I'm grateful to you,' he added.

He shrugged. 'Expect me to call you in about a month's time. I'm not promising I'll have what you're asking for by then, but I'll give you a progress report.'

Anton again thanked him before turning to leave. He merely nodded in response and looked down. So far it had been a much easier process than Anton had anticipated, and when he telephoned Franz to tell him what he'd achieved he was naturally pleased.

'Well done, Anton. Let's hope we don't have to wait more than a month to hear something positive.'

'And how are you feeling?'

'Oh, I still get a few aches and pains. All part of getting old, I suppose, but I don't feel as tired as I did.'

It was a little less than four weeks later when the officer telephoned Anton.

'Herr Lehár, it's Lieutenant Veats here.'

'Yes, hello.' Already he felt tense about what the lieutenant might be about to say next.

'I have the following information for you; Fritz Löhner-Beda was transferred to Monowitz concentration camp last October.'

'And where is that?'

'Let me see… It's in Poland. This is outside the Reich so no inmates are entitled to send or receive letters.'

'Really?' He was genuinely shocked rather than seeking to argue.

'I don't make the rules, Herr Lehár.'

'I'm sorry. Is there anything you can do to find out how he is at the moment? I would like to be able to give my brother some reassurance that he's as well as can be expected.'

'I have sent an enquiry already but I cannot say how long it will be before I receive any reply.'

'And the others?'

'I've established that his wife and children were deported

out of the Reich to Minsk. What has happened to them since I cannot tell you but I'm prepared to make further enquiries.'

'Thank you.'

Lieutenant Veats coughed and Anton sensed that he was about to deliver some bad news. 'Herr Treumann and his wife were deported to Theresienstadt concentration camp. I regret to inform you that they are both dead.'

Anton was stunned. 'I see...' was the best he could muster.

'I have no information on the circumstances of their deaths, merely the dates. Frau Treumann died on the twenty-ninth of September last and Herr Treumann on the fifth of March. I will be in touch with you again if I have anything further to report. Good day.'

What he had just been told left Anton reeling and he shook his head in dismay.

'Has it been bad news?' Emilie asked him.

'The very worst. Both Louis and his wife are dead.'

'Oh, how terrible!'

'The officer couldn't tell me how they died, only when. Stefanie's been gone six months but Louis only died three weeks ago. I dread having to break this news to Franz. He'll be devastated, I know he will.'

'Do you think it might even be best not to tell him? I mean, he's been getting better and this could send him downhill again.'

'I can't lie to him about something as serious as this. Even if I were to try, he might well see through my deception. No, he deserves to know the truth, dreadful though it is. I must telephone him immediately. The longer I leave it, the harder it will become.'

'And what about Fritz and his family?'

'All the officer could tell me was that they'd been sent to concentration camps outside the Reich so aren't even entitled to send or receive mail.'

'But that's monstrous!'

'Everything that's been done to the Jews is monstrous. It will shame the German nation for ever.'

Picking up the telephone to give Franz this grim news reminded Anton intensely of the letters he'd had to write in the Great War informing parents that their beloved son was dead, or missing, presumed dead. If anything, this was worse, because Franz was his brother and he would be speaking to him rather than merely sending a letter.

'Hello, Franz, it's me, Anton. I'm afraid I have some very sad news for you...'

By the time he'd finished passing on the information Lieutenant Veats had given him, he worried that the line had gone dead and that Franz might not have heard everything he'd said. 'Hello, Franz, hello, can you hear me, are you still there?'

'... Yes, I'm here. What you've just told me has been like a knife to my heart. I just don't understand how this could have happened.'

'Nor I, but the chances are they were kept in dreadful conditions and not fed properly.'

'You mean, they might have starved to death like poor Victor?'

'That or some contagious condition carried them off. Perhaps even typhoid or cholera.'

'And I suppose we may never know what's happened to poor Fritz and his family?'

'The officer said he was making further enquiries. I expect he'll come back to me again quite soon.'

'You know, it feels to me as if the Germans as good as killed Louis and Stefanie, just as they as good as killed Victor,' Franz said, with a bitter edge to his voice.

'And to me. I'm really so sorry, Franz. Try not to take it too badly.'

'Easier said than done, dear brother, especially when everything that's happened makes me feel guilty for having ever sucked up to Hitler.'

'But you only did it to protect Sophie. Don't forget that.'

'Yes, but that wasn't the only reason. I was flattered, too, and proud to have won such recognition when some people I could mention were only too happy to denigrate my work as artistically inferior.'

'Just don't be too hard on yourself.'

'I'll try not to be.'

By the beginning of June, Anton had heard nothing further from Lieutenant Veats and assumed his further enquiries had been unproductive. Meanwhile, not long after he'd told Franz the dreadful news of Louis Treumann's death, Franz had suffered a relapse and taken to his bed again. Inevitably, Anton saw one as being the consequence of the other, and out of concern for Franz's welfare, he and Emilie had visited Ischl for a few days in late April. Franz perked up a little upon their arrival, even getting up for a few hours each day while they were there. A week or so after their return to Vienna, though, Sophie told Anton on the telephone that he'd taken to his bed yet again.

At the same time, the war was also going from bad to worse with the Afrika Korps having been driven out of their last toe-hold in North Africa, and with Russia in the ascendancy on the eastern front. Rationing, too, was beginning to bite in a way it hadn't before, though one small consolation was that there'd been no repetition of the air raid of the previous September.

Anton then made his monthly visit to SS headquarters. Naturally, as he made his way there he wondered if he might be seeing Lieutenant Veats again and what he might be able to tell him.

'Ah, Herr Lehár, do come in.' It was indeed him. 'I apologise for not having been in touch with you again. Until last week I had no more news for you, but then I finally received a response to my enquiry. I'm afraid it's more bad news. Do sit down.'

He wasn't prepared to make eye contact with Anton, preferring to look nervously at a piece of paper in front of him. 'Herr Löhner-Beda died last December and his wife and children are also dead. Again, I have no details as to how this happened. I'm sorry.'

Shock, horror, anger; all these emotions surged through Anton. 'How could this be?' he spluttered. 'How could this be?'

'I've already told you. I do not know.'

The remainder of their short session together was like a blur to Anton and he left the SS Headquarters in a state of utter gloom. It had been bad enough having to tell Franz of the deaths of the Treumanns; now he knew having to give him this awful news as well would be especially difficult.

'I don't want to tell him this over the telephone,' he said to Emilie. 'It seems too cowardly. I really think I should tell him face to face.'

'As you wish, but are you really sure he needs to know at all? He's already gone back to his bed and this... Well, it could kill him.'

'I must take that risk. Of course, it'll be hard and I don't want to hurt him. Yet to withhold such a truth would be disrespectful. He's not a child and he's entitled to know what's happened to Fritz and his family, immensely painful though that is.'

'But look, if you were to telephone it's more than likely that Sophie will answer. You could give her the news and let her have the final word on how Franz should be told.'

'If I do that, she'll more than likely say that she'll tell him. But I can't be sure she'd mean it. No, I just think this has to come from me.'

'At least let's go to Ischl together, then. You really shouldn't do this on your own.'

The following day, they boarded an early morning train to Ischl. It was cloudy and this soon turned to rain, though by the time they reached their destination this was beginning to ease off. As they approached Franz's villa, Anton felt the same sort of trepidation he remembered from his fighting days before going into action. There was certainly a part of him which would have gladly turned back and his legs felt weak.

'Are you all right?' Emilie asked, sensing that something was wrong.

'No, I hate having to do this, I really do.'

'Then it's still not too late to just return to Vienna.'

'No! This must be done.'

It was Sophie who came to the door after I'd rung the bell and, of course, she was surprised to see them.

'Why didn't you let us know you were coming?' she asked.

'Because I need to give Franz some dreadful news and I decided I can only do that to his face. You see, Fritz and his entire family are dead.'

She put her hand to her mouth in shock. 'Oh God, that's too terrible for words. If you tell Franz it will make him even more unwell.'

'I realise that but I don't believe this should be kept from him. He's entitled to know the truth.'

'Oh, very well, I suppose you're right. He's in bed, of course. If you find him asleep, please don't disturb him.'

'I won't.'

When Anton entered the bedroom, Franz was sitting up in bed, looking old and sickly. 'Anton, what brings you here without warning? I heard voices downstairs and wondered who it might be.'

Anton had already made up his mind to come straight to the point. 'I'm the bearer of more grave news, I'm afraid, Franz. I could have just telephoned, could have left it to Sophie to tell you, but I just felt that would have been cowardly.'

'Are you trying to tell me that Fritz is dead?'

'Yes, I'm sorry, Franz, he died last December. Worse than that, Helene and their two daughters are dead as well.'

Franz shook his head and then put a hand to his eyes before beginning to tremble. When he took his hand away, Anton could see tears in his eyes and then he sobbed.

'How could this be?' he wailed. 'How could this be?'

'The officer couldn't or wouldn't tell me how they died. As with Louis and Stefanie I expect it was a combination of neglect and disease.' Anton in fact had dark thoughts that it could well have been more brutal than that, but he certainly wasn't about to share these with Franz.

He now laid his head back on the pillow, once more bringing a hand across his eyes. He was still crying.

'I'll never get over this. Never, never, never!'

At this moment Sophie, who'd clearly been listening at the door, rushed forward, and sitting on the bed, put her arms around Franz. 'I know it's terrible but try not to distress yourself too much, my love.'

'I feel responsible for their deaths. I should have done more.'

'You did what you could. You mustn't blame yourself,' Anton said. 'I'm just sorry to be the bearer of such dreadfully painful news.'

'At least you had the courage to tell me the truth. I'm grateful for that, dear brother. Now I need to rest.'

50

April 30th 1945

The climactic battle for Berlin had by now been waging for fourteen days. Although it could be said from a Nazi perspective that the struggle to defend Germany's capital city against the feared communist red army of Joseph Stalin had been heroic, total defeat was now inevitable. In his bunker, Hitler had also been informed that Russian troops were closing in and could not be held at bay for very much longer.

In his private office at the heart of the bunker, Hitler was alone with his wife of less than two days, Eva Braun. There was a gramophone in the corner of the room, which was playing the aria 'I'm always smiling' from *The Land of Smiles*, sung by Richard Tauber.

As defeat had followed defeat in the last months of the war, Hitler had increasingly sought solace in Franz's music to an almost obsessive degree, indifferent to the irony that many of the singers of his music had been Jewish. Now, in a state of complete despair, he walked over to the gramophone and switched it off for the last time.

Eva then took a cyanide capsule from the pocket of her dress before looking into his eyes and placing her free hand in one of his.

'My darling husband. I love you now and for eternity. We

shall shortly meet again in the afterlife, where we shall be together, forever.'

'My beloved wife, thank you for all your loyalty during our time together. Now, let us both choose eternal peace over torture and public degradation at the hands of the Bolsheviks.'

They exchanged a brief, passionate kiss, before Eva brought the cyanide capsule up to her mouth and bit onto it. For a moment she continued to stand in front of him as the cyanide started to swirl inside her body. Then she coughed, agonisingly, several times, and fell dead at his feet.

Hitler then immediately took a revolver out of his desk drawer and put it to his right temple.

Meanwhile, two Nazi guards were standing outside Hitler's office. Upon hearing the sound of a gunshot, they stepped into it, only to discover Hitler and Eva's bodies lying on the floor.

'We must follow our great leader's orders for the final time by burning his body and that of his wife,' one of the guards said before beginning to break down in tears.

'He will always be my hero,' said the other before giving an emphatic Nazi salute. '*Heil Hitler!*'

51

May 1945

Broken by the deaths of so many Jewish friends and colleagues, Franz spent most of the next two years in bed with one illness or the other, the worst being pneumonia, which came close to killing him. He was clearly afflicted, too, by a deep melancholia which, while entirely understandable, surely made his poor health worse.

All the while, Germany came ever closer to losing the war, bringing in its wake more severe rationing and, worst of all, bombing. It began in earnest in June 1944, once Allied Forces had invaded Normandy, and then continued relentlessly. As a consequence, Anton and Emilie had to spend many nights in a shelter, fearful that their apartment would be obliterated. That this fate had not befallen them by the beginning of March 1945 was due to the raids being concentrated on industrial targets on the fringes of the city.

They had started to make a habit of spending one week every month with Franz and Sophie in Bad Ischl, far away from the raids that were devastating Vienna. Sophie was certainly grateful for their company as well as the support they both offered her in helping to look after Franz. His health also began to improve somewhat along with his mood as he spent longer periods out of bed. Sometimes, indeed, he even managed to get dressed, so that in the summer months, when it was dry and warm enough, he could venture into the garden.

Anton and Emilie's days in Ischl cannot be said to have been happy ones, but at least they were companionable. Certainly, they found pleasure in listening to gramophone recordings of Franz's music, and in playing cards in the evening with Sophie. Occasionally, Franz would even join them in this activity, though for the most part he went to sleep immediately after supper. It was a time, Anton supposed, for sombre reflection. However, they seldom talked about the war and avoided the fraught subject of the Jewish persecution and all it had led to as if it was the plague.

In early March, Anton was due to report to SS Headquarters. By this time it was increasingly obvious that the war was likely to come to an end within a matter of weeks, leading him to think that this could well be the last occasion on which he would have to present himself. It was Lieutenant Veats whom he had continued to see on every previous visit and it was no different on this occasion. Up until now he had been consistently polite but never willing to interact with him on any sort of emotional level. On this occasion, though, for the first and last time, as they were never destined to meet again, he showed a different side to his personality.

'Well, you'll be pleased at the prospect of never having to do this again, I'm sure.'

'Are you suggesting the war's lost?' Anton wasn't yet quite certain that this wasn't some kind of trap.

'Of course it's lost. In fact if I were you, I'd take yourself off to Ischl and not bother to come back. It's going to get nasty here once the Russians arrive, which I'm sure they will in a matter of weeks.'

'And what will you do once that happens?'

'Continue to obey orders, of course. But once the surrender comes, let's just say I'd rather be in the hands of either the Americans or the British.'

'That may not be an option for you?'

He shrugged. 'Perhaps not, but I hope to make it an option so I can head west.'

'Well, I wish you luck.'

'Thank you, I expect I'll need it.'

'May I ask you one more question?'

Lieutenant Veats nodded.

'When you told me you had no information on how Louis Treumann and his wife and Fritz Löhner-Beda and his family died, was that a lie?'

He shook his head. 'No, not at all, but I can tell you this: the camps are hell-holes, rife with disease. I've been to more than one of them, including Theresienstadt, and it's no surprise to me that Herr Treumann and his wife died there within months of their incarceration. As for Herr Löhner-Beda and his family, well, by all accounts, conditions in camps in Poland have been even worse than the ones here in the Reich.'

Before Anton left they even shook hands, for all that they had nothing in common. Anton remained a Catholic monarchist who despised the Nazis and all they stood for, whereas he expected Lieutenant Veats to have been totally loyal to the party's ideology. What cruelties he might have been involved in was also something Anton preferred not to speculate upon. At least the lieutenant had always been polite to him and had gone as far as he could to provide the information he'd asked of him. Subsequently, for all Anton knew, he could have died when Vienna was besieged by the Russians, or, if captured by them, marched off to some gulag in Siberia, not unlike the camps in which so many Jews died.

When Anton returned home, he and Emilie had no difficulty in deciding what they should do. Their next visit to Ischl was scheduled for in about a fortnight's time, and once there they would not return until the war was well and truly over and Austria hopefully once again a free nation.

'I don't want to be too alarmist, but the Russians could easily wreak a bloody vengeance on Vienna, burning, looting and raping,' Anton declared to Emilie.

'Then, darling, the sooner we escape from here the better.'

A mere two days later the air raid sirens sent them scurrying for their shelter where they cowered in increasing fear as bombs seemed to be falling all around them. When they emerged into the sunlight the following morning, their apartment block was still standing but many others close by were not. For the first time large parts of central Vienna had been badly damaged and the prospect of more such raids taking place encouraged them to move their plans forward.

Of course, many others had the same idea, and trains were few and far between. Nonetheless, on 16th March, with just Emilie's handbag and two quite small suitcases between them, they managed to board a train heading west. Anton had also managed to speak to Franz on the telephone before their departure to inform him of their plans. He'd made a point of emphasising that they didn't wish to impose on his hospitality for longer than was absolutely necessary.

'You're welcome to stay with us for as long as you need to,' Franz assured him. 'Sophie appreciates your company and my health is continuing to improve. I'm now able to get up and dress myself and then spend most of the day out of bed. I'm finally putting my grief behind me, I hope.'

They had barely been with Franz and Sophie a week, when Allied Forces managed to cross the Rhine in order to invade Germany. Some ten days after that a Russian army invaded Vienna, vindicating their decision to escape when they did, and within another fortnight, the battle for Berlin began. The Third Reich was now in its death throes, but in pleasant spring weather, life in Ischl continued to be as outwardly peaceful as it had ever been. Then one day at the beginning of May, German troops retreating from the east appeared.

'They're Waffen SS,' Anton said, recognising their uniforms. 'The sort of men who might decide to make a last stand here, I'm afraid.'

'But what's the point?' Emilie asked. 'The war's lost and the wireless is reporting that Hitler's dead.'

'Because they're fanatics and may not think they've anything much to lose. Better to go down fighting, in fact, than surrender to the Russians.'

'But the report we've been listening to on the wireless suggests that this part of Austria has been invaded by American forces. Surely they've far less to fear from them?'

'I agree, but they may still see it as their duty to keep fighting.'

Franz and Sophie's house stood less than fifty metres away from a bridge over the river Traun and afforded an excellent view of it. During the course of the day they looked out with growing anxiety from an upstairs window as some of the SS troops took up a position nearby. Then they started to run a cable onto the bridge itself.

'I believe they're mining the bridge. They mean to blow it up!' Anton cried out in alarm. 'If that happens this house could be destroyed by the blast. I need to talk to their officer and see if I can persuade him to stop this madness.'

'Be careful, dearest,' Emilie said. 'If these men are as fanatical as you suggest, they might take you for a traitor.'

'I don't think so. I merely wish to appeal to their officer's better judgement.'

It was a pleasant enough day but still rather chilly, so Anton put on his coat before stepping out of the front door to walk the short distance to where the SS troops had taken up position behind a wall.

'Excuse me,' he called out. 'I need to speak to your officer.'

'What is it you want to say to me?' The question was asked by a man who looked to be about thirty years of age. He was bearded and he could tell from his insignia that he had the rank of a *Hauptmann* (captain).

Anton pointed. 'The house just here is the home of Franz Lehár, the Führer's favourite composer. He's in residence and not at all well. If you mean to blow up this bridge and turn Ischl into a battlefield you will seriously endanger his life and that of his wife. If you must go on fighting when the war's been lost and by all accounts the Führer is dead, I appeal to you to do so elsewhere. Otherwise, simply continue to travel west. I'm sure you'll soon be able to surrender to American troops.'

The officer hesitated to reply. Anton could imagine that he was beset by very mixed emotions, much as he had been when Austria had been forced to surrender at the end of the Great War. Part of him had not wanted to give up the fight and suffer the ignominy of defeat; the other part had been simply relieved to see so much death and suffering brought to an end. He pressed home what he thought was his advantage.

'I tell you, Hitler is dead and the war is lost. We've also heard on the wireless that American troops have entered Austria from the west. Please, I beg of you, do not be the cause of yet more needless destruction. Even if you don't care about an old composer, think of the women and children of this town and their welfare.'

'All right,' the officer said at last. 'We'll leave. My regards to Herr Lehár. My mother has always loved his music.'

Anton then stood and watched as the officer and his men returned to their vehicles and drove away. They hadn't bothered to remove the high explosives they'd put in place on the bridge, or the device and wiring leading to it, but he decided not to remonstrate with them about this. Instead, once they'd gone, he simply fetched a pair of scissors from the house and cut the wire.

For his actions, he received a welcome hug from Emilie along with Franz's warm thanks. 'That was well done, dear brother, I'm immensely grateful to you.'

'I'm just pleased good sense prevailed. There was a moment there when I thought he might refuse to leave.'

Four days later, Germany surrendered unconditionally. Anton thought, though, that he might not live to see the terrible wounds the war had inflicted even begin to heal.

52

Tuesday 1st October 1946

The International Military Tribunal in Nuremburg, having deliberated on its verdicts, was now in the process of delivering its judgements that would send leading Nazis to the gallows.

Amongst those put on trial was Arthur Seyss-Inquart, former Reich Governor of Austria who was led up to the defendants' bench by two American military policemen to face the judges. It fell to the British judge, Norman Birkett, to deliver the court's judgement.

'Arthur Seyss-Inquart, you took part in the last stages of the intrigue that brought about the occupation of Austria, and you became its chancellor when President Miklas resigned rather than sign the law making Austria a province of Germany. Shortly thereafter, you became Reich Governor of Austria when many political opponents of the Nazi regime in that country were sent to concentration camps.

'Subsequently, as Reich Commissioner for the Netherlands you supervised the deportation of one hundred and twenty thousand Dutch Jews to Auschwitz. It is true that some of the excesses were carried out by units that reported to Heinrich Himmler, and that you successfully opposed the scorched-earth orders at the end of the war. Nonetheless, you were a knowing participant in war crimes and crimes against humanity.

'The international military tribunal finds you guilty on counts two, three and four. The sentence of the court is death by hanging.'

Father Bruno Spitzl arrived outside the prison cell of Arthur Seyss-Inquart at Nuremberg's prison about a week later, with an American military policeman, who was one of Seyss-Inquart's guards, at his side. The guard then proceeded to open the door of the cell. As he then entered, Seyss-Inquart, who was sitting despondently in a chair, turned his head towards him.

On seeing the condemned man, Father Spitzl had a sudden and violent attack of nerves. It was the first time he had ever felt this way before hearing a confession. Until now, he had always believed that God would forgive anyone, no matter what they had done, as long as they were truly sorry. But now that he was face to face with a former high-ranking Nazi who had committed what amounted to cold-blooded, genocidal murder on an industrial scale, he began to doubt that even God could forgive sins of such appalling magnitude.

Nevertheless, he took a deep breath and in the calm, measured tones he always used when hearing confession, he said, 'My son, I am Father Bruno Spitzl, the prison chaplain. I understand that you wish to be received back into the Roman Catholic Church and to receive absolution in the sacrament of confession?'

'That is correct. Thank you for coming, Father.'

Father Spitzl then sat next to Seyss-Inquart in order to hear his confession.

For the first time in many years, Seyss-Inquart bowed his

head and uttered the words, 'Bless me, Father, for I have sinned.'

At first, Father Spitzl said nothing. He knew he couldn't treat this as just another confession. After taking a few moments to formulate his thoughts, he began:

'At this point, I would normally ask you, "What are your sins, my son?" And we will come to your sins, even though many of them are already a matter of public record. But first, there is another question I must ask you. It is a question that has plagued my mind for a long time. It's this: why did it happen? Why did Germany, an otherwise marvellous nation, descend to this? Why did your party come to believe, as it did, that the destruction of six million innocent Jewish people could possibly be justified?'

'That seems to me like several questions.'

'Well, I suppose it is.'

Lifting his head and looking Father Spitzl in the eye, Seyss-Inquart said, 'Father, when I received my sentence of death and returned to where I and the other prisoners were being kept while we all waited to hear our verdicts, I told the journalists there that I felt I deserved my punishment. I still feel that. I really cannot explain to you why I did what I did. The best I can say is that at the time I believed it was in the interests of Germany, the country that I love and will continue to love. But Hitler misled us all. He told us things that were not true. He assured us that we could win the war when it was clearly impossible for us to do so against the combined allied forces of the old world and the new world, as well as the Red Army. He also led us to believe that the Jews were contemptible parasites who wished to destroy Germany. I do not believe that any more. It's a nonsense. The Jews are human beings like anyone

314

else. I can only pray for God's forgiveness in believing such terrible nonsense. I do not truly know why I did believe that rubbish. Satan, I'm afraid, came knocking on Germany's door, and I was one of those who let him in...'

He then sighed before continuing. 'I must confess, too, that I was intoxicated by power together with all its trappings. I come from a modest background, and yet, thanks to my belief in the National Socialist cause, became Chancellor of Austria and then ruler of the Netherlands. It was as if I had the power to walk on water and could do no wrong. I was vain, arrogant, deluded...' He lowered his eyes, shaking his head in dismay.

'God will find it in his heart to forgive you, my son,' Father Spitzl responded. As soon as he had uttered those words, he realised that he believed they were true. There really were no limits to God's mercy, and in any case Father Spitzl could see Seyss-Inquart was a broken man, wracked with guilt and shame about what he had done.

'I do hope so, Father. To all murdered by our regime I also wish to beg for God's forgiveness. I know that thousands of innocent men, women and children were sent to their deaths at my orders and I am truly sorry. I know, too, that by my actions I have inflicted shame upon my dear wife and children and wish to beg their forgiveness for what I have done. Admission of my guilt and my acceptance of my punishment are as close as I can come to redemption, not that I don't fear hell's fire. I know I'll always be thought of as an evil villain for...' He fell silent.

'Yes, my son, have you anything else to add?'

'I am referring to my many crimes. As I say, I can only pray for God's mercy. I am a wretched, remorseful sinner.'

Without any qualms or hesitation, Father Spitzl forgave

Seyss-Inquart in the name of the Father, and of the Son, and of the Holy Spirit.

Seyss-Inquart went to his death in the execution chamber at Nuremberg prison at approximately 2.45 in the morning on Wednesday 16th October 1946. His was the last of the executions of Nazi war criminals to be carried out that day.

Those present to witness this were Colonel Burton Andrus, the prison's commandant, a German chaplain, four American military policeman and an American journalist, John Webster. And then, of course, there was the executioner John C. Woods.

As Seyss-Inquart stood at the gallows, not yet hooded, Colonel Andrus asked him if he had anything to say before the sentence of death was carried out.

'Yes, Colonel Andrus... and thank you for this opportunity to speak. I hope that this execution is the last act of the tragedy of the Second World War and the lessons taken from this war will be that peace and understanding should exist between all people and all nations. I believe in Germany!'

John Webster hastily wrote down these last words on a notepad in shorthand, before Andrus nodded at Woods, who promptly placed a white cap over Seyss-Inquart's head. He then stepped back, pulled a lever, and Seyss-Inquart dropped to his death.

'Well done,' Andrus said to Woods. 'That was quick and easy for all concerned, especially him.'

53

'Franz, my dear old friend, how wonderful it is to see you again after all this time.'

Richard Tauber threw his arms around Franz and they embraced. After nine long years this was a reunion which gave them both great pleasure, combined, inevitably, with a good deal of sadness. For Anton's part, he couldn't help thinking that the mixed emotions they all felt, added pathos to the occasion. He could but hope that those many other old friends who had not lived to see this day had found peace in a better place.

Europe was still struggling to recover from a war that had caused so much devastation. Austria in particular had been divided into four zones of occupation, and by choosing to return to live in their farm he and Emilie had placed themselves under de facto Russian rule. There was, though, an Austrian government of sorts and from the summer of 1946 onwards it enjoyed some measure of power. He was therefore reasonably hopeful that in time the occupation would end. On the other hand, rationing was also still very much a fact of life, while the country was a poor shadow of what it had been prior to Anschluss, never mind the Great War.

The war had also diminished Franz's wealth rather than destroyed it, in early 1946 Franz and Sophie had been able to afford to visit Zurich for private medical treatment. Now, the following year, with the coming of spring, along with Anton and Emilie they had come to the city on holiday; the first Emilie and Anton had enjoyed since their visit to Budapest four years previously. It was also an ideal opportunity for a reunion between Richard and Franz, which they had been seeking to achieve for some time.

Anton's first reaction on seeing Richard again was one of shock as the years had certainly taken their toll, although he thought his much younger English wife, Diana, still as attractive as he remembered her. Franz, too, was certainly frail and looked all his seventy-seven years. Yet, in comparison with the bedridden state in which he had endured most of the last two years of the war, he had made a significant recovery. In contrast, Sophie, who had devoted so much of her failing energy to his care during the latter years of the war, had aged considerably since its ending. Despite being some eight years younger, she now looked almost as old as Franz.

An arrangement had been made for them all to meet for lunch at one of Zurich's finest restaurants, the Kronenhalle. As they then took their seats in surroundings that spoke loudly of wealth and privilege, and Anton looked at the menu, he was struck by the variety of what was on offer.

'This is a revelation after the diet we have to exist on in Austria,' he declared.

'It's pretty bad in England, too, you know,' Richard responded with a grin. 'People are beginning to grumble about rationing still being in place two years after the end of the war. If that's not bad enough there's no sign of it ending, either.'

Richard's looks might be fading, but Anton thought he'd

lost none of his natural charm and still possessed an ebullient personality, along with a presence which seemed to fill the room they were now sitting in.

'I have a little surprise for you, Richard,' Franz said.

'Oh yes?'

'While here in Zurich, I've accepted an invitation to conduct the Tonhalle orchestra tomorrow evening. The performance will take place at the studio of Radio Beromünster. They're going to be performing overtures and waltzes from my operettas.'

'Congratulations.'

'Thank you. There was a time during the war, when I could barely get out of bed, that I thought I'd never be able to conduct again. Anyway, I mentioned you would also be coming to Zurich to see me and the invitation has been extended to you to sing two or three of your favourite songs from my operettas. I hope you'd be happy to do so?'

Richard smiled at Franz but still shook his head. 'It's kind of them but I came here to see you and to enjoy a few days' rest, not to work.'

'I understand, of course. I've heard it said your voice is not all that it once was?' This was said in a gently teasing voice, which evoked a guffaw from Richard.

'Have you indeed? Well, whoever's been saying such a thing is wrong. I assure you I can still sing as beautifully as I've ever done.'

'So you'll do it then? It will be like old times, after all.'

'Oh, all right, if you insist on twisting my arm.'

The reunion could not be properly celebrated without the ordering of champagne, and once it arrived glasses were duly raised. At this stage, though, no toasts were called for. There seemed to be a tacit agreement that no one would mention it, but everyone present was acutely aware of the absence of those friends who should, but for the now infamous cruelty of the Nazi regime, have been alive and well and able to join them in celebrating this occasion.

Throughout the meal, everyone avoided the subject of the war as well as the horrors it unleashed. Instead, they indulged in a good deal of perfectly understandable nostalgia, either for the now long-gone days before the Great War, or in Richard's case, the optimistic days of the nineteen twenties when he'd begun his wonderful partnership with Franz.

By the time coffee was served, the quantity of champagne and wine they had drunk had loosened tongues and made them all feel more relaxed. Richard had permission from the ladies to light a Havana cigar that would have impressed Winston Churchill. He then began to regale them with an account of his recent trip to America to perform on Broadway in a production of Franz's *The Land of Smiles*, renamed for the supposed benefit of its American audience *Yours Is My Heart*.

'I must confess to you, Franz, that it was a total disaster. The management were utterly incompetent and allowed hacks to make a complete mess of everything. For some reason they decided to set the operetta in Paris rather than Vienna and played around with the wording of the songs in a vulgar and infantile fashion. I realised that it was trash as soon as we began to rehearse, which made me really cross. I threatened to pull out, but against my better judgement was persuaded to carry on.' He paused to puff on his cigar, which induced a cough and a splutter before he was able to continue.

'Anyway, as I was saying, not surprisingly, the whole

production flopped terribly. I got so irate that I refused to perform any longer. I said, "You can tell the audience I have a throat infection. On no account will I go on stage again.""

'It fell to me to have to tell the audience he wasn't well,' Diana added.

'Yes, I'm sorry to have put you through that, darling. I was just so angry. My sincere apologies to you, too, Franz, that the production failed to do your music the justice it deserved.'

'There's no need to apologise, Richard. In fact I'm grateful that you should feel so strongly about the integrity of my oper- ettas. I must also say that I'm happier to see one of my works hacked around than ignored completely, which I'm afraid, in Austria, has been the fate of all of my music since the war ended. I'm afraid I've become tainted as a Nazi sympathiser, indeed some even say a collaborator, though, of course, neither allegation is true.'

'No, it's a slander,' Sophie asserted.

'The trouble stems most of all from that damned present I sent Hitler back in thirty-eight as well as the awards he then gave me. On the face of it, of course it does make me look like a Nazi sympathiser, or, at the very least, someone who was happy to curry favour with Hitler for my own benefit...'

'But that's not the truth of the matter at all,' Anton declared.

'Well, it's not the whole truth. I was pleased that Hitler adored my music and after what happened to poor Fritz I was desperate to protect Sophie. I thought sending a present would encourage him to look favourably on my request for Sophie to be granted Aryan status.'

'And it worked,' Anton added.

'Yes, but I was flattered, too, I can't deny that. What some people now all too easily forget is that at the time Hitler and his party seemed all powerful. There was much talk of a thousand-year Reich. Really, the last thing I envisaged was that it would all end in utter devastation in only seven years.'

'Hindsight, as they say, is a wonderful thing,' Richard commented through a cloud of cigar smoke followed by more coughing.

'Ah, but it's not just that. What's really compounded my supposed crimes is the realisation of what utter monsters Hitler, and those who served his ends, were. People are saying that he was the most evil man who ever drew breath and quite rightly that the Nazis perpetrated the most terrible crime ever when they gassed so many Jews. It's as if I supped with the devil incarnate. I don't suppose I'll ever live it down.'

'Your music will still be your legacy, Franz,' Anton said.

'I do hope so, just so long as it's still performed, even badly performed.' And with that he raised his glass of brandy to Richard and smiled. 'I want to propose a toast to absent friends.'

'To absent friends,' they all said as one, their glasses raised.

'I also have something here I want to share with you all,' Franz added, pulling a piece of paper out of the inside pocket of his jacket. 'I have a letter here from Hermann Leopoldi, the composer who's recently returned to Austria from the USA. He was an inmate of Dachau and Buchenwald at the same time as Fritz. Together, they composed a piece of music, which they called "The Song of Buchenwald". Hermann wrote the music and Fritz the words. Hermann's wife was then able to purchase his freedom. He was one of the lucky ones. Permit me to read the refrain to you.

'Oh Buchenwald, I cannot forget you,
Because you are my fate.
Only he who leaves you can appreciate
How wonderful freedom is!
Oh Buchenwald, we don't cry and complain;
And whatever our destiny may be,
We nevertheless shall say 'yes' to life:
For once the day comes, we shall be free!'

Franz continued, 'Even in adversity, Fritz didn't lose his spirit. It's some comfort to me, too, that according to Hermann he continued to speak warmly of our collaboration and friendship. What's harder to take is the thought that he and his family were murdered. The grief I felt when I knew they, along with Louis and Stefanie Treumann, were all dead nearly killed me. Certainly, I will never be able to think of them without a sense of pain.

'If I was ever tempted to accept the validity of the Nazi regime, I can assure you all that discovering what they had done to so many Jewish friends and colleagues put paid to that for ever. How they could have behaved in the way they did, makes me struggle to still believe there's much goodness in humanity. Perhaps, indeed, we are at heart an evil species. It's a bleak thought, I confess.'

Anton had a picture in his head of the awful pictures he'd seen on newsreels of the inmates of liberated concentration camps, both alive and dead. They were enough to make him think that Franz might well be right. Richard, however, adopted a more optimistic stance.

'All I can say, Franz, is that there's always been evil in the world, but as far as I'm concerned a lot of goodness, too. What's more, on this occasion goodness won and evil was defeated.'

'But only at a terrible price,' Anton countered. 'Too many people in both Germany and Austria had their prejudices indulged and loved it until everything started to fall apart.'

'Well, more fool them. No one around this table was ever a Nazi, or in any way a party to any of the terrible things that were done to the Jews.'

'You escaped, Richard,' Anton said. 'Like Hermann Leopoldi, you were one of the lucky ones. For those of us who saw out the war as part of the Reich, it's hard to shrug off a sense of guilt. I sometimes think that Hitler has tainted the German race for ever.'

'Well, I hope you're wrong in saying that. Germany will learn from what's happened and move forward into a better world, I'm sure of it. And Franz, Anton, as far as I'm concerned, neither of you have anything to reproach yourselves for.'

The debate might have continued, but Franz then said that he was feeling tired so needed to return to his hotel to rest, thus bringing the occasion to an end. The following day, he and Richard met again and went for a walk together before going on to the radio studio, where the broadcast they listened to was enhanced by Richard's wonderfully melodic voice.

'It's a happy ending, don't you think?' Emilie suggested to Anton.

'In a way. I just hope the ghosts of those who perished can forgive us.'

Sadly Franz and Richard never met again. Barely four months later, Sophie died of a heart attack; and the following January,

Richard died of lung cancer.

Anton prayed that future generations would not judge his generation too harshly. It had had to endure not one but two dreadful world wars, which fundamentally changed entire societies. Most people, he thought, including Franz, were in one way or another victims of events and forces over which they had little or no control. They were seduced, exploited, or in the case of the Jews, demonised. Sooner or later, too, millions suffered for it, and none more so, of course, than the Jewish victims of the Holocaust.

Epilogue

24th October 1958

Since his brother's death, Anton had worked tirelessly to preserve and enhance his legacy, rebutting whenever he could what he saw as the unjust accusation that he had been a Nazi sympathiser.

Now on the tenth anniversary of Franz's death, Anton stood in the garden of his villa in Bad Ischl, remembering his brother's life and achievements with a deep sense of pride.

It pleased him, too, that in these ten years, West Germany had achieved, by peaceful economic means, everything, and more, that Hitler's Reich had tried but failed to achieve by violence and military conquest. In 1952 it had also signed a reparations agreement with the State of Israel and since then had paid that country billions of Deutschmarks in order to help this new nation to become a prosperous developed country. Many Israelis had bitterly opposed this agreement, calling the reparations blood money, which perhaps they were. Nonetheless, the money had given West Germany the opportunity, not to achieve redemption - for how could that be possible for such dreadful crimes? - but at least to demonstrate that it recognised how evil it had been and wanted to try to make some kind of amends.

Anton was now an old man, and did not suppose he had very much longer left to live. He still wondered every day how it was possible that the young artist and music-lover, whom Franz had befriended in Vienna on the joyful night of the première of *The Merry Widow*, could have become one of the most abominable murderers in human history.

Somehow, he supposed, the devil had got into him, and into Germany, with the most appalling of consequences. What he remained confident of, though, was that the power of love and music would endure for the good of humankind, and yet help to save it from further catastrophes.

Anton Lehár died on Monday 12th November 1962.

THE END

Author's note

In the autumn of 2019 I was approached by James Essinger, founder of the Conrad Press, to whom I have dedicated this book in conjunction with my wife, with an idea, which he enthusiastically encouraged me to take up . This was that the life of the Austrian composer, Franz Lehar, (1870-1948) and most particularly his association with men like the brilliant lyricist Fritz Lohner-Beda, (1883-1942) the famous singer Richard Tauber, (1891-1948) as well as no less than the Fuhrer himself, Adolf Hitler, (1889-1945) was worthy of a novel. This led me to appreciate that in the course of a career spanning five decades, Franz, who is most associated with *The Merry Widow*, composed many fine operettas, with the support of an array of talented librettists, of whom Fritz was probably the most able.

What I also quickly discovered was that while the Fuhrer lauded the music of the German composer, Richard Wagner, the man whose music he took most pleasure in was Franz. There is also every reason to believe that this began when he was a struggling artist in Vienna before the First World War and continued until his dying hours in his Berlin bunker in 1945. Further, it was apparent to me that nearly all Franz's closest colleagues in the musical world of Vienna were Jewish, including both Fritz Lohner-Beda and Richard Tauber, and that more than that his wife, Sophie, was Jewish, too. I realised, as well, the important role that Franz's younger brother, General

Anton Lehar, (1876-1962) played in his life and decided that the novel should reflect that reality.

By the time of Anchluss in 1938 when Austria was incorporated into the Third Reich, Franz was an old man in declining health, understandably anxious to protect his wife. In the event, the Fuhrer needed little encouragement to grant Sophie honorary Aryan status. More than that he began to heap honours on Franz, but all the while the composer's many Jewish colleagues who had not been able to flee the country, were either sent to concentration camps, amongst them Fritz Lohner-Beda, or forced into hiding. By 1943 all these colleagues were dead , leaving Franz a broken man, who had taken to his bed, although once the Second World War ended his health improved sufficiently to enable him to enjoy a reunion with Richard Tauber.

With this historical background in mind, the novel is very much a work of fiction, which imagines an association between Franz and Hitler in Vienna before the First World War, and then as well Franz's fruitless endeavour, some thirty years later, to appeal to Hitler to spare Jewish colleagues from incarceration in concentration camps. It's undoubtedly the case that Franz tried unsuccessfully to appeal on behalf of Louis Treumann, (1872-1943) who was the first Danilo in *The Merry Widow*, and probably tried to intervene on Fritz's behalf as well, but there is no evidence that any meeting took place between Franz and Hitler at Berchtesgaden.

The novel also puts a human face on Hitler as a struggling artist in Vienna, during which, ironically, it was a Jewish art dealer, Samuel Morgenstern, (1875-1943) who gave him the most support. It was, too, during these years that Hitler came under the influence of the anti-Semitic Mayor of Vienna, Karl Lueger (1844-1910).

In the years following Franz's death, his brother, Anton, did all he could to enhance Franz's legacy, which had to an extent been tarnished by his association with Hitler. Of course, with his Jewish wife as well as Jewish friends and colleagues, Franz was never anti-semitic. It was simply a perfect two-edged sword for him that Hitler adored his music, as on the one hand it enabled him to protect his wife, but at the same time, in order to do so, he had to be careful not to offend Hitler. Notwithstanding Sophie's honorary Aryan status, Nazi officials in Austria still tried to make life difficult for her. It's also true that retreating Nazi soldiers attempted to blow up the bridge in Bad Ischl close to Franz's home in 1945, but as with the supposed meeting at Berchtesgaden between Franz and Hitler, I plead dramatic licence, as there is no evidence that Anton helped to prevent this from happening.

The broad sweep of this novel, covering as it does a period of forty years and more, also puts some of Hitler's principal supporters under the spotlight, including Baldur von Shirach, (1907-1974) who governed Vienna from 1940 to 1945, and his predecessor but one in office, Arthur Seyss-Inquart, (1892-1946). Both men were put on trial at Nuremburg after the war, and after being condemned to death, it is true that Seyss-Inquart received absolution from the prison chaplain.

The great tragedy that lies at the heart of this novel, is, of course, the holocaust and the terrible fate of not just Fritz and Louis but also their families along with that of men like Bela Jenbach (1871-1943) and Victor Leon, (1858-1940) the librettist who starved to death whilst in hiding from the Nazis.

Song of Buchenwald, the title to this novel, was the song created in Buchenwald concentration camp by Fritz and the composer, Hermann Leopoldi, (1888-1959) in 1938. Hermann was lucky that his wife was able to buy his freedom, while poor Fritz was beaten to death for not working hard enough. Poignantly, the song's words still serve as an affirmation of freedom in the face of tyranny.

James Walker February 2023

About the Author

James Walker is a retired lawyer living near Canterbury, Kent. He is married with two sons and five grandchildren. He has had a life long love of history, and has German ancestry on both sides of his family.

Also by James Walker

Ellen's Gold (2012)

My Enemy, My Love (2011)

I Think he was George (2014)

Shamila (2016)

Aliza, my Love (2019)

Ravishment - The first diary of Lady Jane Tremayne (2019)

The Hanging Tree - The second diary thereof (2021)

Falling - The third diary thereof (2022)

Acknowledgements

To James Taylor, with many thanks, for his valuable contribution, both as a proofreader and editor, to the creation of this novel.